"The heat works just fine," a male voice says.

My heart jumps into my throat and I flip around, thinking we have an intruder. My gaze darts all around the store looking for anyone, anything to explain what I thought I heard. I shiver again, realizing I'm alone.

"And so do the lights," the voice adds.

A chill runs down my spine. I feel like I've stepped into the kind of horror movie where the stupid heroine just stands there pleading with the ax murderer not to hurt her instead of getting the heck out of there.

"Who's there?" I do a 360-degree turn and still see no one.

I feel the hairs on the back of my neck rise. Silence. I try the light switch again, but the lights just keep flickering and finally go off completely. I open my mouth to scream for my mother but, just like in all good horror flicks, no sound comes out. I'm frozen to the spot in fear.

Just when I'm sure I'm going to be the lead story on the six o'clock news, I see Uncle Omar across the room, leaning on the bookshelves, his arms crossed in front of him.

"Ohmigod, I'm seeing ghosts again!" I shriek. I blink hard trying to get rid of the apparition.

"Well, I'm not really a ghost, I'm a spirit, but materializing sucks energy out of the air," he says with a grin.

I stare in disbelief. "I...I...uh..."

"Don't worry, I won't slime you," he says, laughing.

I could almost laugh with him if I weren't so freaked out. Just when I'd chalked up my last sighting of him to stress, or exhaustion, or hormones, or whatever, here he is again. Now all my rationalizations go out the window as I look into the seemingly solid face of my mother's dead brother.

Reviews for
CONFESSIONS OF A TEENAGE PSYCHIC

"Caryn has a strong voice; I like her."
~Barbara Shoup, author of ***Everything You Want***

Confessions of a Teenage Psychic

by

Pamela Woods-Jackson

This is a work of fiction. Names, characters, places, and incidents are either the product of the author's imagination or are used fictitiously, and any resemblance to actual persons living or dead, business establishments, events, or locales, is entirely coincidental.

Confessions of a Teenage Psychic

COPYRIGHT 2009 by Pamela Woods-Jackson

All rights reserved. No part of this book may be used or reproduced in any manner whatsoever without written permission of the author or The Wild Rose Press except in the case of brief quotations embodied in critical articles or reviews.
Contact Information: info@thewildrosepress.com

Cover Art by *Tina Lynn*

The Wild Rose Press
PO Box 706
Adams Basin, NY 14410-0706
Visit us at www.thewildrosepress.com

Publishing History:
First Climbing Rose Edition, 2010
Print ISBN 1-60154-770-6

Published in the United States of America

Dedication

To Robert and Caroline, for their love and patience.
And to all my Broad Ripple High School students
who inspired me.

Prologue
April Foolery

I take one last look in my locker, hoping I've got everything. My biology book is shoved in sideways, blocking my algebra book, my sketchbook is buried under some math homework I never turned in, and my color-coded class notebooks are now in a pile on the bottom, next to a wrinkled Texas A&M sweatshirt. It's easier to just keep most of my stuff in my book bag because I don't feel like digging through the clutter most of the time. I sigh, slam the door shut and hurry to class.

"Hi, Caryn!" Emma looks really tired, like she didn't get much sleep last night. "I wanted to ask you..."

"About your algebra test?"

"Yeah, right. Well, I was wondering if, well, if you thought I'd..." She sighs.

I guess she's decided not to ask me if she's actually going to pass it, and instead just looks at me sheepishly and says, "Wish me luck, okay?"

"Sure, good luck," I say, knowing all too well she's going to need it.

Sometimes I wonder, *Why me?* Most days are okay I guess, but, see, I'm fifteen years old and everyone thinks I'm weird because I know stuff. I don't mean smart kinds of stuff, I mean things I have no way of actually knowing, but pick up on anyway. Sometimes it's a gut reaction, sometimes it's just images, like a movie-of-the-week on fast-forward in my brain, but once in a while I just know something and it comes spilling out of my mouth before I can stop it.

"See you in class, Caryn." Emma waves and heads down the hall.

"Yeah, I'm on my way." I stop to readjust my overloaded book bag on my shoulder before following her.

Emma Cartwright is also a sophomore here at Rosslyn High School in Indianapolis. She's popular because she's a pretty redhead with a fun sense of humor and great fashion sense. And all the teachers like her too. She's not at the top of the class like Ashleigh Ko, but she's a solid B student who works hard. Usually. Unfortunately, she's going to flunk that algebra test big time because she spent all last night texting her boyfriend Kevin Marshall.

How do I know that? It's not because she told me. I just know. See, that's what I mean.

"Caryn!"

I turn to see Megan Benedict waving at me and practically running down the hall.

"Finally! Didn't you hear me calling you?" Megan says. She puts her book bag down, balances it between her knees, pulls the ponytail holder off her wrist and ties back her shoulder-length blonde hair. Megan is also new this year at Rosslyn High. She's a transfer from some private school in that ritzy suburb of Belford, but Megan is cool, not at all stuck up like you might think. She once told me she hated that private school, but she really likes it here at Rosslyn with all the different kinds of kids. She sort of eased my way when I first got here, just by being willing to hang out with me when all the other kids thought I was too weird.

"Hey, Megan, what's up?"

"I wanted to know if you were free tonight," Megan says once she's caught her breath.

"Aren't you spending the weekend at your dad's house?"

Megan opens her mouth to answer, stops for a second, and then gets a puzzled look on her face. "Did I already tell you that?"

I shrug and wait for her to go on.

"I'm not going till Saturday."

"Oh, okay."

Megan slaps her forehead when it finally dawns on her. "Geez, Caryn, I *hate* when you do that. Just let *me* tell *you* stuff, even if you already know it. It's so unnerving."

I could have sworn Megan told me about going up to Belford for the weekend, but sometimes I can't tell the difference between what I *know* and what I really know and it gets me in trouble.

Especially with Megan. She can get into a huff quicker than anybody I ever met, but luckily she doesn't hold a grudge. It's a good thing too, because once she found out about my, uh, talent, she made it clear she doesn't want to hear it. So I try really hard to think before I speak, but sometimes it just comes out anyway. Mom says it's because I'm just a kid and I'll learn to control it when I'm older. I hope so, because it can be really embarrassing to be a know-it-all teenager.

Megan turns on her heel and heads into Mrs. York's classroom just as the tardy bell rings. Mrs. York is standing in her doorway and stops me as I walk in right behind Megan.

"Running a little late today, Caryn? You're usually the first one here."

I smile up at her and notice her cheeks are a little flushed. She's an attractive woman about my mom's age, tall and thin but putting on weight around the middle. "How are you feeling, Mrs. York?"

"Oh, much better, thank you." She pauses and I get another one of those puzzled looks I'm so used to.

People always look at me funny when I blurt out

stuff I shouldn't know, which is way too often. There's always this awkward silence, and then I get embarrassed because I know I did it again.

"How did you know I was sick?"

"Um…sorry I'm late," I mumble as I hurry to my seat.

I really should put a filter on my mouth. When one of these things pops into my head it's often out before I can slap a hand over my mouth or bite my tongue. It's sort of like a disconnect between my brain and what's socially acceptable. I have no logical way of knowing that Mrs. York is pregnant, because she doesn't even know for sure yet. She'll be thrilled when she finds out next month, because at age forty, she and Mr. York have all but given up hope of having children.

"How are we doing with *Pride and Prejudice*?" asks Mrs. York when everyone has settled down.

This is my favorite class. It's an elective called Love of Lit, a one-semester course studying some of the most romantic literature ever written. Right now we're about halfway through Jane Austen's famous novel, but we've also read (or reread for some of us) *Romeo and Juliet*, a bunch of Shakespeare's sonnets, *Midsummer Night's Dream* (for contrast to the tragedy of *R&J*), and we're going to read Elizabeth Barrett Browning's sonnets before school is out.

Not everybody is in here because they want to be, though. Like Kensington Marlow, for one. She's using the elective credit to make up for an English class she flunked. And Ashleigh Ko is here because the counselor couldn't find any math electives that she hadn't already aced. And Kevin Marshall hates literature, but got stuck in here because his athletic conditioning class conflicts with every other elective he wanted.

The class has turned out to be a diverse bunch of kids, though, sometimes making it more interesting than the literature we study. Mostly it's sophomores like me and my friends Emma, Megan, and Ashleigh, and some juniors like Kevin, but there's one very studious freshman, Harris Rutherford, who's always sneaking romantic looks at me and creeping me out. And there are a couple of seniors coasting to graduation, like Deana Pruitt. She's the daughter of the school superintendent, and a notorious bulimic.

Then there's Janae Thomas, also a sophomore—tall, gorgeous, African-American with a wardrobe to die for. Everyone calls her "The Voice of Rosslyn High." If you want to know anything that's going on in this school, ask Janae. If you want something spread around school, tell Janae. This class provides her with a steady source of information and she keeps her eyes and ears open at all times.

"What's up with Elizabeth Bennet anyway?" Megan asks the teacher. "Why doesn't that woman just admit she's in love with Mr. Darcy?"

As if delighted that someone is actually reading the book, Mrs. York smiles and says, "She's not initially in love with him, Megan. At what point does Elizabeth realize her dislike of him has turned to love and admiration?"

"After she sees what a big house he lives in!" Naturally Kevin Marshall gets a big laugh from everyone with that remark.

Mrs. York gives him a stern look, surveying the classroom and her uninterested students. Deana has her head down on her desk, Kevin is sideways in his seat talking to a giggling Emma, Ashleigh's doing her math homework, and Janae is staring out the window watching a couple of guys with spring fever cutting classes. I feel sorry for Mrs. York because it's a beautiful day and hardly anyone is listening to her lesson.

Harris slowly raises his hand.

"Yes, Harris?" asks Mrs. York.

Poor Harris. He's like this stereotype geek—short (but he'll grow, trust me), dark hair that doesn't look like he's run a comb through it in days, no fashion sense, and please don't get me started on those black, thick-rimmed glasses that make him look like Clark Kent. Still, the kid's got spunk. He's the only freshman in this class, and yet he always raises his hand and speaks out. He's a straight-A student and usually ends up making the upperclassmen look bad. But things will improve for him in a lot of ways by next year, and I know that for a fact.

"Maybe—" Harris clears his throat when his changing voice breaks. He looks around the room with a panic-stricken look on his face, but gathers his courage and tries again. "Wouldn't it ruin the story if she fell in love with Darcy too early in the book? Maybe Jane Austen wants us to get to know Miss Bennet first."

There are groans from Kevin and a few others, and Harris turns a bright red.

"Excellent observation, Harris," Mrs. York answers with another stern look at the disgruntled kids. "Austen was a master storyteller. She builds suspense by having Elizabeth be surprised when she realizes she's in love with a man she thought she loathed."

"She's pretty stubborn, so she wouldn't even admit to herself that she's attracted to Darcy, let alone tell anyone else. Not even her sister." Janae is still staring out the window but can multi-task with the best of them.

"Very good, Janae, quite right. Any other comments?" Deana suddenly lifts her head and raises her hand. "Deana?"

"May I use the restroom?"

Without waiting for an answer Deana jumps up

from her seat, grabs the hall pass from the hook next to the door, and rushes out of the room.

Mrs. York sighs.

"Hey, Mrs. York, sorry I'm late. Dentist appointment."

It's Quince Adams. He walks in just as Deana dashes out, and hands his late pass to the teacher.

"Have a seat, John," Mrs. York tells him.

Quince takes the seat directly in front of me. He automatically glances at Kensi across the room, which makes me cringe.

Now maybe you're wondering why I call him Quince when Mrs. York calls him John. Which is it? Well, get this—his name really is John Quincy Adams. His dad claims they're descendants of the sixth president of the United States, so he insisted they name the kid after their famous ancestor. But no one calls him John, except maybe the teachers.

He's sixteen, tall and muscular, blond hair, blue eyes, and has charm oozing from every pore. He's a fairly good student, usually making As and Bs, but his real strength is sports. At the last pep rally, Coach Edgemont introduced him as "an all-around star athlete, a slam-dunk for an athletic scholarship to the college of his choice" and the student body went wild. Right now he's just a junior, so he's got some time before the talent scouts start coming around making offers.

Naturally all the girls want to date Quince, but he's been going out with Kensington Marlow since last year.

Everyone calls her Kensi, and for reasons that escape me, she's the most popular girl in school. Maybe it's because she's head cheerleader, or maybe it's because of the sleazy way she dresses.

As it so happens, she's sitting next to her best friend and fellow cheerleader, Salissa Pringle, a slender, attractive girl who always looks really serious. Salissa is Indian, so she's got that dark exotic look all the guys go for. The two of them usually have their heads together, whispering about something. It's enough to make us regular kids paranoid.

Quince casually smiles at me as he sits down, making my heart race wildly, but then he grins at Kensi. She tosses her hair and bats her eyes at him, but once she's sure she's got his undivided attention, she goes back to her conversation with Salissa.

I'm so miserable I could die.

"Okay, everyone, focus," says Mrs. York, trying to regain the class's attention after Quince's grand entrance. "What makes the romantic clash between Elizabeth Bennet and Mr. Darcy so intense?"

"You don't expect a woman in the nineteenth century to argue with a man," I say.

That's me trying to sound confident. I've already finished the book, but even so I don't like speaking out in class because people look at me and I hate drawing attention to myself. It's bad enough that this sixth sense I've got makes kids think I'm weird, or crazy, or both. See, all I really want is to be a normal, everyday teenager, just like all the other kids.

But being psychic is so *not* normal.

Mrs. York gives me a nod, so I relax a little and glance over at Quince, catching him staring at me. Is he staring because I said something smart, or is it because maybe he likes me? Just as I'm engaging in a bit of wishful thinking, there's a knock on the classroom door, and I can tell Mrs. York is about to give up in frustration.

She steps into the hall to talk to Ms. Benedict. She's Megan's mom and a brand new freshman English teacher here at Rosslyn. I guess that's why Megan transferred to this school. Or maybe it had something to do with her parents' divorce a few years back. Anyway, I see Megan slump down in her chair.

"Megan, your mother would like to speak to you," Mrs. York says.

Megan lets out a huge sigh of disgust, gets up from her chair and goes to the door, closing it behind her.

"I wonder what that's all about," Janae whispers to me.

"Megan's still way involved with this uniform policy thing." I was sure everyone already knew that, but if Janae doesn't know then it must be a pretty well-kept secret.

"WHAT? I thought she dropped that!"

"You know Megan. She never lets anything drop."

"Really? Tell me what you know!" Janae leans in closer so she doesn't miss a thing.

When will I ever learn to keep my big mouth shut? Here it is April, I've been in this school since September, and it's like I haven't learned a thing. Who knew the principal's new dress code rules would cause all this trouble? Okay, I did, but did Megan listen to me? She's as stubborn and opinionated as Elizabeth Bennet. It's like she's been on this collision course since school started and there's no stopping her.

When I think back to last September and my first day here...

Chapter 1
New Kid, New School Year

"Class, may I have your attention? I'd like to introduce our new student Caryn Alderson. She just moved here from Houston, Texas," announces the art teacher, Miss Emerson. She looks frazzled, her apron covered in paint, and there's a smudge of blue chalk on her face.

I feel like an idiot, being presented to the class like I'm in elementary school. What next? Will they greet me in unison?

"Hi, Caryn!" all the students say at once.

Great. My sixth sense always kicks in at the most embarrassing moments.

"Caryn," says Miss Emerson after the class settles back to work. "As I told you when we met yesterday, we're already working on our first project of the year. So to get you up to speed quickly, I'll partner you with someone." Miss Emerson looks around the room for a likely victim. "Megan? Megan Benedict, may I have a word with you?"

Megan is absorbed in a pencil drawing on the other side of the room and clearly doesn't want to be disturbed. She groans and rolls her eyes as she gets up from her stool and walks across to the front of the room where I'm still standing next to Miss Emerson. Megan stops in front of me, arms clasped across her chest, glaring at me like I'm her worst nightmare. Right now all I want to do is run—back to my mother, back to Houston, anywhere but here.

"Megan, will you help Caryn get started on this project? You can explain it to her, show her where the supplies are, things like that. Do you mind?"

"No," Megan says, but her body language speaks volumes. She turns and walks toward the supply closet, leaving me to trail behind her like some unwanted puppy.

I guess most kids would be able to tell Megan wasn't happy about Miss Emerson sticking her with the new kid. I'm sensing there's more to her attitude, but I can't home in on it right now. I'm too busy being embarrassed.

"You don't have to, you know," I say to the back of her head. "Show me around and stuff, I mean. I know my way around art rooms."

Megan turns and looks me up and down, making me feel even more insecure. I'm trying not to stare, but I have to admit I'm looking right back. She's what we call a "prep" back in Houston. Her light blonde hair is pulled back into a ponytail, her clothes are Old Navy casual—khaki knee-length cargo shorts, layered blue and white short-sleeved ribbed T-shirts that fit snugly on her slim figure, and sandals that look expensive, like Birkenstocks. I feel self-conscious in my peasant skirt, faded Houston Astros T-shirt, Walmart sandals, and my long brown hair braided down my back (the better to hide the green stripe I dyed into it last spring).

She shrugs. "Miss Emerson has a weird filing system, so I'd better explain it to you. Where have you been, anyway?"

"Been?" Now it's my turn to be confused.

"Duh. It's September," she says and rolls her eyes again. "Way after Labor Day even. School started over three weeks ago, so where have you been?"

"Oh, yeah, my late enrollment. My mom and I just moved here."

"Hm," Megan says, as she carefully pulls pencils, drawing paper, and rulers from the cabinet.

"Come on, I'll tell you what we're doing."

I follow her to the table in the back of the room where she's left her drawing in mid-stroke. "That's really good, what you're working on," I say, glancing over at her sketches. This girl's got talent. It's a fairly detailed drawing of an old building that looks like the pictures I've seen of downtown Indianapolis. I get an instant gut reaction to Megan's artwork and realize how important it is to her. No wonder she didn't want to get stuck showing me around—it's taking her away from what she really wants to be doing.

"Thanks," Megan says, finally smiling. "I love architecture, especially historic buildings."

Now how did I know that? Ugh, here I go again.

"Have you been downtown yet? There's so much to look at." Suddenly the sullen Megan disappears and a different girl emerges, one who lights up just talking about her art.

I smile back. "No, I haven't done much sightseeing yet, but I'd like to." Megan picks up her pencil and goes back to work, so I wait a minute. And then another minute. "So what's the assignment?"

"Oh, sorry," she says, realizing I'm still standing here. "We're supposed to draw a famous building or house or whatever—sketch it in pencil—then construct a miniature of it using all natural materials. No plastic or anything like that."

It sounds easy enough. I like art, but I don't know if I'm crazy about architecture. Still, Megan's enthusiasm is contagious. Miss Emerson told me when I agreed to enroll in the art program that we'd do all kinds of projects, so I let myself be talked into joining this class in the hopes of doing some actual watercolor painting. Since it's a longer class just after lunch, I have lots of time to either prove myself or screw up. And all I want right now is to somehow fit in, even if I don't like the project. Screwing up isn't an option.

"So what are you going to draw?" Megan is talking and sketching at the same time, although she's not paying much attention to the conversation.

The only famous building I can think of is the Alamo in San Antonio. Okay, I know I'm from Houston, but every self-respecting Texas kid has either been to the Alamo or at least studied it in school. One summer a few years ago, right around the Fourth of July (which is my birthday, by the way), Dad and Michael surprised me with a trip to San Antonio. We did all the usual stuff—walked around the River Walk, ate Mexican food till we were about to explode, and of course visited The Alamo. It's now a museum with lots of stuff from that famous siege in 1836, but what I remembered most was that this really old, historical fort was completely surrounded by modern skyscrapers, creating a weird mix of old and new.

"Did you hear me?" Megan asks. "Hello?"

"Oh, sorry, my mind wandered."

"What are you going to draw?"

"I think I might do The Alamo. You know, in Texas."

"Weird." Megan screws up her face as she does some sophisticated pencil shading on her building.

Just what I need—to be thought of as weird by the first kid I meet in this new school. "Well, I really don't know much about Indiana," I reply with a shrug. "So I should probably go with someplace I've actually been."

I realize I'm giving Megan more information than she wants, since she's already become re-absorbed in her own project. I sit down next to her with a piece of drawing paper and a freshly sharpened pencil and try to sketch The Alamo. Instead, my mind wanders back to that trip to San

Antonio with my dad. I really miss him.

Guy McNamara and my mom were never a couple. They met at a wild college party one night while he was an undergrad and she was going for her masters, so I was the result of some experimenting Dad said he was doing at the time. Mom gave me her last name, but Dad has always been important in my life, and luckily my parents are good friends as well as co-parents.

One spring in elementary school Dad encouraged me to try out for little league softball and I somehow made the team. The coach tried me in every possible position but nothing worked. I struck out every other time I got up to bat—which was less and less as the season progressed—and eventually I ended up so far in the outfield that I spent my time catching butterflies instead of fly balls. Dad never missed a single one of my games, though, giving me lots of encouragement.

After that disastrous season ended and I vowed never to step foot on a softball field again, Dad tried to boost my spirits by taking me to an actual Major League Baseball game. Soon he and I became huge baseball fans and spent many nights watching the Astros play on TV or even taking in high school games around town. Michael Ferguson, Dad's partner, is a high school teacher, so he kept us clued in as to schedules and stuff.

I sigh. Dad's still in Houston and I know I won't get to see him again till next summer.

I glance at the wall clock and realize there are just a few minutes left in the class and I haven't accomplished a thing. My paper is still blank. Megan looks over at it, frowns, and starts gathering her supplies to put away.

"Come on, there are drawers in the cabinet for each of us, so I'll show you which one you can use."

I pick up my things and follow her back to the

cabinet. I'll bet Megan thinks I should have been placed in the beginner art class, since I don't have anything to show for myself after wasting an entire class period. After seeing Megan's artwork, I think maybe I should be too.

"So why did you move here?" Megan asks, after we store our projects.

"My mom and her partner Sybil just opened a bookstore in Rosslyn Village."

"Her *partner?*" Megan looks startled.

I quickly realize how that sounds.

"*Business* partner!" I'm not ready to tell her about Dad and Michael, but I really don't want her getting the wrong idea about my mom.

But then Megan surprises me. "Whatever. My mom's best friend Emily lives with her partner. She's this hotshot realtor and she helped Mom find a house she could afford on a teacher's salary."

This is news. Maybe my psychic radar is off, but judging by the way she's dressed I was just sure Megan was from one of those society families—you know, Mom does lunch and charities, Dad runs a corporation.

"Do you like coffee?" Megan's checking the classroom clock with her watch, waiting for the bell, but then she suddenly looks over at me and smiles.

"Um, yes..." I answer, startled by yet another change of subject.

"Great! A bunch of us usually go to Peterson's after school for frozen lattes. You can come if you want to." Megan heaves her book bag onto her shoulder as she waits for both my answer and the dismissal bell. I guess she notices my hesitation because she says, "Listen, I know what it's like to be new here. Come on, it'll be fun."

I'm nervous, but I smile back at Megan. "I'd really like to go. What's Peterson's?"

"DUH. Peterson's Coffee Emporium—huge chain

of coffee houses in Indiana. There's one right down the street from school." Megan is now looking at me like I'm the most clueless girl on the planet. Maybe I am.

"Oh." Brilliant response, Caryn. I blush and look down at my shoes.

"We all meet in front of school, walk over, then Mom picks me up in about an hour after she gets her work done." Megan drops her book bag down again with a thud, stretches her fingers, and rubs her shoulder where the strap was cutting into it.

A light bulb flash goes off in my head. "Oh, yeah, your mom's the new English teacher." I instantly wish I hadn't let that slip out since I forgot nobody has introduced me to her. But in my mind I can see her mom standing before a class of unruly freshmen on the first day of school, and I can feel her panic because things didn't go very well.

"How do you know about my mom if you just got here?" Megan looks puzzled. "Aren't you a sophomore? Mom teaches freshmen."

Megan frowns at me and I struggle for a plausible explanation when really there isn't one. "Uh, I saw her classroom when the counselor showed me around school yesterday."

Megan looks skeptical, her brow furrowed.

"So she and your dad are divorced, huh?" I figure if I change the subject she'll forget I said that.

"Yeah. Yours?" She hoists her book bag onto her shoulder again.

Fortunately, the bell rings before I can answer, so I scurry out of the room, heading for algebra. Unfortunately, I can't remember the room number, so I have to stop and fumble in my book bag for my crumpled schedule, enduring dirty looks from kids who barely avoid bumping into me. I scrutinize it, try to remember how I got there yesterday, and head off into the crush of students in the hallway.

Well, maybe I've made one friend, if I haven't given too much away.

I promise myself I'll do better when I meet Megan and her friends for coffee after school.

See, I don't want what happened at school in Houston to end up sabotaging my social life here. I was always a little odd anyway, at least the other kids thought so, since I was forever blurting out stuff about them that I'd forgotten they hadn't told me yet. When I was a little kid it wasn't such a big deal, because all little kids say stupid stuff. As I got older my intuition began to cramp my social life. No kid likes a know-it-all, and that's what they all thought I was.

It first started when I was about five years old and one day for no apparent reason I said to my mom, "Daddy's on the phone."

"No, he isn't, Caryn," Mom had said patiently. "The phone didn't ring."

"Daddy's calling you!" I remember Mom giving me an exasperated look, and then sure enough, the phone rang.

"Hello?" Mom's eyes got all wide and she gave me this look of surprise as she turned back to the phone and said, "Guy, did you tell Caryn you were going to call me?" Then I got yet another one of those looks.

After she finished her conversation, Mom asked, "Caryn, how did you know Daddy was going to call—*before* the phone rang?"

I just shrugged my shoulders and went back to playing with my dolls. After that, it got to be a joke in the family—I always knew when the phone was going to ring and who was on the other end. From predicting phone calls I graduated to accurately foretelling events, and pretty soon everyone in the family knew I had "The Gift" as Sybil put it.

But I'd either managed to keep my abilities

under wraps through eighth grade, or else the other kids were too clueless to pick up on it, because no one outside of the immediate family knew about me. When I started ninth grade at a new high school, though, things went south in a hurry. I kept blurting out information without thinking. Why? New kids, new surroundings, maybe I'd just gotten used to getting away with that when I was younger, but high school kids are a lot less forgiving. I'd say stuff about students and teachers in front of everyone, and at first I just got the weird stares I'm used to, but pretty soon kids were looking at me suspiciously all the time. When I really messed up was in history class one day in November.

"Hey, Caryn," whispered a girl in class. "Can I borrow your notes from last week when I was absent?"

"I'm sorry about your dad," was my idiotic response. She looked at me funny, so naturally, I made it worse. "Sorry he's sick. Heart attack, right?"

With a look somewhere between shock and anger, she gasped. "How did you know that? I didn't tell anyone!"

After that, my reputation as a weirdo grew, completely ruining my social life. No one wanted anything to do with "the witch" as they started calling me. For a while I laughed it off, but by spring, I had no friends left and I was totally miserable. That's when I dyed the green stripe down the middle of my hair and started wearing it loose and unkempt. I figured if they were going to call me a witch I might as well look the part.

Except for making fun of my hair, kids continued to ignore me for the rest of the school year, which is why I was ready and willing to move to Indianapolis with my mom. I hoped a fresh start here would erase the pain of freshman year and put me on a better social path.

That's why I have to watch what I say in front of Megan and her friends. If I start to let stuff slip out uncensored, pretty soon I'll end up an outcast again. I just want to be normal, doing all the things normal kids take for granted—friends, homework, extracurricular activities—you know, NORMAL. I wish I could just forget I'm psychic.

Chapter 2
Caffeine Rush

I spot Megan standing on the street corner outside school that afternoon and hesitantly walk over to join her. Even though she was nice to me today in art class, I'm still the new girl and my insecurities make me wonder if I'd really been expected to come or if it was just a pity-invite.

"Hi," Megan says, looking surprised.

"You did say *today* after school, right? For coffee?"

"Oh, yeah," she says, like she's just remembered she asked me to join them.

She turns away and continues watching for her friends to emerge from the school building.

"I wasn't sure if you'd really come," she adds without looking at me.

I'm not sure whether to stay or go, but while I hesitate, Megan glances over my head and waves both arms. I turn around and see two girls heading toward us.

"Hey, Megan!" shouts one.

"Can we hurry and go?" asks the other one. "I'm meeting Kevin."

"And who's this?" asks the first one, staring at me. This girl is very pretty, part Asian, with long black hair and dark eyes. I wistfully admire the rhinestone-studded T-shirt she's wearing, take another look at my faded Astros shirt, and wish I'd chosen something else for my first day at a new school.

"Emma, Ashleigh, this is Caryn Alderson,"

Confessions of a Teenage Psychic

Megan says, motioning toward the two girls to show me which one is which. "She just moved here from Texas. She's going with us."

I guess that means I'm staying, but I'm still nervous about trying to fit in. At the moment I'm not sure I do.

Emma has a pretty oval face and light-brown curly hair tucked behind pierced ears. With her crisp white blouse, flowered cotton skirt, black Mary Janes, and a small string of pearls at her throat, she's sort of a throwback to another era. But I have to admit it works for her.

"Aren't you in my English class?" Emma asks, interrupting my thoughts.

"I've got Mrs. Renfrow fifth period. Is that your class?"

"Yeah. Mrs. Renfrow is pretty boring, but at least it's easier than math," Emma says with a moan.

Megan nods in agreement. "I can't do math either."

"If you two would just study a little," says Ashleigh, shaking her head. "It's not all that hard."

"So you take honors geometry, right? And play violin?" That just pops into my head and out of my mouth before I can stop and think. I press my lips together—too late—and brace myself for her reaction.

Ashleigh looks a little surprised. "Yeah, I'm an Asian cliché—good at math and first chair in the orchestra. Who told you?"

"Lucky guess," I say. "You seem smart."

Be cool, Caryn, you just met these girls.

"She IS smart," Emma says. "She's the—"

"Valedictorian," I finish, but then want to clap my hands over my mouth.

"Well, not yet, but she will be." Emma gives me a puzzled look.

Quickly changing the subject I ask, "Are we waiting for anyone else?"

"No, this is it. Sometimes other kids just show up there, but it's usually pretty crowded, so we'd better go if we want a decent table," Megan says as she pushes the Walk button on the street signal.

The light finally changes and we all cross the busy street, heading toward Rosslyn Village. That's what the locals call it, although I don't know if the name is really official. Actually it's just an odd assortment of little shops, trendy restaurants, and nightclubs for the over-twenty-one crowd. And of course plenty of places where kids like to hang out too, like the coffee shop and a fast-food restaurant.

Peterson's Coffee Emporium is an easy one-block walk from school, situated on a corner (and taking up most of the city block) next door to a pizza place and across the street from a consignment clothing store. I don't know why I didn't notice Peterson's before, because Mom and I have eaten in that pizza place. Megan, Emma, Ashleigh, and I walk in and I follow them straight to the counter to place our orders. They all seem to be buying frozen lattes, and wanting to fit in I do the same, despite the fact that I'd rather have an herbal iced tea.

I look around while I wait and a sudden flash in my head tells me that this hasn't always been a coffee shop. I see a pool table and bar that used to be here. But it's definitely a coffee shop now, decorated with cozy tables-for-two scattered around the room, but also lots of large leather-upholstered booths lining the walls. There's an old Tiffany chandelier hanging from the ceiling in the middle of the room where the pool table probably was, and the eclectic posters on the walls are supposed to look like they came from a garage sale.

"Over here!" Megan leads us all to a large circular booth in the corner.

We slide in, one after another, and I start sipping my latte. Slowly, because too much caffeine gives me a head rush, and if there's one thing I don't need it's to be even more wired.

"Is anyone going to the homecoming game Friday night?" Emma asks.

"I am!" Megan answers, and then adds for my benefit, "It's not that I care about football really, but I want to go to the dance afterward, and you can't go to the dance unless you go to the game."

Weird rule. I take another sip of the latte and then push it aside. "A homecoming dance after a football game? How does that work?"

"It's like a mixer," Megan explains. "No one really dresses up. Everyone just goes to the game and then to the dance in the school cafeteria. Wanna go with?" she suddenly asks me.

I'm a little surprised, being the new kid and all, but before I can answer, Emma jumps up and hurries to the door as two good-looking guys walk in. And I mean these two boys are HOT! Emma kisses the dark-haired one on the cheek, links her arm in his, and leads him to our table. The other boy goes to the counter and places an order.

"Scoot over." Emma nudges everyone to make room for the newcomers. "This is Kevin Marshall," she says to me. Her boyfriend I assume, and I don't need to be psychic to figure that out.

"And you are...?" he asks me.

"Caryn Alderson, new to town, new to Rosslyn High." I start to offer my hand to shake, but there isn't enough room at the table to even stretch it out, so in embarrassment I pretend I just meant to grab my latte.

"Mind if I sit down?" asks the other boy, balancing three iced teas. He hands one of them to Kevin and takes a sip from one of the other two.

Did I say he was hot? That doesn't begin to

describe him. He's tall, probably over six feet, and very muscular in an athletic sort of way. He keeps running his fingers through his surfer-blond hair, and he's dressed prep-style—golf shirt, belted khaki shorts, loafers. You know, the clean-cut all-American type.

He can't be that thirsty. I glance around the room to see who else might be joining us.

"Everyone shove over again," Emma orders. "Caryn, this is John, but no one calls him that."

He awkwardly tries to juggle the iced teas in order to shake hands with me, but grins at me endearingly when he realizes he can't do it. I can feel my heart start to flutter.

"Everyone calls me Quince," he says in a clear, deep voice.

He has an easy-going charm, the kind that makes girls fall instantly in love, and I am already sure I'm going to be one of them. Sometimes guys like that are players—they like to play with girls' hearts for a while and then dump them when they get bored. But my instincts tell me Quince isn't like that. This guy seems genuine and I like him immediately.

"Hi," I say, looking him directly in the eyes. He has the most beautiful blue eyes I've ever seen.

"So where did you come from?" he asks me, squeezing into the booth.

I'm so busy staring I almost forget to answer him. He grins at me expectantly.

"Uh, Houston," I finally reply. "My mom owns a bookstore." I can't stop looking at him. He's just so darned cute.

"Cool. You coming to the game Friday?" My heart skips another beat.

"Quince here is the star quarterback, number seventeen, and Rosslyn is favored to beat Newton Tech by a whole lot." Kevin laughs as he playfully elbows Quince. "I'm his favorite receiver."

Usually I'm just a baseball fan, but suddenly football seems very interesting. Just as I'm about to open my mouth and say I'll be at the game with Megan, the door opens and in walks a girl who looks like she's just stepped off the cover of a fashion magazine. She's tall, slender, wearing an impossibly short skirt and extremely high heels, and has cascading brunette hair which she keeps tossing over her shoulder. All eyes turn to watch her as she makes her grand entrance and I get a sick feeling in the pit of my stomach when I see the smitten look on Quince's face and realize this is who he's waiting for.

Quince slides purposefully out of the booth and walks over to greet her with a hug. He casually takes her hand and leads her back to our table, but there's no way we can squeeze in one more person.

"Kensi, this is Caryn," Quince says, never taking his eyes off her. "Caryn's new at school," he says, beaming at her and squeezing her hand.

She pushes her hair back with her sunglasses, nods in my direction like a queen barely acknowledging a subject, gives my outfit the once over, and says, "Nice to meet you."

Yeah, right.

She turns to Quince and coos, "I don't think there's room at this table, hon. Let's get our own." Quince happily follows her across the room to a table for two, leaving the rest of us to watch them go.

"They're like the signature couple of the junior class," Emma sighs.

"They're such a cliché," snaps Ashleigh. "Varsity cheerleader dating the quarterback. Gimme a break!"

"Well, I think they're cute," Emma shoots back as she grins up at Kevin. "Almost as cute as us."

"So they've been going out since last spring?" I ask half-heartedly. In my misery I forget no one told me that yet.

"Wow, you catch on fast," responds Megan. "Yeah, they started going out after one of Quince's baseball games last May. Right after he hit that grand slam."

Ashleigh must take my frown for confusion, because she jumps in to clarify. "Oh, yeah, Quince is the star of both the football and baseball teams."

Megan takes a big, loud slurp of her latte and adds, "So what I hear is, Kensi supposedly kept the cheerleaders yelling for an eternity after he crossed home plate, until Quince personally went over and thanked her. But I didn't go to Rosslyn last year, so I'm just telling you."

"I guess Quince not only won the game that day but Kensi's heart," Emma sighs again.

My eyes follow Quince and Kensington to their darkened corner of the shop. I don't know if it's curiosity or the green-eyed monster that makes me stare, but when I realize I'm being rude, I try glancing around the room like I'm just taking in the ambience or something. Curiosity gets the better of me, though, and my gaze eventually drifts back to the two of them. Kensi is leaning on the table practically in Quince's face, batting her eyelashes and flipping her hair. Now, honestly, what guy wouldn't think that kind of behavior was enticing?

As I watch them, my heart sinks. How can I compete with HER? I've never had a boyfriend, but this feeling in the pit of my stomach tells me it must be a very painful experience. How can I be reacting like this to a guy I just met?

I come out of my reverie when I hear bells ringing and wonder if it's the Universe sending me a wakeup call. Fortunately it's just someone's cell phone.

"Hi, Mom," says Megan after she pulls her phone out of her handbag. "Okay, I'll be right out."

She flips the phone closed. "I've gotta go."

"I'll go out with you," I tell her. "I'm supposed to go over to my mom's store and help out after school."

Emma, Ashleigh, and Kevin all have to get up to let us out, but then they sit right back down again, obviously not ready to leave.

"Nice meeting you," I say to all of them as I follow Megan out the door.

"Nice to meet you too, Caryn," Emma calls after me. "Don't forget about Friday night!"

"Don't worry, I'll be there," I call back.

Emma smiles at me before turning her attention back to Kevin. Having her repeat Megan's invitation makes me feel more welcome, like maybe I'll fit in here after all.

"Where's your mom's store?" Megan asks as we walk outside in the late afternoon heat. She scans up and down the street looking for her mother's car. "Do you need a ride?"

"It's only about a block and half that way," I answer, pointing north. "You should stop by sometime. It's called Sybil and Starshine's New Age Bookstore." Maybe I shouldn't tell her that—about its being a New Age bookstore. It's got to sound weird to someone like Megan who seems so, well, normal.

"Sybil and Starshine?" she repeats. "Is that your mom's name?"

"Okay, her name is Bethany Alderson, but they thought Starshine sounded more like the owner of a New Age store."

I can tell Megan is having mixed feelings about that information. Not that I can read her mind, but anyone could figure that out from her lifted eyebrows and forced smile. Just then a soccer-mom-style SUV pulls up alongside the sidewalk.

"Mom, this is Caryn Alderson," Megan says, as she opens the door and throws in her backpack.

"She's new to school. Her mom owns some kind of New Age-y store here in the Village."

"Nice to meet you, Caryn," says Megan's mom with a smile. "I'll try to stop by soon and meet your mother. Megan, we've got to go. Honey has been alone way too long." Megan hops into the passenger side of her mom's car.

"What kind of dog is Honey?" I ask, picturing the cutest little yellow dog. Again the puzzled look from Megan. When will I remember that mental images don't necessarily mean anyone has actually mentioned something in the conversation?

"Mixed breed—we got her from a shelter back in July," Megan answers.

Ms. Benedict smiles at me as she presses the turn signal and pulls out into traffic. Megan sticks her head out the window, waves and shouts, "See you tomorrow!"

"That went well," I say wryly to myself, hoping I haven't completely blown it. I really want this school to work out. Now if I could just learn to think before blurting stuff out.

****

Mom's store is in an old red-brick building that's been renovated recently and now houses four different shops. Ours is the second to the last, right next to a bed and bath shop on one side and between a florist and a sandwich shop on the other. Fifty years ago, this building was a dry goods store (whatever that is), but the landlord assured Mom and Sybil that everything inside is completely modern—new electrical wiring, heating and air conditioning, and fresh insulation. To me, the shop still has an old-timey feel with large picture windows, a beveled-glass door, and antique doorknobs, like something you'd see on *Leave It to Beaver*. I stand on the sidewalk and admire the newly painted sign on the front window:

Sybil and Starshine's New Age Bookstore
All welcome! Books, Crystals, Tarots, Candles
Open 10-6 Monday through Saturday

I walk in, setting the bells above the old-fashioned wooden door to tinkling. I spot Sybil behind the counter, but before I can ask where Mom is, she tilts her head toward the book section where my mother stands patiently waiting on a customer.

"Mrs. Solomon," Sybil informs me quietly. "She's looking for just the right spiritual guidance to assist her and her husband with their financial difficulties."

I nod, hop up on a stool behind the counter, and pull my math book out of my book bag. While fumbling for a pencil, I can hear my mother talking to the customer.

"Mrs. Solomon, I believe this book might be of help."

"Oh, that looks like just the thing," Mrs. Solomon says as she looks at the back cover and thumbs through the book. "My husband and I…"

"In addition to the book, perhaps you would like to consult with Sybil, who's skilled in numerology," Mom suggests.

"Well, maybe." Mrs. Soloman clasps the book to her chest, seeming uncomfortable with that idea.

Sybil walks over to the woman and introduces herself. Mrs. Soloman frowns slightly, but shakes Sybil's hand.

"I think I could assist you, dear, if I just knew your birthday and that of your husband," Sybil offers.

Mrs. Soloman still looks uncertain. Sybil always knows when someone needs a little encouragement, so to keep the customer interested, she adds, "And the stars tell me your difficulties will be over in about three months."

I snap my head up from my math book at that

remark and signal my mother across the room. Luckily Mrs. Soloman has her back to me and doesn't see me waving my arms in the air like I'm trying to hail a cab. When I catch Mom's eye, I point to Sybil, shake my head and hold up six fingers. She winks at me and pokes Sybil, who sees me frantically waving six fingers in the air. Sybil nods and calmly turns back to the customer.

"Or definitely within six months, dear," Sybil amends soothingly.

I smile to myself and get back to my homework.

Fifteen minutes later, Mom's customer pays for her book, as well as some candles, and walks out the door with a smile on her face.

"Another satisfied customer," Mom says cheerfully. "And thanks for your help, Caryn."

"We make a great team," I say as I high-five her. "All three of us."

"If they only knew who the real psychic was!" Sybil laughs.

Sybil Smythe is in her sixties, short, round, and has bleached blonde hair (this week). She wears way too much makeup and bling, her long flowing skirts only exaggerate her abundant size, and she drinks a lot of espresso, giving her a kind of nervous energy. Despite her eccentric appearance, her heart is the size of Texas, which is where she met my mom.

After earning a master's degree in business and with a baby in tow (me), Mom was working in an old-fashioned corner bookstore where the owners appreciated her business sense but didn't want to pay her much for it. My dad helped out whenever he could, sometimes financially and sometimes just taking over childcare duties, but he was a struggling actor/student, and pretty cash-poor himself. Mom has what she always calls "intuitive good sense." She's not really psychic like me, but I definitely inherited some of my abilities from her. Anyway,

Mom spent downtime at the bookstore reading about astrology, numerology, spirituality, tarot cards—you know, all the stuff that makes up New Age thought—and really getting into it. So when Sybil happened into the store one day and Mom waited on her, it was like their friendship was meant to be.

Sybil managed a loyal clientele doing numerology readings in a shop not far from the corner bookstore, but luckily she didn't have to live on the pittance she earned. She had a string of loving ex-boyfriends and ex-husbands who were always willing to help her out financially. One of those ex-boyfriends had been a wealthy Texas oilman who left her a big chunk of cash in his will.

Sybil with the money, and my mom with the business savvy, eventually decided to open a metaphysical bookstore in Houston, in a neighborhood similar to Rosslyn Village. Things went along pretty well for a while, despite how different Mom and Sybil are. They weren't getting rich, but they were keeping the business afloat and drawing in customers.

But after a while, crime started to increase in the area around their store, and a couple of times Mom was pretty scared going home late at night. They didn't ever get robbed or anything, but when a man was shot in front of the convenience store across the street, Mom and Sybil began searching around for someplace to relocate. After doing some serious online research, they decided on Indianapolis. So here we are. Their store just opened Labor Day weekend, and already they're attracting new customers. Word of mouth is pretty good advertising—especially since the real thing costs too much money.

Sybil still does the occasional numerology reading in the back room, but mostly she says she's retired from all that. She'd rather spend her free time (and her dead boyfriend's money) flying off to visit friends or vacationing in exotic locations.

Oh yeah, and that little hint I gave Sybil? I can't explain it. Stuff just comes to me, sometimes in mental pictures and sometimes just thoughts that randomly pop into my head. I'm almost always right. *Almost?* Fair enough. No one is perfect. Am I ever wrong? Not usually about other people, but when it comes to my own life, I have to live it as it happens, day by day, just like everybody else. No hints, no advance warnings. Kind of annoying really, since I can use all the insight I can get.

"How was your first day at school?" Mom asks.

"Okay," I say. "I may have made a new friend."

"Who's that?"

"Her name is Megan, and she introduced me to some other kids too. She seems nice."

"So why do I detect hesitation?" Mom raises an eyebrow.

I wince a little. "She kept looking at me funny when I'd say strange things. Why do I do that, Mom? Why can't I learn to keep quiet?"

"You have to be who you are, Caryn. Who you've always been."

"You always say that. But I won't have any friends if they find out what I can do." I sigh.

"Just be yourself, honey, and they'll learn to love you."

Mom gives me a hug. I always feel so safe in her arms.

Chapter 3
At The Hop on Friday

I join Megan at the school's football stadium for the homecoming game against Newton Technical High School. It's a pretty warm evening, and there's still plenty of daylight for a seven o'clock kickoff, so I tell Mom I can just walk to the school from our apartment.

I admit I sort of dawdle on the way. I don't get football anyway, and I'm also still feeling some insecurity with these new kids. So I end up missing most of the first quarter, and as a result the bleachers are already crowded with both students and parents when I arrive.

I spot Megan near the top of the stands sitting next to Emma, so I walk up the steps to join them. Emma is dressed in a cute little blue cotton skirt with a matching blouse over a camisole and a string of pearls around her neck—you know, like she went to school in the 1950s or something. Megan has on expensive-looking jeans and a Rosslyn High T-shirt, and her hair is tied into a ponytail with red and black spirit ribbons (Rossyln school colors, of course). There I am in faded Levis and my trademark Houston Astros T-shirt, which makes me feel underdressed and self-conscious all over again. I wish I'd changed clothes after school.

Before I can do much more brooding about my wardrobe, though, Megan grabs my arm and jerks me into a seat next to her.

"You're blocking the view," she shouts above the crowd noise.

There's a great deal of excitement among the fans, and I suppose the game is going well, because the Rosslyn cheerleaders are waving their pom-poms in the air, keeping the fans stirred up with enthusiasm. I spot number seventeen in formation on the field and at the same time I see Kensi cheering wildly on the sidelines as he snaps the ball. Quince's mind is clearly on the game, Kensi's focus seems to be on how good she looks cheerleading, and all I can think about is Quince, wondering what he sees in her. I try to watch the game, but pretty soon my thoughts kind of wander off just about the time Kevin Marshall carries the ball on a long run downfield.

"And now it's time to crown the Homecoming King and Queen, Quince Adams and Caryn Alderson. Kids, take the floor for your first dance as royalty!"

****

"Great game, huh?" Megan says. I look up at the scoreboard flashing the final score as people are leaving their seats.

"Um, yeah, I guess," I mumble in embarrassment.

"Did you see that run Kevin made? Over fifty yards for a touchdown!" Emma is gushing, the color rising in her cheeks every time she talks about her boyfriend.

"That was great," I say, trying to pretend I'd been paying attention.

Emma begins picking her way gingerly down the bleacher steps, trying to avoid getting spilled soda and popcorn on her black Mary Janes. Megan is right behind her, and I'm following Megan. There's a large crowd of kids already heading toward the dance in the cafeteria, but suddenly I get a sick feeling. It might be that popcorn I ate, but more likely it's a premonition, the kind that feels like a sucker punch to the stomach. I don't want to go inside.

"Are you okay?" Megan looks concerned. "You look kinda pale."

"Um, I don't like crowds," I tell her. And that part is true.

Whenever I find myself in a crowd of people, I get way too much information. I can look at an adult's face and hear the fight she had with her husband, or a kid reaches down to tie a shoelace and I see him arguing with his mother in the store about the brand of shoes, or I see a man's tattoo and watch him wince in pain as his girlfriend's name is etched into his arm. Stuff that's mundane, stuff that's intense, but definitely stuff I don't want or need to know about total strangers.

I don't confide my tingly fears to Megan, though. Instead I try to casually ask, "Where do the football guys go after a game?"

"The locker room, silly," Megan says. "Why would you ask that out of nowhere?"

I don't have a logical answer, but my gut is telling me something is going to go terribly wrong tonight.

The school cafeteria is already getting pretty crowded after the homecoming game. The Rosslyn High Wranglers defeated the Newton Tech Arrows by a score of 31-3, so everyone at the Homecoming Dance is in high spirits. From what I can learn as I overhear kids talking about it, Quince threw three touchdown passes (two of them to Kevin Marshall), ran a quarterback sneak into the end zone for a fourth score, and finally led the team to the ten yard line where the place kicker nailed the field goal. Newton Tech was lucky to even get their lone field goal, because they spent most of the game inside their own fifty yard line.

Megan is in a hurry to get inside and keeps

dragging me along, so I never do get to catch my breath after that premonition.

Megan, Emma, and I show the door chaperones our game ticket stubs, and when we walk in we see how crowded the dance floor already is. To my surprise, the only festive thing on the school cafeteria's institutional green walls is the banner the cheerleaders hung at lunch which reads "GO WRANGLERS—SLING THE ARROWS!" I guess homecoming isn't as big a deal here as it was in Houston.

"It's way too hot in here," Emma complains. "Too many people, and I don't even think the AC is turned on!"

"It's on." Megan puts her hands on her hips and looks at Emma impatiently. "Come on, don't be a wuss."

"I'm gonna sit right here and wait till Kevin comes!" Emma plops herself down at the chaperone's table near the door.

"The football team won't be here for ages, Emma. They have to change and stuff."

Emma is staying where she is, her arms crossed over her chest, and is all but daring Megan to try to change her mind. Megan throws up her hands and begins searching the crowd for someone else to talk to.

"There's Ashleigh!" she exclaims. She grabs me by the arm and drags me over to where Ashleigh is dancing. I'm beginning to feel like a rag doll with no will of my own, being dragged around by a determined Megan.

"Hi, Ash," shouts Megan as we get closer. "Who's your friend?"

Ashleigh waves at us, but her attention is all on the hottie she's dancing with.

"I think he's a senior," I say to Megan over the music. He's a senior, all right, but I didn't tell her I'd never seen him before an image flashed in my mind of him posing for his senior photo.

The music is pretty loud and it's hard to hear conversation, but that doesn't stop Megan.

"Emma's waiting for the football team," Megan shouts to Ashleigh, who nods in response, "so we're gonna go get something to drink."

I assume "we" means me, so I again follow Megan, this time to a table in the back of the cafeteria, which is loaded with water, sodas, chips, pretzels, and cookies. I take a diet soda as Megan grabs a bottled water, and then we finally stop moving long enough to look around a little.

"This is so new to me," she confides. It's easier to talk where we're standing now, next to the refreshment table, away from the DJ and crowd noise. "We did things way different at Willowby Prep."

This is the first time Megan has attempted more than a superficial conversation with me, so I listen eagerly. "Why did you leave private school?"

"My grades sucked, I kept getting in fights with kids and teachers, and they threatened to expel me. My dad didn't want to pay for an expensive school anymore if I was flunking out. Then my mom got a job here."

"So you were acting out because of your parents' divorce?"

"That's what they tell me," Megan says with a shrug. "I like it better here anyhow. The art program is great!"

"Isn't your dad like some kind of CEO?"

"Yeah, how'd you know?" Megan asks with a surprised look on her face.

I shrug and look away. Good question. Maybe it was that flash in my head like a picture being taken, one where Mr. Benedict is standing in front of a large corporate building, smiling as he shakes hands with some important-looking official. Megan looks as uncomfortable as I feel, so I'm glad when she changes the subject.

"So where is your dad, Caryn? Are your parents divorced?"

"Still in Texas. They were never married. They met in college and I was what Mom calls a 'surprise.'"

"So why didn't they get married?" Megan waits for an answer, but I *really* don't want to get into it right now.

Fortunately at that moment we hear clapping and cheering from the cafeteria entrance and turn to see what's happening. The football players are making their grand entrance, with Quince leading the way, while the students shout their approval.

Quince is all cleaned up from the game, wearing khaki shorts and a white golf shirt, his hair still wet from his shower. My heart starts pounding as I watch him walk in with his teammates. He smiles modestly at all his adoring classmates, even though he's the star of the night and has every right to boast.

As I watch Quince accept congratulations from his fellow students, I get that creepy feeling inside me again. It's hard to explain, but it's the difference between an intense gut reaction and the flood of random information I get just from walking through the mall. I've learned it's best not to ignore my psychic instincts, but I try to push it away anyway, hoping for once I'm wrong.

"Do you think we could get close enough to talk to Quince?" I ask Megan.

"We can try," she says. We begin pushing our way through the crowd and eventually she gets close enough to call out to him.

"Hey, Quince, great game!" Megan shouts as she motions him over.

Confessions of a Teenage Psychic

Quince spots her and breaks ranks with his teammates to come over to us.

"Quince, do you remember Caryn?" Megan asks.

"Sure," he says, smiling at me. "From Peterson's the other day, right?"

I feel my palms get sweaty. "That's right."

My heart begins to beat very fast. I guess that's what people mean by calling someone a "heartthrob." I so want to ask him to dance, but I don't know what the protocol is at this school—if girls ever ask guys to dance or if they just have to wait to be invited.

"Would you like to dance, Caryn?"

It was like he could read *my* mind. My heart is pounding wildly. I nod and follow him out onto the dance floor. It's the Electric Slide, so technically no one really needs a partner, but just standing next to Quince makes my pulse race. Soon nearly everyone at the dance is out on the floor, enjoying the fun.

The song ends way too soon, followed by a slow song. Quince gingerly puts his arm around me, keeping a polite distance as he lightly holds my waist. I'm just beginning to enjoy *really* dancing with him, when I hear an irritated voice behind us.

"May I cut in?" says Kensi, her hands on her hips.

She's still in her cheerleading outfit and is surrounded by the other varsity cheerleaders, who must have come in after the football players when I was too distracted with Quince to notice. The question she oh-so-politely asks is just a formality, because she pulls Quince toward her, throws her arms around his neck, and begins swaying to the music.

"Do you mind?" Quince asks me over the top of her head.

Yes I mind! But I shake my head and back away.

I look around the room realizing I've abandoned my friends in the heat of the moment. I finally see Megan dancing with Jeremy Harper, a cute sophomore boy I recognize from my English class. He's a little taller than Megan, his brown hair tied back in a short ponytail, and he's wearing pressed jeans with a tucked-in Colts T-shirt. Emma is dancing *this*close with Kevin, who now has on a clean Rosslyn jersey with black jeans, and Ashleigh is still with the same tall, redheaded senior. I stand there alone in the middle of the crowded dance floor feeling like a total outcast.

I try to act cool as I walk over to the drink table again, wondering how many sodas I can consume before I explode, and pretend to busy myself with making my selection. I feel a tap on my shoulder and turn around to look down on a dorky little freshman.

"Hi, I'm Harris," he says, offering his hand to shake.

"Caryn," I answer, cautiously shaking his hand.

"Would you like to dance?"

Okay, I have some quick decision-making to do. What would be worse for my image? Dance with a freshman who's half-a-head shorter than me, or stand here alone like a dork? I suck in my breath and opt for the dance.

And you have to hand it to the little guy—he has guts, asking an upperclassman to dance with him. Despite his nerdy appearance, I begin to get good vibes about Harris. A picture flashes through my mind, showing me he'll improve in a couple of years—and he does have sort of a cute little crooked smile. The DJ is playing a rap number that doesn't require me to actually stand close to Harris who, it turns out, definitely has some moves, so I hope my reputation won't be too tarnished. I attempt to look cool by balancing the soda in one hand while faking steps on the dance floor, pretending all the while that Harris is my number one choice of a dance partner.

And wouldn't you know it? When the song ends, Harris and I stop right next to Quince and Kensi.

"Hi again," I say as cheerfully as I can.

"Hi, yourself," responds Quince with a smile.

Kensi shoots me a condescending look and gives Harris a sneer. "You two look so cute," she snarks.

I can feel my face turning beet red. Then she turns back to Quince and says loudly enough for my benefit, "Are you ready to go yet, babe? My folks have that big after-party set to start at eleven."

"Oh, yeah, sure." Quince shrugs and gives me a look that says, "What can I do?"

Panic strikes me. NO! They can't leave! This time it isn't pure jealousy on my part, it's a twisting pain in my stomach telling me that if Quince gets in the car with Kensi something bad is going to happen to him.

I grab his arm. "Do you have to leave NOW?" I realize I sound ridiculous, but I don't care. I'm a girl on a mission.

I must have freaked him out or something, though, because he pulls his arm away and my soda spills all over his shirt.

"Geez! What is the matter with you?" Quince shouts as he tries to wipe the dark soda off his clean, white shirt.

"You clumsy idiot!" Kensi yells at me. "Caryn Alderson, you're a loser! Come on, Quince, let's get out of here. My friends are waiting."

"Quince, I'm so sorry. Let me get you a towel or something," I beg, trying to stall for time.

My heart sinks as he looks at me in sheer disgust, but I guess at the same time he must be realizing that the shirt is a mess.

Through gritted teeth, Quince says to Kensi, "You go on and I'll meet you there. I've gotta go change my shirt."

I wish I was invisible right now, but even though he's angry with me, I hope again that he doesn't get in the car with her. They quickly leave the dance floor, Quince dabbing at his soiled shirt. Without giving poor Harris another thought, I go find Megan.

"Megan," I say when I finally locate her in the crowd. "I just did the stupidest thing."

I tell her about the spilled soda. "Come outside with me. I've got to make sure Quince doesn't get into Kensi's car."

"What? Why?" Megan looks skeptical. "First you spill soda on him, now you want to stop him from going with Kensi? Are you jealous of her?"

I don't answer, but this time *she* follows *me* outside to the parking lot, just in time to see Kensi's yellow VW pull onto the busy street in front of the school.

Kensi is driving with her cell phone pressed to her ear, with two of her cheerleader buddies in the backseat, and Salissa Pringle in the front passenger seat where I guess Quince would've been sitting. Kensi hits the gas hard and speeds off down the street going way too fast. Dad always says no one should drive when they're angry, because that's when they do stupid stuff.

I look around and see Quince walking along the sidewalk next to the street, talking on his cell phone.

He may be mad at me, but at least he's not in her car.

CRASH! Everyone turns to look in the direction of the sound. I swallow hard when I realize Kensi's car has been hit broadside by an SUV because she ran the red light. There is a frozen moment of shock, then Quince runs into the street.

"Ohmigod! Did you see that?" Megan screams.

People are running everywhere, trying to get a

look at the accident and its victims, offer help, whatever. Megan pulls out her cell phone and dials 9-1-1. Quince is pulling on the driver's side door, but it must be stuck. The two girls in the backseat are screaming, but I've got to hope that if they can yell they're okay. The man driving the SUV has gotten out of his car looking dazed, but he isn't hurt and neither is his car.

Finally we hear sirens in the distance.

I'm shaking all over and tears are coming to my eyes. I can't believe I didn't see the danger to Kensi ahead of time too. To my immense relief, Kensi is finally able to get her door open and stumble out of the car. I don't like the girl, but I don't wish her any harm. She hugs Quince and he walks her around to the passenger side where the door is completely bashed in. Salissa doesn't look too good, blood everywhere, but I hear her muttering something, so at least she's conscious.

"Wow! If that had been Quince riding shotgun..." Megan doesn't finish the sentence. She turns to face me. "What was that you said about keeping Quince from getting into Kensi's car?"

I can't find the words to answer her. I just thank the Universe that no one was killed or seriously injured in the accident. We wait while the paramedics pry the door open, place Salissa onto a stretcher and ease her into the ambulance. Lights and sirens go screaming down the street, and the crowd finally begins to disperse. I say a silent prayer for Salissa's recovery and start walking home.

****

Mom and I live in a two-bedroom apartment about three blocks north of our store, which makes it about six blocks from school. All the lights are off when I let myself in, except Mom has thoughtfully turned on the lamp next to my bed. I tiptoe across the hall and peek into her room, but she's fast asleep. I sigh, wanting to tell her what's happened, but I decide it'll keep till morning. Still, I wish I had someone to talk to right now.

I can't even e-mail anyone. My mother says she doesn't believe in high-tech stuff. Well, okay she believes in it, she just doesn't want it in our house. She *claims* all those electronics suck the energy out of the room, but I know it's really because that stuff costs a lot of money. Neither of us has a cell phone, but we do have a landline with an answering machine. We have a microwave, because it came with the apartment, but there's no computer so I have to either use one at school or go to the public library. And we have one old TV hooked up to the cable line that came with the apartment, but no DVD player. Mom says it's important for both of us to be in touch with the Universe, and we can't do that if something is beeping or ringing 24/7. I let her pretend her reasons are spiritual and not financial.

So at a time when most kids would send an e-mail or text someone about what just happened, I'm faced with silence. I flop down on my bed and try to think my way through all the evening's events on my own, but I can't focus. Something is distracting me. I look over at the nightstand next to my bed and see a letter propped up against the lamp, addressed to me. It's from my dad!

I eagerly rip open the envelope and begin reading.

Dear Care Bear:

Things are pretty busy here, but I miss you and hope you are doing well up there in the frozen north. (Ha ha! Just my little joke!) I'm now working the day shift at the country club, earning good tips from the "ladies who lunch," so I have my nights free for acting gigs. I just got a small part at an Equity theatre in downtown Houston, and I'm doing all kinds of radio voice-over spots, which helps pay the bills. It's a good thing Michael has a real job and is willing to support me in my dream, because I'd never make it on my own as a waiter/actor.

We both hope you're making new friends and feeling more at home in Indianapolis. Your room here with us is always ready for you, should you want to come for a visit. Know that I love you and wish you well.

Love, Dad

Tears come to my eyes as I read and reread the letter. Michael teaches high school biology and my dad's acting career is just starting to take off, so they won't be able to come up here for a visit any time soon, if at all. They've made a good life for themselves in Houston despite being total opposites of each other—Michael so practical and Dad so creative.

I carefully fold up my father's letter and put it back in its envelope. Since I can't send e-mail anyway, I don't think there's anything more special than getting snail mail with my name on it and an old-fashioned stamp on the outside. I set the letter on my nightstand and, promising myself I'll write him back tomorrow, turn off the light and go to sleep.

Chapter 4
Trick or Treat

Kensi's car accident was all anyone at school could talk about that next week. The two cheerleaders in the backseat had been wearing their seat belts, so they weren't seriously hurt, but they were seriously scared. Kensington had a concussion and some bruises, but basically she was okay. Salissa was the one hurt the worst, suffering a broken leg and collarbone, but she came back to school on crutches three weeks later to a hero's welcome.

As for Quince, he was pretty shaken up. If he'd been in that car his football season and maybe his scholarship chances would be over. I was sure everyone was still thinking I was a big dork for spilling that soda on him, but my clumsiness was seen as a lucky coincidence. All the kids were saying that if I hadn't doused poor Quince...well, you get the idea.

Now I'm really starting to like it at Rosslyn. Most of all I'm in awe of the way the seasons actually change in Indiana. In Texas, it's just warm all the time, but in mid-October here, the air is cool and the leaves are changing into gorgeous shades of red, yellow, and brown. Halloween is coming, and I really can see the frost on the pumpkin, like the poem says. I'm thrilled at the sight of my breath in the cool air, and revel in the fact that I need to wear a light jacket to school.

"What are you doing for Halloween next weekend?" Megan asks me after school, a couple of weeks after homecoming.

"Nothing that I know of." I'm searching my increasingly cluttered and messy locker for my English book. "What'd you have in mind?"

I find my book and yank it out, knocking two other books onto the floor along with it, narrowly missing Megan's toes.

"Oh, sorry." It seems I'm doomed to be clumsy.

Megan, when she's got something on her mind, doesn't pay attention to little things like tumbling books, although she does pull her feet out of the line of fire.

"The PTA is having a carnival in the school parking lot Saturday afternoon. It's a fundraiser, but it should be lots of fun and everyone's going to be there. My mom got roped into taking tickets at the gate, so she's making me run one of the booths. Wanna help?" Megan's eyes are all lit up with excitement.

I think about it for a minute. Running a dunking booth or apple-bobbing contest doesn't sound too bad.

"What would I be doing?"

Megan now looks embarrassed, and I don't think that's a good sign. "Well, really..." she begins, and then hesitates.

Megan isn't meeting my eyes, which is setting off alarm bells in my head. *Oh, no, she wants me to do something really stupid, like be the bearded lady.*

"We need someone to be Madame Wilhelmina. She's the fortuneteller. Would you mind?"

I'm leaning down to pick my books up off the floor and the shock of that question causes me to trip and land on top of them.

"Ouch!" I say.

"Are you okay?" Megan asks as she helps me up.

The look on her face says she thinks I'm the biggest klutz in school, and frankly I'm starting to agree. As I get to my feet and attempt to compose myself, I realize I need to do some fast talking to get out of this one.

"Fortuneteller?" *I mean, really.* "Why ME?"

"I just think you'd be good at it," she says with a shrug. "You kinda look the part anyway, what with that long dark hair and green stripe in it. All you need is a flowing caftan with a turban and you're set."

"Megan!" Visions of me dressed like some crazy gypsy lady reading a crystal ball pop into my head and make me cringe. "The fortuneteller? Couldn't I be in charge of the dunking booth or something?"

"All the other booths are covered, but no one wanted to do this one."

I wonder why. Duh.

"So can you do it?"

Okay, this might just be some weird coincidence, but Mom always says there are no such things as coincidences, that things happen for a reason. I'm really confused, so I stall for time.

"I need to talk to my mother about this, but I'll let you know."

I gather my books and jacket and hurry out the door. I hope Megan doesn't think I'm rude, but this is a pretty uncomfortable spot to be in.

Fortuneteller? No way. I might as well announce to the world that I'm a psychic freak and be done with it.

I walk down the sidewalk outside of school, stop at the intersection and push the Walk button. I need to talk to Mom and get her advice on how to gracefully decline this offer without alienating Megan. It's chilly outside and I realize in my rush to get out of the building that I haven't even put my jacket on, so I hurriedly slip into it. The light is taking forever to change, and my only thought is to get to Mom's store and plead for help.

I guess I'm pretty distracted with both the jacket and the stoplight when out of the corner of my eye I catch a glimpse of a good-looking young man in an olive-drab T-shirt standing on the street corner. He looks familiar, although I'm certain we've never met. He waves at me and I half-heartedly wave back. I tap my foot, impatient for the light to change.

You know how you can just feel it when someone is staring at you? Well, I sneak a look again and sure enough the guy is still there, grinning at me, like we're long-lost best friends or something.

Who is that guy? Do I know him?

I start getting goose bumps all over. Uncle Omar! No way, it couldn't be! Uncle Omar?

I swallow hard, blink, look again, but this time he isn't there. Did I imagine it? I look up and down the street, behind me, and back again where I just saw him, thinking whoever the guy is must still be close by, but he's gone. No one could disappear that quickly, but there has to be a logical explanation. The light finally turns to Walk and I'm so freaked out I run all the way to Mom's store, arriving breathless and stuttering.

"Caryn, what's wrong?" Mom is busy reorganizing some sale items on a shelf near the front window, pushing the hard-to-sell items forward and arranging them in an attractive display. She looks up in alarm as I hurry in and shut the door so hard the bells jangle wildly. "You look as if you've seen a ghost."

"I...I..." My heart is beating so fast I could be getting a great cardio workout if I weren't standing still.

"Calm down, Caryn. Take a deep breath."

I try, but it doesn't help. "I saw Uncle Omar!" I finally sputter.

Mom looks way too calm. "Caryn, that's nonsense. Omar is dead."

"I *know* he's dead, but I swear I just saw him. Just now—on the street corner. He waved at me!" I'm jumping up and down, hugging myself with nervous jitters.

"Caryn, you must be mistaken. Your Uncle Omar died before you were born. You never met him."

"I've seen pictures! And I know what I just saw! It was Uncle Omar!"

I desperately need for my mother to believe me, or at least to convince me for sure that I'm hallucinating.

Omar Alderson was my mother's much older half-brother. She was just a little girl when he enlisted in the Army during the Vietnam War, and then he died in combat six months later when he stepped on a land mine. He was only twenty years old. There were lots of pictures of him in photo albums that I looked at as a little kid. He was a tall blond with brooding good looks, who resembled Mom a little. My favorite picture is the one Mom keeps in her bedroom—Uncle Omar grinning into the camera as one of his buddies snapped a photo just before they shipped out. He's wearing Army fatigues and a green T-shirt, with his dog tags prominently displayed on a chain around his neck.

"MOM!" I gasp as the realization hits me full force. "It was him, just like in that picture on your dresser!"

"Omar?" Mom looks perplexed as she tries to make sense of what I'm saying. "But he's been dead for years. How can you have seen him today?"

I don't know. My long-dead uncle? It's just my imagination. It has to be. Or is it?

"Now I'm seeing DEAD people? What's wrong with me?" I cover my face with my hands like I'm really going to be able to shut out the visions.

Mom pulls my hands away from my face.

"There's nothing wrong with you. But I can't understand..." Her voice trails off as she drops my hands and stands lost in thought. "Is it possible you really did see him?"

"If I did, I'm being haunted!" I wail, throwing my hands in the air.

"I don't think 'haunted' is the right word. Did he talk to you?"

"Ohmigod, are you crazy, Mom? It's bad enough I'm seeing ghosts, but *please* tell me I can't talk to them!"

"I don't know, Caryn. You're pretty psychic. But this is definitely a new development." Mom gives my shoulders a squeeze.

"Am I gonna be hounded by ghosts like that lady in the TV show? You might as well commit me to the loony bin right now, because everyone at school will think I'm nuts! *I* think I'm nuts!" I bury my head on her shoulder, shaking, as tears come to my eyes.

"Caryn, I don't think—" she starts, but just then the bells over the door jingle.

Mom releases me and I turn away, hurriedly trying to wipe away the tears as Megan and her mother walk into the store.

"May I help you?" Mom stands up straight, smoothes her work apron and is immediately back in store-owner mode.

I remember she hasn't met them yet.

I swallow hard, making sure I don't sound like I'm still blubbering, and force myself to smile.

"Mom, this is my friend Megan Benedict from school, and her mother Ms. Benedict who teaches at Rosslyn High." I motion toward Mom. "This is my mom, Bethany Alderson."

"Pleased to meet you, Ms. Benedict," my mother says, offering her hand.

"Please, call me Susan." She and Mom shake hands.

Mom smiles at her. "I'd be glad to show you around the store. Is there something in particular you're looking for?"

Megan has already wandered off, finding her way to the display case toward the back of the store.

"No, thank you," Ms. Benedict says. "I just came to speak to you about the Halloween Carnival next Saturday. Caryn, did you get a chance to talk to your mother about it?"

I clear my throat, hoping Mom will get my hint. "No, not yet," I mutter. I try conveying a *NO!* look to Mom, but she doesn't pick up on it.

"The school PTA is having a fundraiser and we need help staffing some of the booths. Megan thought Caryn would be a good choice for the fortunetelling booth." Ms. Benedict shifts her large overstuffed leather handbag, which probably doubles as a briefcase, to her other shoulder. She's tall, slender, mid-forties, and with such dark brown hair I wonder how Megan turned out blonde.

Mom gets an amused look on her face but says nothing, which I guess Ms. Benedict mistakes for hesitancy.

"Of course, the PTA would provide all the costuming and props," Ms. Benedict is quick to add.

Mom has to turn aside to keep Ms. Benedict from seeing her snicker. In spite of myself, I'm almost laughing too.

"Caryn," Mom says with that telling smirk still on her face. "Is this something you'd like to do?" I have to admire her restraint.

I look from Mom to Ms. Benedict and realize I'm stuck. "Sure," I say reluctantly. "I guess. What would I have to do?"

"Oh, it's all just for fun," Ms. Benedict reassures us. "All you need to do is show up and the carnival committee will take care of the rest."

"Hey, Mom, look at this!" Megan calls from

across the room. "Aren't these necklaces gorgeous?"

She's pointing to the crystals in the glass display case. For the first time, Ms. Benedict looks around the store and realizes this is not your regular type of bookstore.

"Interesting place you have here," she says politely. Then it dawns on her and she blushes. "Oh, you must find it amusing, me asking Caryn to play the part of the fortuneteller. I suppose you already have an interest in..." She pauses, still taking it all in. "I mean crystal balls and such. I hope you didn't think..."

"No, Susan, of course not. You haven't been in here before, so how could you know?" Mom has a really cool way of putting people at ease.

"Have you been in this sort of business long?" Susan asks, carefully sniffing an aroma-therapy candle.

Mom gives her a friendly smile. "My business partner and I moved our store here from Houston just last month. Business has been good so far."

Ms. Benedict nods and smiles as she continues to look around. She puts down the candle and picks up a music box and I get a sudden visual of her at an elementary school art fair, Megan on stage accepting first prize, Ms. Benedict applauding proudly in the audience. I don't see Mr. Benedict anywhere. I snap out of my head when she puts the music box back on the shelf and looks around for Megan.

"Well, I'm sure Caryn will be an outstanding Madame Wilhelmina." Ms. Benedict turns to where her daughter is still browsing and calls out, "Come on, Megan, we've got to go home and let the dog out."

Ms. Benedict opens the door. "Nice meeting you, Bethany."

"But, Mom, can't I buy..." Megan begins, but her mother gives her a stern look so she shrugs and waves goodbye to me as her mother hustles her out of the store.

After they're gone, I turn back to Mom. "How am I supposed to pull this off?"

"Just keep in mind that no one actually expects you to predict futures." Mom pats my shoulder.

"But what if I accidentally say something that's really gonna happen?"

"Then they'll think it's a lucky guess." Mom smiles at me. "Relax, Caryn. Like Susan said, it's all just for fun. You might even enjoy yourself!"

I roll my eyes and gaze out the window that faces onto the street, lost in thought. Suddenly I do a double-take as I could swear Uncle Omar is strolling by, waving and grinning at me. As I watch in surprise he slowly disappears.

I pull my jacket hoodie over my head, look away, and decide to think about something normal. Pizza. That's pretty normal.

"Hey, Mom, let's order from Jerry's Pizzeria!" I shout as cheerfully as I can.

****

It's Saturday and the weather is perfect for an outdoor carnival in October. It's crowded with lots of kids from school, as well as their parents and younger siblings.

All sorts of booths are set up. The games of chance are all rigged of course, but no one cares because the profits are going to benefit the school. Megan is conducting the cakewalk with great success, especially since all the cakes have been donated by a well-known bakery in town. There's a dunking booth where students are lined up for an opportunity to plunge Principal MacGregor into a water tank. Kensi Marlow has a big handmade sign outside of a tent that reads, "Two kisses for a buck!" Naturally there's a long line of cute boys ready to pay a dollar for the kisses. What they're really getting is chocolate, but they don't know that until after they pay their money and go into the tent where she swears them to silence.

Coach Edgemont and his football players are hustling people with the football toss and an opportunity to win a big stuffed bear. Needless to say, it's set up to be harder than it looks, and even Peyton Manning himself might miss. And there are the usual carnival activities of face painting, apple bobbing, pumpkin carving, and lots of junk food sold for inflated prices.

Then there's my tent, "Madame Wilhelmina, Fortuneteller Extraordinaire." I feel ridiculous enough in the oversized caftan the PTA has provided for me, but I drew the line at wearing a turban. I opt for letting my hair hang loose around my shoulders, accentuating the green stripe that has yet to fade after all these months.

Yeah, it's every bit as bad as I imagined. I'm seated in a folding chair next to a card table covered with a gypsy-style fringed cloth, with a white plastic folding chair opposite me for my clients. For props I have a crystal ball and some worn-out tarot cards, but I can't decide if it would look better if I pretend to use them or just let them lay on the table for effect.

Don't take this so seriously. It's for a good cause.

People are paying five dollars each for my predictions, a higher price than any of the other booths, so I feel obligated to play my part well. My first customer, Emma Cartwright, waltzes in as butterflies dance in my stomach.

"Hi, Caryn. Oh, I mean Madame Wilhelmina," she says with a giggle. She takes the seat across from me and stretches her right palm on the table in front of me. "What's my fortune?"

"Madame Wilhelmina doesn't read palms," I say in a deep voice. "She only gazes into the future."

At that I pretend to look into the crystal ball.

What can I tell her that won't give too much away about my real abilities?

"What do you see?" She peers into the crystal ball like there's really something in there.

"Um," I hesitate.

Okay, Caryn, just go for it. "You're going to attend a dance with a young man, a football player." There. That's not so hard.

Emma looks up at me, beaming. "Wow! Kevin's going to ask me to the Christmas dance?"

"This is what Madame Wilhelmina sees," I reply, trying to stay in character. *And yes, he's going to ask you.* I smile to myself because in my mind I can see her in a slow-dance with Kevin, swaying in time to the lyrics, "Chestnuts roasting on an open fire..."

Emma happily dances out of the tent and in comes my next customer, Harris Rutherford. How ridiculous could I look in front of a freshman? I begin to relax, realizing I can pull this gig off and maybe even have some fun with it.

"I want to know if Angie Morrison's ever gonna go out with me."

I feel bad for him, but nope. She's a very popular freshman who thinks dorky Harris is far beneath her. Still, I kinda like the kid and don't want to hurt his feelings.

"Madame Wilhelmina sees great success for your future in the academic realm, but recommends you postpone romance while you concentrate on making straight As."

I can tell he's disappointed, but he finally grins, shrugs, shakes hands with me and gets up to leave.

I have a long line of customers for the rest of the afternoon, as word spreads that I'm the best Madame Wilhelmina the carnival has ever had. My uneasiness disappears as I confidently make predictions that I know are true but could easily be passed off as lucky guesses, like my mom said. Late in the day I look up in surprise as Megan walks in.

"All the cakes are sold out," she explains. "So I wanted to see what all the fuss is about. Everyone says you're really good. So what's my prediction?"

I pull back, think for a minute, hesitate. She's tapping her foot impatiently, waiting for me to read her outstretched palm. I ignore her hand and pretend to look at the tarot cards laid out in front of me. What can I tell her that's true but not too outlandish?

Oh, of course! "You are going to get new shoes," I say in my fortuneteller voice. "Soon."

"That's it?" she asks incredulously. "Shoes?"

"Madame Wilhelmina sees new shoes in your immediate future." I bow my head in fake modesty.

Megan throws up her hands just as Quince walks in.

"Don't waste your money," she tells him as she walks out.

He looks puzzled as Megan flies past him, but then grins and plops himself down in the chair opposite me. "You aren't going to throw a soda on me, are you?" he says.

I'm relieved to see that he's forgiven me for my social gaffe last month, and I determine to give him a good reading to try to make up for it.

"Madame Wilhelmina is above pranks!" I say, back in character.

I'm not sure my psychic abilities will stay on track as I stare into Quince's sparkling blue eyes, but I guess it doesn't matter anyway. No one at the carnival is taking me seriously. Quince looks at me intently and I feel sure he's going to ask me about his love life, a question I don't want to answer because I still don't get what he sees in Kensi.

"Tell me about my future," he says with a grin. Well, at least he didn't ask about *her*.

I pretend to gaze into the crystal ball, trying to

decide whether to tell him about school or athletics—anything but his relationship with Kensi. As usual, whenever Quince is in the vicinity, my pulse starts to race. I try to look calm, even if I don't feel it.

I look up from the crystal ball, smile at Quince, and open my mouth to speak. To my shock, there's a kindly looking gentleman standing behind him, even though I didn't hear anyone else come in. My mouth drops open. Quince just sits there expectantly while I stare at the man over his shoulder.

"Well? What great things do you see for me?" Quince is getting impatient and begins drumming his fingers on the table and I realize he doesn't see anyone else in the tent.

The man is in his 60s with thinning grey hair, thick glasses, and is wearing an old-fashioned yellow cardigan sweater. I blink, thinking my eyes are playing tricks on me, look back into the crystal ball and lift my eyes again, but the old man is still here. I can even smell the smoke from the pipe he takes out of his mouth before he speaks to me.

"Tell him his mother's going to be okay, that the doctors will get her diabetes under control." His voice sounds kind and full of concern.

I look from the man back to Quince, who obviously doesn't see or hear a thing.

"Hello-o-o? Still waiting," Quince says.

"You…you will be a great…athlete," I stammer.

"Duh. Tell me something I don't know." Quince fakes a big yawn.

"Go ahead, tell him," urges the gentleman.

I bend my head over the crystal ball and mutter under my breath, "I can't. He'll think I'm nuts."

"What did you say?" Quince asks.

"I said I can't see anything else," I answer in my regular voice.

"That's lame. I thought you were supposed to be

good at this."

"Caryn, I'm Quince's Grandpa Adams. I know him and I know he needs to hear this," my unusual visitor insists.

How the heck does he know my name? His intent stare sends a chill down my spine and I pull the caftan tighter around me.

"Okay," I finally whisper, just wishing him gone. I draw a deep breath and look up at Quince. "Your mother has been sick but she's going to be okay. I mean her diabetes."

Quince stares at me in stunned silence, but after what seems like an eternity he stammers, "How...how did you know that she has diabetes? Who told you that?"

"I don't know," I mumble, embarrassed. How can I tell him it was his dead grandfather?

"Who?" Now he's pounding the table, anger creeping into his voice.

"I...I'm sorry, I just..." That's when I notice Quince's grandfather is gone. The smell of pipe tobacco has also vanished and suddenly I feel overheated instead of cold. I blush.

"That's NOT funny!" Quince says, his face reddening. "Someone told you so you could look good doing this stupid fortunetelling thing. You're either really mean or you're some kind of freak!"

He stands up so fast that he knocks the chair over, and storms out of the tent.

I sit there in shock. What just happened? What possessed me to say something like that? "Possessed" is the operative word here. Was Quince's Grandpa Adams ever really here? I have no idea, and no one to blame but myself.

I decide I've had enough of Madame Wilhelmina. I want to go out and try to enjoy the rest of the carnival as Caryn, in my regular, teenage clothes. I also want to apologize to Quince if I can find him—

like that will do any good. Hopefully I'll be able to salvage some of my reputation if I go back to being just a regular fifteen-year-old girl.

And normal fifteen-year-old girls don't predict the future or talk to the dead.

Chapter 5
Turkeys and True Confessions

It's a hot summer day and I'm walking on a beautiful beach in Galveston, Texas. I kick the sand with my bare toes as I stroll along and check for seashells, enjoying the warmth of the bright sunshine on my face. I look over in the distance, cup my hand over my eyes to block the glare, and see Quince running toward me on the beach...

"Caryn, we have to go to the store!"

"Huh?" *There's no store on the beach.*

"Caryn, did you hear me?"

I moan and pull the covers over my head. Just as I start drifting back to that romantic walk in the sand, something shakes the bed. I turn over onto my back and crack open one eye to see my mother standing over me.

"Caryn, are you awake? We've got to get to the store."

"It's too early to go shopping," I mumble.

"No, *our* store," Mom says, throwing the covers off me.

"It's Sunday. Can't I sleep in for once?" I groan, pulling the pillow over my head, hoping to get back to that Galveston beach.

"No. We need to do inventory while the shop is closed. We have to get ready for the Christmas shopping rush." Mom hesitates and then asks, "There will be a Christmas shopping rush at our store, right?"

"Yes," I tell her. "But it won't start till after Thanksgiving, so let me sleep."

"Well, then we need to get busy. Get up because Sybil will be here in half an hour to pick us up." Mom opens the window blinds, letting in the early morning sunlight.

"Why didn't you tell me this last night?" I grouse as I squint in the bright light. "And why is Sybil picking us up?"

"It's cold outside, hon, and my car won't start—again. So dress warmly."

"I WAS warm!" How I wish I really was on that beach.

****

There's been a light frost on this mid-November Sunday morning, and being from south Texas, all I own is a denim jacket and a gray hooded sweatshirt, neither of which is going to keep me very warm. It never gets really cold in Houston, and I arrived in Indiana two months ago with plenty of spring- and summer-wear but nothing in the way of winter clothing. Mom has promised to take me to the consignment store and buy me a winter coat, and I figure I'll need some gloves and a hat as well, but today I'll have to make do with what I've got.

The crisp autumn weather of October was a pleasure, but now serious winter is setting in and I'm just plain cold. Being rudely awakened on a Sunday morning hasn't improved my mood either. I grudgingly get up and put on as many clothes as I can. Sybil picks us up and drives us the three blocks to the shop, car heater turned up full blast.

Mom opens the door to Sybil and Starshine's New Age Bookstore but keeps the Closed sign turned to the outside. She flips on the lights, rubs her hands together, and goes to check the thermostat. I wrap my arms tightly around myself and hop up and down, trying to stay warm until the heat kicks on.

Sybil waltzes into the store wrapped in an oversized wool shawl, oblivious to the chill. She immediately heads to the back storeroom, calling out, "Anyone for espresso?"

"Just hot tea for us, Sybil," Mom answers. "Caryn, can you take an inventory of the books?" Mom hands me a clipboard with a printed list of all the books we sell. "Just write down next to each title how many copies we have of each, or make note if we're sold out. Sybil and I will be in the storeroom counting boxes of candles."

"It's still cold in here."

Mom ignores my whining as she heads to the back to join Sybil. I wonder how soon that tea will be ready so I can get warmed up.

"Caryn, dear, I appreciate your help," Sybil calls in a cheery voice, "and don't forget—Christmas shopping is a huge source of revenue!"

Don't I know it. Mom has impressed upon me the fact that if the store doesn't show a profit by the end of the first year, we're closing up and moving back to Houston. Right now that doesn't sound like a bad idea. I shiver, exhale, and realize I can see my breath. Amazing! That never happens in Texas. Still, the heat hasn't come up in the store yet, so I go over to have another look at the thermostat. It's set at sixty-five, but for some reason the actual temperature is hovering around fifty.

"Mom! You need to call the landlord. The heater isn't working." I fiddle with the On/Off switch. "And the lights are flickering too," I call out, as I notice them dimming and brightening several times.

"The heat works just fine," a male voice says. My heart jumps into my throat and I flip around, thinking we have an intruder. My gaze darts all around the store looking for anyone, anything to explain what I thought I heard. I shiver again, realizing I'm alone.

"And so do the lights," the voice adds.

A chill runs down my spine. I feel like I've

stepped into the kind of horror movie where the stupid heroine just stands there pleading with the ax murderer not to hurt her instead of getting the heck out of there.

"Who's there?" I do a 360-degree turn and still see no one.

I feel the hairs on the back of my neck rise. Silence. I try the light switch again, but the lights just keep flickering and finally go off completely. I open my mouth to scream for my mother but, just like in all good horror flicks, no sound comes out. I'm frozen to the spot in fear.

Just when I'm sure I'm going to be the lead story on the six o'clock news, I see Uncle Omar across the room, leaning on the bookshelves, his arms crossed in front of him.

"Ohmigod, I'm seeing ghosts again!" I shriek. I blink hard trying to get rid of the apparition.

"Well, I'm not really a ghost, I'm a spirit, but materializing sucks energy out of the air," he says with a grin.

I stare in disbelief. "I...I...uh..."

"Don't worry, I won't slime you," he says, laughing.

I could almost laugh with him if I weren't so freaked out. Just when I'd chalked up my last sighting of him to stress, or exhaustion, or hormones, or whatever, here he is again. Now all my rationalizations go out the window as I look into the seemingly solid face of my mother's dead brother. And he *is* solid—I can't see through him or anything. It's almost like, if I'd dared to reach out, I'd touch skin. At that thought, I wrap my jacket tightly around myself and hold on for dear life.

"What do you want? Why are you haunting me?" The voice I'd intended to sound fierce comes out in a squeak.

"I want your attention."

"You got it." I'm shivering, but I don't know if it's from cold or fear.

"Don't look so scared, Caryn. I've come to give you a message." His voice sounds really kind, oddly enough, considering I'm talking to...whatever.

"From the Great Beyond?"

He shrugs. "Sure. What'd ya think? I'm bringing messages from Yahoo?"

Wouldn't you know my dead uncle would have the Alderson offbeat sense of humor?

Uncle Omar unfolds his arms and takes a ghostly step toward me. "Seriously, Caryn, here's the thing. You've got a gift and you need to start using it."

I instinctively back up. "But I don't want the gift!" I say. "I just wanna be normal."

He stops and puts his hands on his hips, like any exasperated grownup might do. "So be normal. You just have to let go of your fears."

Like it's that easy. I'm still backing up, but now I've bumped into the cash register and realize I can't go any farther. I try to compose myself and look him in the face, but I'm still quaking. "The only thing I'm scared of is talking to dead people!"

Uncle Omar winks at me. "Aw, come on. Am I that bad? I'm just here to help you."

"I don't want any help!" I close my eyes, hoping he'll be gone when I open them. He's not.

"Too bad, 'cause you're stuck with me. Orders, you know." Uncle Omar grins and points up.

Naturally I look up too, but all I see is an old light fixture that needs dusting.

I huff out a sigh. "But it's completely unnerving every time I see someone who's not really there!" I'm arguing with the spirit of my dead uncle like it's the most common thing in the world.

This is nuts! Cue the Twilight Zone *music!*

"You aren't crazy," he says, as if he can read my

mind. "Look at it this way—some people sing or act or play piano. That's their talent. Your talent is you see spirits, and you know things."

As if it's that simple. "Kids think I'm a freak," I grumble. "Like Quince. He won't even speak to me anymore."

"He will, don't worry. Just be yourself, and your friends will accept you."

"But..." I start to say, and then he's gone.

Just like that I'm alone again. I blink, rub my eyes, and look around the store—everything is back to normal. The lights have stopped flickering and suddenly the room is perfectly warm.

"MOM! SYBIL!"

They both come running out of the storeroom. "What's the matter?" my mother asks, her eyes wide.

"Mom! Didn't you see him? He was standing right there!" I point to the bookshelf where moments before I'd been talking to a ghost.

"Who, Caryn?" She walks over to the door and checks to make sure it's still locked. "No one's here but the three of us."

"Uncle Omar!" I insist. "He was here! Talking to me!"

My mother looks a lot less surprised than I would've liked. "Omar? Here? You spoke to him?" How can she be so calm?

"I had a conversation with a ghost, Mom! You're acting like it's nothing!"

"No, it's not *nothing*, but I really don't know what you want me to say." Mom wraps me in her arms, making me feel safe again. "You're shaking," she whispers. "Come sit down."

I allow myself to be led to a chair and collapse into it, relieved that the worst is over.

"Our little psychic medium," coos Sybil. "Bethany, your little girl here is growing into her powers."

I roll my eyes. "The next thing I know, you'll be trying to send me off to Hogwarts!"

They just aren't taking this seriously. I stand up, grab the clipboard, and stomp over to the bookshelves to start the inventory, shedding my sweatshirt as I go. Suddenly it's very warm in the store.

****

A couple of hours later, Mom comes out of the storeroom and says, "I've had enough tea. Caryn, would you mind making a Peterson's run? Sybil? Do you want anything from Peterson's?"

Sybil calls back, "Well, I've got to watch my girlish figure, but bring me a sticky bun and a latte."

I put my sweatshirt back on, pocketing the money Mom gives me, and slip out the front door headed around the block to Peterson's. It's now about noon and the sun has come out, warming the air considerably, but it still isn't what I'd call balmy. People are out and about in Rosslyn Village—parents with babies in strollers, couples arm-in-arm, storekeepers sweeping walkways. Everyone is taking in the brisk fresh air or just enjoying the sunshine. I smile and breathe in the autumn crispness.

Everything is perfectly normal.

But it isn't normal. I shudder and try to forget my encounter with Uncle Omar as I walk quickly into Peterson's Coffee Emporium.

It's crowded inside, nearly every table filled, the perfect weather for hot coffee. I walk up to the counter and give the barista my order, then because I know she had a fight with her boyfriend this morning and she's in a bad mood, I let my gaze wander around the store, trying to avoid the negative feelings the barista is dispensing with every order.

In a booth in the back a pretty teenage girl is having a heated discussion with the teenage boy who's frowning at her. Barbie and Ken, I dub them. She's a brunette with a sporty ponytail and designer jeans, a white long-sleeved turtleneck, and a pink sweater tied around her shoulders. He has perfectly groomed blond hair, chiseled features, and a golf sweater worn over a stiffly-starched collared shirt.

I try not to pry, but I know they are breaking up due to his wandering eye. I feel like I'm eavesdropping, even though I can't hear a word they're saying. I turn my back on them and pretend to look at the display rack of assorted coffees and teas for sale, still trying to tune out the barista's bad mood and the argument in the corner.

"Hey Caryn!"

I turn to see Megan walking in with a young woman I don't recognize. "Caryn, this is my sister Caroline."

Caroline offers her hand. She's about twenty-five and looks like an older version of Megan—petite, slender, strawberry-blonde hair, warm smile. "Nice to meet you, Caryn...?"

"Alderson," I finish for her as I shake her hand.

"Oh, you're the new girl from Texas," Caroline says.

"And you're the ad executive," I answer, then bite my lip. Did Megan tell me that?

Caroline looks a bit surprised, but then smiles and says, "Well, that's a slight exaggeration, but I do work for an ad agency."

"And your other sister—is she sleeping in?" I ask. Naturally both Megan and Caroline look surprised at that question.

Filter your mouth, Caryn! That vision of the piano-playing sister was only in your head.

"When did I..." Megan starts, then shrugs.

"Oh, Allie never gets up before noon on Sundays," Caroline says with a laugh. "Megan, I'm going to go get our coffee."

Confessions of a Teenage Psychic

"Okay." Turning back to me, Megan says, "Caroline and I were out for a walk but we got cold. What are you doing today?"

"Helping my mom with store inventory."

"Yo, Megan Benedict!" Barbie across the room is calling and waving enthusiastically.

"Ohmigod, Annabeth!" squeals Megan.

Barbie/Annabeth jumps out of her chair and runs toward us, hugging Megan like a long-lost friend.

"Annabeth Walton, what are you doing here in Rosslyn Village? Slumming?"

She's breaking up with her boyfriend and didn't want to be seen by any of her school friends.

"Oh, we were just in the area. I was having coffee with Josh." She tilts her head in his direction. Lowering her voice, she adds, "It's not going well."

"What happened? You two seemed so happy," Megan says sympathetically. She glances over at Josh still at the corner table, glowering and sipping his coffee.

At first Annabeth frowns, but then she shakes it off and says, "It's no big deal. It's just so great to see you, Megan. Who's this?"

Megan slaps her forehead. "I'm so rude. This is Caryn Alderson from school. Her mom has a new bookstore in Rosslyn Village. And Caryn, this is Annabeth Walton, a friend from Willowby Prep. That guy over there is Josh Kennedy, but he goes to Belford High School. They're an item."

"Not anymore," I say a little too loudly. I notice the surprised look on Annabeth's face.

"Well, if it isn't Rosslyn High's very own fortuneteller," says a sarcastic voice behind me. I turn around to see Quince and Kevin standing there.

Is everybody in town here today?

Peterson's must be THE place to be on a Sunday morning, because the already-crowded coffee shop is getting busier by the minute. And now Quince is here, and obviously still mad at me.

"Hi," I say, trying to sound casual. "What brings you guys in here?"

"Dude—coffee!" Kevin gives Quince a high-five.

"I just got back from visiting my grandfather's grave with my mom," Quince says, in a more serious tone. "And Kevin came by my house, so..." He shrugs and turns away from me.

Once again I really, *really* wish I'd ignored Grandpa Adams and kept my big mouth shut about Quince's mother, because all I want is to be back in his good graces.

"Who are you and what do you mean by 'fortuneteller'?" Annabeth demands, facing Quince.

Quince and Annabeth glare at one another. Finally he jerks his thumb at me and says, "Caryn here. She thinks she's some kind of psychic."

"Really?" Annabeth turns to face me. "Really?"

I wish I could just melt into the floor or something. Quince hates me and now Annabeth is going to think I'm weird, or crazy, or both.

Megan rolls her eyes. "Quince is just mad because of something Caryn told him at the Halloween Carnival while she was playing the fortuneteller. Quince, get over it! That was weeks ago."

"It was mean." Quince folds his arms and backs away from me.

Suddenly I feel a cold chill, like I'm standing under a vent, which I'm not. I look around trying to find the source of the air blast, like an open door or window or something. Nothing. I shiver, but no one else seems to feel the draft and Megan is even taking off her jacket.

"Tell Quince I liked the flowers he put on my grave this morning," says a disembodied voice in my right ear. I swat at my head as if at a mosquito. "Tell him," urges the voice.

I know that voice. Who…? Oh no! Quince's Grandpa Adams!

"I can't," I say under my breath. I feel like a secret agent talking into a hidden earphone, but the way the other kids are staring at me I know I'm not being cool.

"Can't what?" Quince asks.

"I, uh, can't…stay." How embarrassing, to be caught talking to Quince's dead grandfather—again!

"See?" Quince turns triumphantly to both Megan and Annabeth. "She's weird." He goes off to rejoin Kevin without giving me a backward glance.

I don't know which is worse—the pain of his rejection, or knowing I hurt him with what I blurted out about his mother back in October. But I'm not about to make it worse by telling him what I know about the flowers on his grandfather's grave.

"Order for Alderson!" Perfect timing.

"I gotta go," I say to Megan as I hurry to the counter to pick up my order. Remembering my manners, I turn back around and say, "Nice to meet you Annabeth. Megan, tell your sister it was good to meet her too."

I leave Peterson's as quickly as I can, balancing a box with two cups of coffee, one cup of hot tea, and three sweet rolls.

Just when I think I've made my escape and I'm safely outside in the fresh air again, I feel a tap on my shoulder.

"Seriously, Caryn, can you *really* predict things?" It's Annabeth.

I sigh. Her again.

I readjust the box and try to keep it from spilling. "What I *really* do is make people mad."

Annabeth blocks my path so that I'm forced to listen to her. "But you know stuff, like about me and Josh."

"Lucky guess," I say, wishing she would just get out of my way so I can get back to the shop.

"But I hadn't even met you yet! How did you know?" Her eyes are intent, determined. She's like a dog with a bone.

"Anybody could see you two were breaking up because he cheated on you," I say. In my hurry to get away from her I completely forget she didn't mention that part.

"How did you know *that*? I didn't tell you." Her gaze flickers to the coffee-shop window. "And you weren't close enough to hear what we were saying."

Maybe it's the fact that my sweatshirt is unzipped and I'm getting cold; maybe it's the fact that the expensive designer coffee is getting cold too; maybe it's the fact that I've never seen this girl before, don't go to school with her, and never expect to see her again; or maybe I'm just tired of keeping a filter on my mouth. Maybe it's all of the above, but I sort of snap.

"Yes," I say, louder than necessary. "I'm psychic, okay? And no, nobody told me your boyfriend is a cheat. I just *know* stuff."

As Annabeth's mouth drops open, I hurry off down the street.

****

It's the Wednesday before Thanksgiving and business in the store is pretty slow. That isn't too surprising, though, since most people are making preparations for tomorrow's feast. The big shopping rush always comes the Friday after Thanksgiving. I'm in the store behind the cash register as usual after school, but I have plenty of time to get my homework done since there aren't any customers right now. Mom is in the storeroom doing some bookkeeping and Sybil has already left to spend the long holiday weekend with jet-setting friends in Florida.

I yawn and try to focus on math, always a challenge at best. I get up from the stool behind the counter, stretch my arms over my head and try to shake the sleepiness off. It isn't working, because every time I look at that math book, my mind drifts. So I'm relieved when I hear the bell over the door jingle, announcing a customer.

To my surprise, in walks Annabeth Walton along with two girls I've never seen before. The look on my face must speak volumes.

"Didn't think you'd ever see me again, did you?" Annabeth says, grinning.

"Well, no, I..."

"I called Megan and asked her where this store was, so here I am." She turns to her friends. "See? I told you she'd be here."

The two girls are definitely an odd assortment. One looks like a Megan-clone from prep school—tall, slender, long brown hair, pricey clothes. The other girl is what you'd call Goth—spiked blonde hair, black jeans with a long-sleeved, black T-shirt sporting a Megadeth logo on the front, piercings on every available body space, and a tattoo on the back of her neck that I can't quite make out. Now *she* looks like she belongs in this store, but Annabeth and the other girl...

"Oh, sorry," Annabeth says, when she notices my stare. "These are my friends, Mel and Syd."

"Nice to meet you," I say.

"Mel"—Annabeth says, pointing to Goth-girl—"goes to my church, and so does Syd, but I also know her from school."

"Hey, Annabeth, we're going down to Peterson's," Syd says. "Meet us there when you're done."

The two of them wave at her and walk out of the store, leaving me standing face-to-face with Annabeth. I try to smile, wishing desperately I'd kept my mouth shut at Petersen's that day.

"Don't look so scared." Annabeth glances around the shop. "Interesting store. Ooooh, are those crystals?" She walks over to the display case and begins gawking at the jewelry. "Can I look at that sapphire?"

I follow her to the display case and open the cabinet door, lifting out the necklace she indicated. "This one?"

Annabeth nods.

"It's $49.95 plus tax," I say in my most business-like tone.

"Sapphires are for spirituality, and that amethyst over there—it's for inner peace, right?" Annabeth holds up the necklace to the light and admires the color.

I'm surprised at her knowledge of their purpose, but all I can do is nod.

She puts the necklace back down on its velvet case. "You're a snob, Caryn Alderson."

"Huh? I'm...what?"

"You think that just because I live in Belford and go to a private school that *I'm* stuck up, but you're the one that's the snob."

Well, that really hurts, because in fact she's right. I wrote her off the minute I left Petersen's that Sunday, thinking she was just some bored, rich preppie looking for excitement. Yet here she is, acting all sincere.

"I'm sorry. I just didn't expect to ever see you again, and I really didn't expect you to be into crystals and things."

Annabeth shrugs. "I'm really into spiritual stuff, and I think you're interesting. Megan said you were cool, and I was hoping we could be friends."

"But you live in Belford, and I—"

"—have a lot in common with me, no matter what you think." Like I said, dog with a bone.

"I'll prove it to you. What are you doing at six o'clock tomorrow morning?"

I look at her in surprise. "Sleeping in, hopefully, since it's a holiday."

"Exactly—a holiday where lots of people go hungry. So get your lazy bones out of bed and come with us to the Loving Sisters Shelter downtown. A group of kids from my church meets there every Thanksgiving to help cook and serve a meal to homeless people."

That blows me away. I never in a million years would have pictured Barbie serving turkey dinner to the homeless, but here she is, not only totally involved but nudging me to help out as well. I agree, give her my home address so they can pick me up at the crack of dawn (UGH!), and then sell her that sapphire necklace she was admiring.

****

So it turns out that Annabeth belongs to a kind of liberal non-church, where they spend less time sitting in the pews and lots more time doing community service. Again, totally not what I'd expected from a private school kid like her, but I'm starting to realize I need to quit stereotyping people. Friends like Mel and Syd sure prove I was wrong about her. I guess I fit into Annabeth's world more than I realize.

It's hard dragging myself out of bed in the cold pre-dawn on a school holiday. Mel is a junior and has a driver's license, so she picks us all up in an old Ford Taurus and drives us to downtown Indianapolis.

I'm not sure what to expect, but the experience turns out to be totally worth it. By noon on Thanksgiving I'm up to my elbows in turkey, cornbread dressing, gravy, and cranberry sauce, helping cook and serve a meal for hundreds. Now it's two hours later and the cleanup volunteers are arriving, so our shift is over and we're free to leave.

"Did I prove myself yet?" Annabeth asks me as we walk out to Mel's car. "Still think I'm stuck up?"

"No." I feel guilty for my pre-judgment of her. "This was probably the coolest Thanksgiving I've ever spent. Thanks for asking me."

Annabeth smiles as we cross the parking lot. "What are your plans for the rest of the day?"

"My mom's cooking us a turkey dinner, and I hope she taped the Thanksgiving Day Parade for me," I respond.

"So can I ask you something?"

Please don't ask me about your boyfriend. "Okay. What?"

"That guy Quince, why's he so mad at you?"

Relieved, I take in Annabeth's calm expression, and hope I can trust her.

"I was supposed to be telling Quince's fortune at the Halloween Carnival, but his dead grandfather showed up and told me about Quince's mom being sick and how she was going to be okay. And when I told Quince, he freaked. I swear I'm not making this up."

Annabeth's eyes get real wide. "Wow! I knew you were psychic, but I didn't know you could see spirits."

Me, neither. "Aren't you going to tell me how creepy that is?" I brace myself.

But Annabeth laughs, surprising me yet again. "Why do you keep it all such a big secret? If Megan knew..."

"You CAN'T tell Megan!" A lump is rising in my throat. "If she finds out, then everyone at school will think I'm the biggest freak on the planet. Not that they don't already."

Annabeth shakes her head, patting me on the back. "You think you've got Megan figured out, like you did me. But you were wrong about me, and maybe you're wrong about her."

I hunch a shoulder. "I don't know. I mean, what if she blabs to everyone? You know Megan usually speaks her mind."

"But it's so cool what you can do," Annabeth argues.

I must look truly panic-stricken, though, because she shrugs. "So, talked to Elvis lately?"

In spite of myself, I laugh.

Chapter 6
Jingle Bells

"Hey, Caryn, look what I got!" Megan says with a giggle.

It's the first Monday in December and Megan has come to school wearing a brand new pair of Jimmy Choos with a matching handbag. Her new stepmother went on a shopping spree last month and spent over two thousand dollars for her birthday present.

"At the Halloween Carnival—you made me so mad when all you said was I'd get new shoes. But boy were you right!"

"Nice," I say as I admire them. "Do you see much of your dad?"

"Not really. He's pretty busy with work, and anyway he won't let me bring my dog to his house in Belford, so I don't go up there too often." Despite Megan's bravado, I can tell she's hurt by that.

As I listen to her talk, I hear her dad voicing his disapproval of her dog, and I feel her pain at his rejection. I also see her stepmother too busy with her society luncheons and shopping to spend much time with Megan. I decide to change the subject. "Are you wearing those expensive new shoes to the Christmas dance?"

"If I get a date I am."

"Don't worry, you'll get one. Jeremy?"

Megan just giggles again.

I look over and see Quince walk by on his way to his locker. He nods to Megan and pretends I'm invisible.

"Hi, Quince," Megan says. "How's your mom?"

Quince shoots *me* a dirty look, but to Megan he says, "Better. The doctors think they have her blood sugar under control."

Sure enough, it's just like his grandfather said. I watch him walk off down the hall toward Kensi, only to feel the usual stab of jealousy when I see the two of them holding hands.

Get over it, Caryn. He's with HER. And he thinks you're a freak.

The tardy bell has rung and Megan and I hurry to class, sophomore English taught by the head of the English Department, Mrs. Renfrow. She's a nice lady, sort of plump and dowdy-looking, sometimes strict, but she's taught us a lot. The semester is ending in a couple of weeks, so we have to wind up our unit on poetry and get ready for final exams.

The kids aren't paying much attention to the lesson, though, because the Christmas semi-formal is next Saturday night and that's all anyone can talk about. Who's going with who, who isn't going, what everyone is wearing, the DJ, the decorations, and so on. I don't have a date, and the event is couples only, so it's an understatement to say I feel left out. At this point I'd even accept an invitation from Harris Rutherford. Well, maybe.

"Class," says Mrs. Renfrow. "Let's open our textbooks to page 445 and continue our study of Shakespeare's sonnets." She opens her book, but there's so much talking in the room, no one is paying attention.

"Quiet!" Emma shouts from across the room. "You guys are so rude!"

"Thank you, Emma, but I'll take it from here," says Mrs. Renfrow. "Class, we still have work to do before we start reviewing for the final, so let's begin."

I'm not in the mood for iambic pentameter, but I

open my book anyway and stare blankly at the page. Visions of sugarplums—well, okay, the Sugarplum Dance—pop into my head and I suddenly feel very sorry for myself. I look around the classroom and see most of the students pretending to read their textbooks. But Jeremy Harper is crouched down in his seat, secretly sending a text message from his cell phone.

He's asking Megan to the dance.

She casually glances at her phone propped up behind her textbook, and then looks over at Jeremy and nods. I smile.

At least she gets to go.

Following English class is lunch, so I'm heading to the cafeteria when Megan catches up to me.

"Jeremy asked me to the dance! You were right. How did you know?"

I'm always right—at least about other people. I wish I could predict my own life as accurately. I shrug and just say, "I'm happy for you."

Jeremy ends up behind us in the pizza line and he and Megan giggle at one another all the way to the cash register. *Good grief.*

"Hey, Caryn, got a date for the dance?" Jeremy asks.

Now how does a girl gracefully answer a question like that? If I say yes, it's a lie, and if I say no, it makes me look like a loser.

"Caryn's weighing her options," Megan says.

"Well, here's another option," Jeremy suggests. "My friend Mark Evans needs a date. Interested? We could double date."

Great. A pity fix-up.

"Cool!" Megan turns to me excitedly. "How 'bout it, Caryn?"

I'm obviously in no position to refuse, but this is a little embarrassing—being set up with a guy no one wants to date. Pretty lame. Still, I realize I have no choice if I want to go to the dance, and I *really* want to go.

"Okay, tell Mark I'll do it. IF he calls me and asks me himself."

Jeremy grins at Megan and goes off to join his friends at their usual table. Unwritten rule—no girls allowed. I look wistfully over as Jeremy sits down next to Quince, but then follow Megan across the cafeteria to our regular table. Emma Cartwright and Ashleigh Ko are already there, deep in discussion about their dresses for the dance.

"Don't tell me, let me guess," I say as I sit down. *Okay, I'm not guessing, but they don't need to know that.* "Emma, you're wearing a retro-looking formal dress with a pearl choker necklace, and Ashleigh, you've got a new red satin dress with a mandarin collar."

They both stare at me in complete surprise.

"Have you been spying on us?" Emma asks suspiciously.

"No, I just guessed." I'm backpedaling now, but those two are pretty predictable. Emma is seriously into the Audrey Hepburn look and Ashleigh is determined not to let anyone forget her Asian heritage.

"Caryn just got asked to the dance," Megan announces as she picks the pepperoni off her pizza.

Emma raises an eyebrow at me. "Really? Who?"

"You don't have to act so surprised. Mark Evans, friend of Jeremy Harper's," I reply.

"Mark?" Ashleigh sounds dubious. "He's in my geometry class and he never says a word."

"Maybe he doesn't like math," I say.

This doesn't sound good, though. How can I spend an entire evening with a guy who can't string two words together?

"Who's your date, Ashleigh?" Megan asks. Everyone knows she has one. She always does.

"Connor Stevenson. Senior, good looking, and unattached."

"The guy you were dancing with at homecoming?" Megan asks. "Caryn said he was a senior." She looks over at me like she's waiting for an explanation of how I knew.

"I'm going with Kevin," Emma gushes. "Come to think of it, Caryn, isn't that what you told me at Halloween?"

They all turn to look at me. Gulp. *How do I get out of this one?*

"I was better at that fortunetelling thing than I thought I'd be," I say with a smile. "So tell me about that dress, Emma. What shoes did you pick out?"

Once channeled in the direction of fashion, Emma is on a roll. She doesn't stop talking until the lunch bell rings and we leave the cafeteria for afternoon classes. For Megan and me, that means art class. Losing myself in a watercolor seems like a good idea right now. Anything to take my mind off Quince, his date with Kensi, and my fix-up with the sophomore class loser.

Speaking of dresses, what will I wear to the dance? All the other girls have been planning their wardrobes for weeks, and Megan will be wearing those expensive shoes along with some new dress I'm sure her stepmother will buy her. I don't own many dresses, and definitely nothing that passes for semi-formal, so I desperately need my mother's help.

I hurry to the shop after school to tell her the news.

****

Mark actually did call me that night and prompted by Jeremy (I could hear his voice in the background), asked me to be his date to the Sugarplum Dance. That may have been more words than he'd spoken in years, but I accepted his invitation. I already knew Quince would be there with Kensi because they were nominated for Nutcracker Prince and Snow Queen, and I hoped I'd be able to talk to him. Maybe in a social setting like that, Quince would be in a more forgiving mood. At least I hoped so.

As for what to wear, Mom solved that problem. She took me to the consignment store not far from her shop, and we found a dress that the shopkeeper promised had only been worn once. It was blue polished cotton with red velvet trim around the hem and waistband, sleeveless with a rounded neck and full skirt that hit just above my knees. The dress fit me perfectly and was affordable, so Mom bought it. When the subject of shoes came up, Sybil gave me a crisp one hundred dollar bill and told me to go buy whatever I wanted.

****

It's Saturday night and my stomach is filled with butterflies. I'm excited about the dance, but I'm also nervous about seeing Quince. At least I get to go, and maybe I'll get a chance to talk to him. With the new dress, new shoes, and a crystal necklace borrowed from Mom's store, I think I look pretty good as Megan, Jeremy and Mark arrive to pick me up at the apartment.

Megan is wearing a gorgeous, green satin tea-length gown that must have set her stepmother back another thousand or so. Instead of the Jimmy Choos, she has yet another new pair of expensive shoes, dyed to match the dress. Mark and Jeremy both look pretty good too, wearing suits, ties, and freshly polished dress shoes.

Mark is living up to his reputation of having little to say. He's tall and skinny with scraggly brown hair that keeps falling into his eyes, and he rarely smiles either. Compared to him, Harris Rutherford looks like a fashion icon. Mark plays french horn in the school orchestra, and according to

Ashleigh, it's the only time he ever makes any kind of sound.

Mark looks as uncomfortable about this date—apparently having been pressured into it by Jeremy—as I feel, so I'm pretty sure we're off to a bad start when he can barely manage to say hi to my mother. She asks him several questions about school, the orchestra, his parents, but he just shrugs each time and inches his way toward the door.

Megan is impatient to get going but that works in everyone's favor this time, since Mark's non-communication is getting awkward.

"Come on, guys, let's go or we'll be REALLY late!" Megan has her hand on the doorknob, ready to bolt.

With a sigh of relief, I wrap my silk shawl around my shoulders and the four of us leave for the dance. We have to ride with Ms. Benedict because nobody is old enough to drive yet, but it's only six blocks. Mark's silence and Megan's chatter manage to cancel each other out. Ms. Benedict is one of the faculty chaperones, so she lets us out in front of the school before parking the car.

"Have fun, kids," she says as we climb out one by one.

Megan faces her mother with hands on her hips and says in all seriousness, "Mom, parents are to be *seen* and not heard! Don't talk to me during the dance."

Ms. Benedict just smiles and waves at us as she pulls away from the curb. I guess you could say she's pretty tolerant when Megan cops an attitude.

Megan is right about us needing to get here early—there are lots of kids already milling around and the dance floor is getting crowded, even though the DJ hasn't started playing the *real* music yet. So far there's nothing but instrumental Christmas music coming from a CD player.

The theme of the dance goes along with *The Nutcracker*, so the decorations in the gym include gigantic toys, candy canes, snowflakes hung from the support beams, and even miniature nutcracker key chains for party favors. The dance committee—whoever they are—did a great job setting this up.

The minute we walk in the door, Megan and Jeremy take off in search of Emma and Kevin, leaving me standing alone with a nonverbal Mark.

"Where should we sit?" I ask.

He mumbles something and leads me to some chairs set up alongside the back wall near the folded-up bleachers.

This is going to be a long evening.

I try every kind of small talk I can think of, but the most I get from Mark is yeah or okay.

Finally in frustration I stand up and blurt out, "Just because you think you have ugly teeth is no reason to never open your mouth and talk!"

For once, Mark's mouth drops open and I'm sure he's wondering how I knew that. I wish I could explain it, but it's just one of those random thoughts that comes flying out of my mouth. Before Mark can mumble one more monosyllable in response, the DJ starts playing dance music and kids jump into action. I take Mark's hand and drag him out onto the dance floor so we won't look like total losers sitting by ourselves.

Quince and Kensi walk in fashionably late, dressed like the royalty they expect to be crowned, her red and green silk dress color-coordinated with his holiday coat and tie. It's amazing how good looks, popularity, and charisma can draw others like magnets, and once they're out on the dance floor, everyone clusters around them. Green with envy, I watch the two of them smiling and dancing *this*close.

I try to smile at Quince while he's focused on *her*, but he deliberately looks in the other direction.

My heart sinks, so I determine here and now to do something—anything—to get him to at least speak to me again. I maneuver Mark over to where Quince and Kensi are dancing and deliberately bump into Quince.

"Excuse me," I say.

Quince rolls his eyes at yet another example of my clumsiness. He starts to back away but I get between him and Kensi and stand my ground. I can almost feel Kensington's angry glare behind me.

"Quince, could I talk to you a minute?"

"Now?"

"Hello! Dancing here," Kensi says a little too loudly.

"Please," I beg him, not even looking at her.

Quince opens his mouth like he's about to tell me to back off, but I must look pretty pathetic because he finally says, "Okay. Meet me at the refreshment table after this song, and it'd better be important."

He turns his attention back to Kensi, who smiles insincerely at me and walks Quince to the other side of the dance floor.

After the song is finished, I tell Mark I'm going for a soda. He doesn't seem concerned at all that I'm making excuses to go talk to another guy, and he heads off looking for Jeremy. Quince drops Kensi off next to Ashleigh and Connor, and walks over to the refreshment table where I'm waiting for him.

"What do you want?" Quince isn't going to make this easy for me.

"I...I know it's been a while but, well, I'm really sorry for what I said at the Halloween Carnival."

"That was totally bogus what you said about my mother," he says, scowling at me.

"I know and I'm sorry," I say again.

The look on Quince's face says he doesn't buy my apology. "And who told you my mother was sick anyway? It's private family stuff."

Not wanting to get into the hows and whys of it all, I simply say, "Can you forgive me and be friends again?"

It's Christmas time and maybe the holiday spirit is getting to him, or maybe he knows a sincere apology when he hears it, but anyway he shrugs and runs his fingers through his hair. "Whatever."

It's the nicest thing he's said to me in weeks. I smile at him, my heart pounding wildly as I reach out to touch his hand.

Quince quickly pulls away. "Kensi's waiting. See ya." And off he goes to find her, leaving me standing there alone.

Well, at least we're back to speaking again.

****

I hadn't seen or talked to Annabeth since Thanksgiving, but Megan surprised me the Saturday before Christmas by calling and asking if I wanted to go to the mall with her and Annabeth. A bona fide offer to do normal teenage stuff—without spirits, drama, or psychic premonitions—was something I couldn't pass up. Also I wanted to buy Mom a Christmas present with the money Dad sent me, and frankly I had no idea how I was going to do that unless someone gave me a ride. Megan's sister Caroline offered to drive us. It seemed as if the Universe was aligning to solve my problem for me.

Malls are exciting places to be during the Christmas shopping season, even though I don't usually like crowds. I tell myself to tune out the unwanted information, sing a song maybe or focus on a cute pair of shoes, but some of it gets through anyway. There's a hot guy who's about to surprise his girlfriend with an engagement ring for Christmas. A little girl just told her daddy she wants a kitten, and even though he told her no, I see him going to the shelter next week to get one. There's the sweetest elderly couple walking along hand-in-hand about to celebrate their golden wedding anniversary on December 25. And I see a grandmotherly woman, who I'm pretty sure isn't of this world, walking alongside her daughter and granddaughter as they window shop. Like I said, I can't tune everything out, but at least I'm getting happy vibes here at the mall today.

Tinsel, twinkling lights, and ornaments dangle in the walkways and rafters, while decorated trees and wreaths adorn every store entrance. Then of course there are the department store aisles that are crammed with extra display tables of merchandise, all with suggestions for the perfect gift. Seasonal music is getting shoppers in the mood to open their pocketbooks, and in a convenient, central location, Santa sits on a throne in the middle of a miniature North Pole, surrounded by bored young women dressed as elves.

The line of little kids trying to sit on Santa's lap snakes halfway down the mall, and some of the kids are tired and cranky. Still, I love all the holiday sounds—even screaming kids—and smells of gingerbread and peppermint. The mall has the blown-in, fake snow surrounding Santa's Village, something I was used to in Houston, but outdoors the real stuff is sitting on the ground. This is the first time in all my life I've seen real snow in December.

Megan, Annabeth, and I walk up and down the crowded mall, peeking into store windows and shoving past hawkers in the temporary kiosks. I'm having a hard time trying to decide what to buy for my mother. The choices may be unlimited, but my budget isn't.

"Any suggestions?" I ask them.

"Moms always like perfume and stuff like that," Megan says. "Or we could go into the bath store and look at some of those scented soaps."

"Okay. Which way?" It's my first time in this mall and I'm turned around.

"I think we passed it." Annabeth looks up at the sign on the sporting goods store behind us.

"Ohmigod, do you two see what I see?" Megan exclaims, pointing across the mall.

"What?" All I can see are hordes of busy shoppers.

"It's Kensington Marlow!"

"So?" I ask, annoyed at the thought that my rival—even though she might not realize she's my rival—is breathing the same airspace as I am. "I imagine she practically lives at the mall."

Still, my curiosity gets the better of me and I look in the direction Megan is pointing. Sure enough, there's Kensi, but she isn't alone. She's walking arm-in-arm with a very attractive guy, occasionally leaning her head on his shoulder, laughing as he whispers in her ear. He even leans over and kisses her on the cheek as they stroll along.

"Who's Kensington Marlow and why do we care?" Annabeth asks.

"She's Quince Adams' girlfriend, and that is NOT Quince!" Megan says.

"He's a college student," I say, too dazed by Kensi's betrayal to think what I'm saying.

"He is? How do you know?" Megan asks me. I see Annabeth give me a knowing look.

"Um, he just looks older than high school," I hedge. Still, we all realize that Kensi is cheating on Quince, big time.

Then a weird sensation comes over me. It's like everyone in the mall is playing a game of freeze-tag and instantly all movement, voices, noise, and music seem to stop while a thought swirls in my head. In my gut I feel a gnawing sensation and I blurt out, "Quince is here—in the mall!" *So much for keeping my psychic premonitions to myself.*

"Where?" Megan searches the crowd. "I don't see him."

Neither do I at the moment, but my radar tells me he's definitely here. "Quince is going to see Kensi with that college guy!"

"So let him. Seriously, I'd think you'd be happy if Quince found out his girlfriend is cheating on him," Annabeth says.

I wonder if she's right. "I don't know..."

"Well, I say we find him and tell him," Annabeth finally says, narrowing her eyes at me.

I have to stop and think a minute. True, if Quince sees Kensi with the other guy, they might break up, but I refuse to be the reason he finds out. I just got back in his good graces and I want to keep it that way.

"I kinda feel bad for the guy, though," Annabeth goes on. "I know what it's like to have a cheating Significant Other and I'd sure want to know if I were him."

"This mall is way crowded today," Megan says. "We'll never find him anyway."

"He's at the food court," I say.

"Huh? How can you possibly know that?"

Maybe I misread my gut reaction? "Well, I'm hungry, so if I'm wrong, we can just get something to eat. Come on."

"Maybe Kensi is with a—friend or something," Megan says charitably as we push our way through the crowd toward the food court.

"They looked pretty friendly all right," Annabeth says.

I scan the seating area, and sure enough, there's Quince over by the pizza place, shoving a piece of pepperoni in his face and laughing at something Kevin Marshall is saying. The three of us walk over, standing in just the right spot to block Quince's view of the mall corridor.

"Hi guys," I say cheerfully. "What are you doing here?"

It seems like a harmless opening. Kevin gives me his usual look that says Duh! and answers by pointing to the pizza. He probably thinks I'm the most clueless girl on the planet.

"No, I mean are you here shopping or what?" I ask, hoping to seem a little less foolish.

"I've gotta buy something for my mom," Quince says, and I bite my tongue when an image of her at the doctor's office pops into my head. I push it away, though, and make myself focus on the here and now. "And Kevin's meeting Emma in a little while."

"Do you guys remember Annabeth Walton?" Megan asks. "From Peterson's last month? I used to go to school with her when I lived in Belford."

"Cool," says Quince, taking another bite of pizza.

"Hey, Quince! Guess who else is here at the mall today," Annabeth teases.

I freeze. *Brace yourself.*

So imagine my surprise when Kensi herself shows up at that very minute—alone—and plants a big kiss on Quince's forehead. He blushes, grins, and then takes a large swig of soda to cover his embarrassment.

Why that little sneak! I look around for the guy she was so cozy with, but he's nowhere in sight. She must have seen Quince and temporarily ditched the new squeeze. I guess my dad's favorite cliché applies after all—the best defense is a good offense.

"Hey, Quince!" Kensi is gushing a little too much if you ask me. "Buying me something pretty for Christmas?"

I want to smack her. She turns to Megan and me, gives us her usual high-and-mighty once-over, and then does the same to Annabeth, whose preppy appearance must seem like a real threat to Kensi.

"Who's this?"

"No one you know, from Willowby Prep," says Annabeth, giving Kensi the exact same snarky head-to-toe inspection. "I'm an old friend of Megan's and a new friend of Caryn's."

The two of them glare at each other, both refusing to be the first to back down. I stifle a giggle. It's pretty funny realizing Kensi has met her match in Annabeth.

"How sweet," Kensi finally says. "Well, you kids have fun. I've got to go meet somebody and finish shopping."

Somebody indeed.

"Meet who?" Quince asks, but it's too late, because Kensington has already walked away.

Annabeth clears her throat loudly and turns to face me, all but daring me to speak up. I wouldn't be able to get the words out about Kensi, even if I wanted to, because I always find myself tongue-tied whenever Quince is around. Fortunately, Emma Cartwright appears and saves me from being put in that awkward position.

"Hey, you two"—she greets me and Megan—"and girl-I-don't-know"—to Annabeth. "Looks like the party started without me."

You can always count on Emma to lighten the mood.

Kevin pulls up another chair, while Megan introduces Annabeth to Emma.

"Aw, come on, sit down," Kevin coaxes us. "We don't bite."

The rest of the afternoon is lots of fun. Quince is laughing and joking with all of us, but I feel like he's warming up to me in particular. Maybe he's truly moved past the carnival incident, or maybe he's just like every other guy with a short memory. Whichever is the case, I'm happy.

The mall Christmas music is playing loudly in

our ears, but the sound of Quince's easy laughter is all the music I want to hear.

****

Mom and I are invited to a Christmas Eve candlelight service at Annabeth's church. She promised us it would be nontraditional, and she's true to her word. We sing lots of the usual Christmas carols—"It Came Upon a Midnight Clear," "Silent Night," "Oh Come All Ye Faithful"—but instead of the regular religious readings, we light candles in the name of ending hunger, achieving world peace, and providing homes for all the people living on the streets. Pretty lofty goals really, but I feel completely in tune with them.

I'm also feeling a kinship with others attending the service, especially when I look around the sanctuary and see people I know. Annabeth is with her parents and a guy I assume is her older brother, and they're sitting next to two other families that include Mel and Syd. Annabeth smiles at me, and Mel and Syd wave as well. I feel all warm and fuzzy as I sing "Silent Night" (okay, a little off-key). At the end of the service, I eagerly hold my lit candle along with everyone else as we walk out one at a time, doing what the minister says is "carrying the light of peace into the world."

****

Christmas Day dawns clear and very cold, with the sun causing the snow on the ground to glisten like brightly colored gems. I saw storybooks when I was a little kid that looked like what's outside my bedroom window, but instead of just a pretty drawing, the snow is very real and it's seriously frigid out there.

I close the curtains and wrap a blanket around myself, shivering with cold. I walk into the living room, where it's usually a little warmer, and huddle on the sofa as Mom comes out of the kitchen. The coffee and blueberry muffins create a delicious aroma, but even though my stomach is growling, I'm too cold to get up off the sofa and go sit at the breakfast table.

"Come on, Caryn, if you eat something you'll warm up," Mom urges.

"Can you bring it to me in here? I'm so cold."

I don't think I'll ever get warm again, and I worry since it's only December that the weather will get colder before it gets warmer. I pull the blanket tighter around me and feel sorry for myself. I don't want to ruin Christmas for Mom, but I'm cold and miserable.

We have a small fir tree sitting on a table in the corner of the living room. We found it at a Christmas tree lot's going-out-of-business sale and saved it from becoming kindling just two days ago. We decorated it with some old ornaments Mom has been saving since my childhood and some from hers, including one Uncle Omar made by hand, and then we added a few crystals from the store—the flawed ones that didn't sell. I found an old string of tree lights in the backroom at the store, so I strung those on it as well. All in all, the little tree looks pretty festive.

"A Charlie Brown tree," Mom dubbed it.

Under the table where the tree sits are several gifts. I selected some scented soaps for Mom from the bath store in the mall and carefully wrapped the box in tissue paper and tied it with leftover red knitting yarn and a "To Mom from Caryn" tag.

A large box is addressed to me from Mom, and she insists I open it first. I disentangle myself from the blanket and carefully remove the ribbon and bow. Then the excitement gets to me and I rip the wrapping paper off like a little kid. The box is from Lacy's Department Store. I give my mother a surprised look.

"Open it," she urges me.

I pull out a gorgeous, knee-length winter coat. It's grey wool with black buttons, a hood, and has a pair of matching gloves stuffed in its pockets. Tears come to my eyes as I stand up and try it on. It's so warm!

"Mom..." I sputter.

"It was on sale so I splurged. Just like you said, our store made money during the Christmas rush," she says, beaming.

I walk over and give her a big hug.

"Now open the present from your dad."

Dad sent me a knitted cap with a matching scarf, plus a pair of winter snow boots. Michael also sent a gift—a gorgeous pink cashmere sweater with a new pair of jeans. And Sybil's gift tops it all off—the coolest pair of earrings I've ever seen, with an attached IOU to take me to get my ears pierced.

"This is the best Christmas ever!" I gush.

Mom snaps a picture of me displaying my new finery.

"Answer the phone, Mom. I'm too overwhelmed to talk," I say, admiring myself in the living room mirror.

Mom rolls her eyes, walks over to the phone and holds her hand over it until it rings, then picks it up.

"Merry Christmas!" she exclaims into the receiver. "Yes, she's here. Nice job, Guy. Here, I'll let you talk to her yourself." She hands me the phone.

"Hi, Dad! It's so good to hear your voice."

Chapter 7
A New Year

New Year's Eve is usually a grownups' holiday. I didn't expect to do anything except stay home with Mom and watch the ball drop in Times Square on TV, but Megan called me a few days after Christmas and said she was having a sleepover that night and invited me to come.

Megan lives with her mother and older sister Allie in a small, three-bedroom house about two miles from school (and a mile or so from our apartment) in a nice, quaint area of Rosslyn Village. Caroline, the older sister I met back in November, lives in an apartment somewhere nearby.

I ring the doorbell, eagerly anticipating the fun this evening, pillow and sleeping bag in hand. I'm greeted by a cute little yellow dog jumping up and down as Megan lets me into the house.

"Honey, get down," Megan scolds. "Sorry. I hope you like dogs, 'cause Honey won't leave us alone."

"Sure I like dogs, and I've heard you talk about her," I say, bending down to scratch Honey's ears.

I've never owned a dog, but I've always wished for one, and this one is really cute. She's wagging her tail contentedly while I stroke her back and pat her head. "How are you, girl?"

I can hear Emma, Ashleigh, and Annabeth in the kitchen as Megan takes my stuff to her bedroom. I'm excited as I join the other girls making microwave popcorn and opening cans of soda. It's been a long time since I've been invited to a sleepover, especially after my disastrous freshman year. I feel so lucky to have made new friends in Indianapolis, friends who keep overlooking my many social gaffes.

"Can you believe we're gonna be all alone till after midnight?" Emma exclaims. "Ms. Benedict has a DATE, if you can believe, and Megan's sister is out too."

An image of Allie standing next to an attractive young man at a wedding pops into my head. "With that college professor?" I ask without thinking.

"Huh?" Ashleigh asks.

"I mean, cool, that we're on our own tonight," I quickly say.

"So girls," Emma says. "We've got movies, junk food, CDs, lots to keep us busy. And then we'll turn on TV about eleven thirty to watch Times Square in New York."

"Maybe we could do more than just veg and pig out," Ashleigh says with a frown. She pulls open a soda tab and the liquid spurts out and bubbles over the can.

"But it's tradition to watch the ball drop!" Emma exclaims, handing Ashleigh a towel.

"It's New Year's Eve. We should do something different besides watch TV. We always watch movies. Why don't we play a game?" Ashleigh dries off the soda can, mops a spot off the floor, and tosses the towel on the counter.

"Like one of your math games? No, thanks," Emma says.

"Hey I know!" Annabeth, who is carefully opening a hot bag of microwave popcorn, casts a sly look in my direction. "How 'bout we get out the Ouija board?"

Uh-oh. What's she up to?

"Or what about Monopoly? Hey, Megan," Ashleigh calls into the bedroom. "You got a Monopoly game? I'll be the banker!"

"I think some of the pieces went missing, or else Honey chewed them up," Megan calls back.

Annabeth, once focused on something, isn't about to let the other girls change the subject. "I still like the Ouija board idea. What about you, Caryn?" She faces me directly, her eyes widening at me.

Emma and Ashleigh watch silently as I fidget. I glare at Annabeth but say as calmly as I can through clenched teeth, "My mom doesn't let me play with those."

"Your mom isn't here," Annabeth shoots back.

My palms start to sweat. Emma and Ashleigh are looking at us wide-eyed, like we have a big secret, which of course we do. Instead of explaining, I grab Annabeth's arm and pull her into the living room.

"What are you trying to do to me?" I ask her when we're out of earshot.

"What do you think? Let the truth out." She pulls her arm away from my grasp.

"With a Ouija board? Those things are dangerous—dark spirits and all. You know I can't—" I shake my head in disbelief that Annabeth would betray my confidence like this.

"Can't what? Be honest about yourself?" Annabeth asks, folding her arms.

"No. Well, yeah, but the truth will lose me all my friends," I say, fear edging my voice.

"If they don't accept you then you need new friends," Annabeth says. "*I* accepted you, didn't I?"

I groan. She has a point, but if you ask me, her timing is all off. We're supposed to just be having fun on New Year's Eve, and here's Annabeth trying to ruin it for me.

"Then if you won't do the Ouija board, we should think of something else. Some other way to let them in on your secret," Annabeth says, tapping one finger against her lips thoughtfully.

We? Something else? I don't like the sound of that either.

"Come on, Annabeth, you're freaking everyone out and I don't want to tell anyone else about my secret." I head back to the kitchen hoping for once Annabeth will let something go.

"Hey, what's up with you two?" Ashleigh sounds exasperated with us. "What's the big secret?"

"Nothing." I shoot Annabeth a warning look. "What movies have you got?" I pretend to be absorbed in the selection of DVDs Emma brought as she flicks through the cases.

"The usual. *27 Dresses, The Devil Wears Prada, Bewitched, Pride and Prejudice.*"

"Boring chick flicks," Annabeth says with a fake yawn.

"So you got any better ideas?" Emma challenges her.

"I do," Megan says as she returns to the kitchen, Honey playfully jumping on her legs. "Come on, you guys, it's too cramped in this kitchen. Let's go to the living room. We can play cards if you don't want to watch movies."

"Hearts?" Emma asks. "I'm good at that game."

That sounds innocent enough to me. Maybe Annabeth will let the whole psychic thing drop.

"Hey! I know a game called Ninety-nine. How 'bout it?" Ashleigh suggests.

"NO numbers games!" Emma stomps her foot. "It's easy for you but not for the rest of us."

"Well, at least it's something different," Ashleigh mutters. "We always play Hearts."

"Hey, what do you guys want on your pizza?" Megan retrieves her cell phone from the coffee table. "Pepperoni, veggies, what?"

"Both," Ashleigh says. "Symmetrically divided in half."

Megan has the pizza place on speed dial, so she

punches in the number and places our order. "They said they're running behind tonight because of the holiday, so it'll be awhile. Can we make do with popcorn?"

We all nod. There's limited sofa space in the small living room, so I sit down on the floor and begin playing with the dog who, just like Megan said, wants to be in the middle of the action. Pretty soon, all the other girls are sitting on the floor too, laughing and playing keep-away with Honey as she wrestles for her favorite stuffed toy.

"So what are we doing? Movie, cards, what?" Megan strokes Honey's head after her dog is finally tired of the game and plops down on the floor.

"Let's play Hearts!" Emma insists. "Everyone knows that game."

"We should. We play it enough," Megan says.

"You are SO terrible at that game anyway. Go Fish is about your speed," Ashleigh snipes.

"It is NOT!" Emma pouts.

"Maybe playing cards isn't such a good idea," Megan says, frowning.

Megan is right, because Emma and Ashleigh are still glaring at each other, and if we want to have any fun at all tonight we have to keep those two from arguing.

"I still say we get out the Ouija board!" Annabeth smiles conspiratorially.

Suddenly the focus is off Emma and Ashleigh and centered on me and Annabeth. There's a long, uncomfortable silence with everyone hoping the tension between me and Annabeth eases. It doesn't. I must have a panic-stricken look on my face, since I'm sure my social life is about to go up in flames and I'm on the verge of being friendless again. Suddenly all four of them are looking at me like I've seen a ghost. And this time I haven't.

"Caryn, what's wrong?" Megan looks intently

Confessions of a Teenage Psychic

into my face. "You're pale. Do you feel okay?"

I can't say a word, so I grab my can of soda and swallow a big, long gulp. No one speaks. Even Honey senses something is wrong and climbs onto my lap in sympathy. I stroke her fur and try to regain my composure.

Megan looks from me to Annabeth, then to Emma and Ashleigh who are clueless. "Will one of you guys PLEASE tell me what's going on?" Megan says, scowling.

Annabeth waits for me to speak up, but of course I don't, or can't. "Yeah, okay," she says with a shrug. "There's something about Caryn you don't know, and if she doesn't tell you, I will. Seriously, Caryn, it's time they knew."

"What's the big secret, Caryn? Are you some kind of ax murderer?" Ashleigh giggles at her own joke, but no one else is laughing. "Well, it can't be that bad, whatever it is."

I scan their faces and feel tears stinging my eyes. Can I trust these girls with the truth? Will they laugh at me, or worse—quit being my friends? Or maybe, just maybe, will they accept me for who I am? Annabeth did, so maybe they will too. But I still can't get the words out, and we all sit there in an uncomfortable silence.

"See, Caryn here, she's psychic," Annabeth finally says.

"What?" Megan exclaims. "No way!"

Ashleigh tilts her head. "Like Psychic Hotline fake-psychic or really psychic?" she asks. At least she knows there's a difference.

"Ohmigod, it's all starting to make sense!" Megan slaps her forehead. "When you knew Kensi was going to have that car accident, the school carnival, knowing Quince was in the mall in December. Wow! Now I get it! But, hey, why didn't you just say so?"

"Because I don't want to end up with friends who think I'm a weirdo, or no friends at all, like in Houston."

"You didn't trust us?" Megan sounds incredulous.

"Well, I..." I stammer, surprised. I'd spent so much time fearing their rejection, I hadn't considered they might be annoyed with me.

"And how come Annabeth knew and we didn't?" Ashleigh looks indignant.

I shrug, embarrassed. "Last November I blurted out the truth to Annabeth because I didn't know her and never thought I'd see her again."

"So, can you, like, really predict the future?" Emma asks, wide-eyed.

I look from Emma to Ashleigh to Megan who are all staring at me. Emma looks stunned, Ashleigh disbelieving, and Megan excited. But not one of them looks like she hates me. "Uh-huh."

"Cool! You really *are* Madame Wilhelmina! Does Janae Thomas know? She'll freak!" Really, Megan is getting a little carried away.

"If you tell Janae, it'll be all over school in a nanosecond," Ashleigh says matter-of-factly.

"So tell us our futures!" Megan squeals, thrusting her palm out in front of me.

"The part I said at the carnival about reading palms? I really can't. But..."

They're all looking at me expectantly. I know I've been blurting out stuff accidentally all semester, but here they are, actually asking me to do it and I don't know what to say. And I don't know if it's such a great idea anyway, since I never know exactly what's going to pop into my head and come out of my mouth. Sometimes it's like I'm floating up on the ceiling watching myself babble about someone's life, and from up there I can't make myself shut up.

I sigh. "Are you sure you really wanna know?

'Cause I'm almost always right, and sometimes people don't want to hear all that stuff."

Ashleigh is the only one who looks hesitant, but the other girls nod enthusiastically.

"Go on, Caryn. Show 'em your stuff." Annabeth has a huge grin on her face, as if she's my psychic agent or something.

I have to laugh in spite of myself. "Well, okay, but just remember you asked. Who's first?"

"Me!" Emma waves her hand in the air.

"Well, you probably won't like this, but you're going to be elected president of the student council."

To say Emma is very startled is a huge understatement. "No way! I HATE politics, and I'd never run. You're *so* wrong."

I just shrug my shoulders and don't say anything else, but my instincts tell me I'm dead-on.

"Do Megan next," Emma says. "Let's see if you say anything about her that makes sense."

Megan nods, so I take a deep breath. "Okay, Megan, first of all, your sister's getting married in the new year."

"Allie? Not a chance!"

"Not her, the other one."

"Caroline? I doubt it. Her boyfriend got dumped by his fiancée on their wedding day last summer, so I'm pretty sure he's not ready." Megan shakes her head.

"Well, she is, and you're going to be in the wedding. But there's more." I pause, because the rest of Megan's prediction gives me serious qualms and I don't even know why or where it's coming from. "I really don't understand this part, but I just know you're going to be in the middle of something huge at school, and it's going to affect lots of lives."

"Hmmm," is all Megan says.

But now I'm on a roll, so I point to Ashleigh. "You already know you're gonna be valedictorian."

"Duh," she says.

"But you're off to some Ivy League college after graduation."

"Yeah, right. Who's gonna pay for that?" Ashleigh is more than a little skeptical.

"I don't know, but there's a full-ride scholarship in there somewhere," I say as she squints at me. "Really, it'll happen."

"What about Annabeth?" Megan asks.

Since Annabeth got me into all this, I like being able to turn the tables on her. I face the other girls. "Well, first of all she's going to make honor roll this spring."

"You have GOT to be kidding. Annabeth?" Megan smirks.

"Yes, Annabeth, because she'll be motivated, and I'm not saying about what. And that's not all." I point a finger at her. "You're going to have to make a choice later in the spring, and it won't be easy because of the people involved."

For once, Annabeth's eyes get real wide and I know I've taken her by surprise.

"I hate to be the voice of reason here..."

"No, you don't, Ashleigh," Emma says.

"But does anyone really buy all this mumbo-jumbo? Caryn hasn't said one single thing that can be proven."

Well, Ashleigh is right of course. It's hard to prove something that has yet to happen, despite how confident I feel in my predictions.

"You just haven't seen her in action." Annabeth always seemed to be my champion.

"None of you have to believe me if you don't want to, but Megan, your mom's on the phone."

"Huh? It's not ringing." Naturally, the phone rings about half a minute later. "OHMIGOD, you're too weird!" Megan fairly shouts at me as she reaches for her phone.

"Hello? Yeah, Mom, we're fine." Megan rolls her eyes and then gives me a questioning glance. "I ordered a pizza. It's okay, you have fun. Love you too. Bye."

"Okay, Ashleigh, there's your proof!" says a grinning Annabeth.

Ashleigh does have a sort of strange look on her face but she just waves her hands and goes into the kitchen for another soda. I guess she doesn't accept something that defies logic.

"Now I've got goose bumps, Caryn," Emma says, hugging herself. "How did you know the phone was going to ring?"

I study my friends' faces intently. At least I hope they're still my friends. "You guys think I'm weird, don't you?"

"Yeah, this is pretty weird," Megan says, a smile creeping onto her face. "And I can't believe I didn't figure it out sooner."

"Wait till I tell Kevin!" Emma exclaims.

More people? "NO! Please, can we just keep this between ourselves?"

"Who'd believe us anyway?" Ashleigh grumbles and gingerly pops open another soda can, taking a swallow when she's sure it isn't going to fizzle over.

Megan is the first to speak after what seems like an eternity. "Maybe you shouldn't just blurt random stuff out, Caryn. It's unnerving. But don't worry, your secret's safe with us. Right?"

"Right," Emma reluctantly agrees.

Ashleigh is silent a moment longer while everyone waits. She does some serious thinking, the kind she probably does when she's working out some complicated math problem, and finally says, "Oh, okay. But it doesn't make any sense."

A thought occurs to Emma. "Hey! You didn't tell us about you. What's in your future?"

I shake my head. "I have no idea. I'm not psychic

about myself."

"Well good, at least you don't know everything," Ashleigh says.

"Now you can answer the door," I tell Megan.

Sure enough, the pizza guy rings the doorbell. Megan gives me another wide-eyed look before getting up to pay for our food.

"Thank goodness. I'm starved." Annabeth goes to the kitchen to retrieve paper plates and napkins.

Emma pops a movie into the DVD player. "Is *27 Dresses* okay with everyone? I guess witches and devils are a bad choice."

Pretty soon we're all eating pizza, guzzling soda, laughing at the film, gossiping, and just doing what normal teenage girls do at a sleepover. Even Ashleigh is starting to come around. For the first time since I moved to Indianapolis, I feel like I can finally relax. I reach over to pat the dog, but she pulls away, growling at an invisible nothing in the corner of the room.

"Be quiet, Honey," Megan says distractedly, turning up the volume on the TV.

The dog is still sniffing and pawing at the floor and I'm a little surprised to see Uncle Omar standing there with his trademark grin, giving me two thumbs up. I smile at him as he slowly fades from view, leaving Honey to go off in search of other prey.

The Universe approves. What a great way to start the new year.

****

When school starts again after winter break, I discover my schedule has changed a little. I still have classes in math, science, English and art, but my first period geography class has been replaced with an elective called Love of Lit being taught by Mrs. Elizabeth York, in a part of the building I haven't been in yet.

I locate the classroom, walk in and smile at the teacher standing by her battered metal desk. I wonder if she's new because I've never seen her before. Mrs. York is about forty years old, attractive for an older woman (my mom would kill me if she heard me say that, since Mom is forty-two), stylishly dressed in a grey pinstripe wool pantsuit with a white camisole and black pumps. She has long reddish-brown hair tied back in a big clip, reading glasses with tiny modern frames, and a large diamond ring on her left hand.

"Do we have assigned seats?" I ask her.

"Not yet. I plan to wait until everyone arrives to determine seating. You are...?"

"Caryn Alderson."

"Nice to meet you, Caryn. Just sit anywhere for now."

I find a desk in the middle of the room and put my book bag on top of it.

"Welcome back, Mrs. York." Janae Thomas claims a desk next to mine and piles her stuff on top of it.

Turning to Janae I whisper, "Where's she been?"

"In the hospital. Missed all of first semester."

A picture of Mr. and Mrs. York in a hospital room with a nurse doing a sonogram flashes into my head, or at least it looks that way based on my extensive viewing of TV hospital dramas. *Oh, I get it. Mrs. York was undergoing treatments for infertility.*

Eek! I slap my head. That really is TMI! Janae looks at me funny.

"Mosquito," I say, pointing to my forehead. Mosquitoes in January? Not in Indianapolis. And Janae doesn't seem to buy it anyway.

More kids filter in and claim seats as Mrs. York greets them. This class is turning out to be a regular Who's Who of Rosslyn High School—Harris Rutherford, top of the freshman class; Emma,

Ashleigh, and Megan grab seats near mine as Janae Thomas, Jeremy Harper, and Mark Evans, sophomores like us, trail in; the junior class is represented by Quince, Kevin Marshall, Salissa Pringle, and Kensington Marlow; plus the seniors, Connor Stevenson and Deana Pruitt.

The bell rings, but kids are still milling around the room chatting. Mrs. York walks out from behind her desk, smiles at the class and says, "Ladies and gentlemen, please find a seat—anywhere for now. Tomorrow I'll make up a seating chart."

The other kids move around and do as they're told, but I decide to stick with the spot I've already chosen.

"Some of you chose to take this class, while others of you got stuck in here because of scheduling problems. Either way, welcome to Love of Lit and I hope we have a productive semester."

Ashleigh raises her hand. "What's this class all about?"

"As the course title would suggest, we'll be studying the great love stories of literature. We'll start with sonnets and then move to *Romeo and Juliet*." Naturally there are groans around the room.

"We read *R&J* freshman year," Kensi says, flipping her hair.

"I'm aware that you've already read it, but I'm sure we'll approach the play differently than you did in Freshman Lit," responds Mrs. York. "Maybe even do some Readers' Theatre."

Ashleigh interrupts again. "Can I go see my counselor? Being in this class is going to look like I goofed off a semester when I fill out college applications."

"See your counselor on your own time, not mine," Mrs. York says sternly. "Now, does everyone have a copy of Elizabeth Barrett Browning's sonnets? If so, let's begin."

I'm starting to like Mrs. York. And I might even like the class if Quince gets assigned a seat next to me. I look over at Kensi across the room and see her in a head-to-head with Salissa, neither of them listening to the teacher.

And if we could get rid of them.

"Mrs. York?" Deana asks, waving her hand wildly in the air. "Can I be excused?"

"Yes, Deana, the pass is on a hook next to the..." but Deana is already out the door with it.

"She always knows where the passes are," Janae explains to the teacher.

The teacher sighs.

****

Mrs. York is as good as her word, and the next day she has a seating chart all drawn up. I thank the Universe when I learn Quince is seated right in front of me, and Kensi's desk is on the far side of the room next to the windows and right by Salissa. The two of them have their heads together whispering most of the time anyway. Harris is sitting on the front row next to Ashleigh, who wasn't allowed to change her schedule but was reassured by her counselor that a literature elective won't hurt her chances of being admitted to a top-notch college. Mrs. York makes the mistake of seating Emma right next to Kevin, and I doubt either of them will get much out of the literature we're going to read, since the only romance they're interested in is their own.

Quince periodically glances over at Kensi. She always smiles in return, but there's something in that smile that says she's holding back. Maybe it's just me thinking that, since I know for a fact she was cheating on Quince in December, but he seems clueless.

The second day of the semester is a cold, dreary January day, and I'm dreading my walk to the store after school. Fortunately, I do have my new coat and accessories to keep me warm, but I still haven't adjusted to temperatures hovering around zero.

"Wanna go to Peterson's?" Megan asks as we gather our belongings from our lockers at the end of the school day.

"Yeah, sure, it's a good day for something hot to drink. But I can't stay long. I have to help my mom in the store."

"I'll meet you there." Megan heads off down the hall but turns around walking backward and calls out, "Emma and Ashleigh are coming too."

I bundle up as best I can, refusing to step foot outdoors until every possible body part is covered. I hoist my heavy book bag onto my shoulder (trying not to think about all the homework I have to do) and head out the front door of the school building.

One block to Peterson's, just one block and you'll be out of the cold.

I duck my head down and walk as fast as I can to the stoplight on the corner, but wouldn't you know it? School buses are exiting the back parking lot—what seems like hundreds of them to my freezing limbs—so the light doesn't turn green until they've all been released. I jump up and down trying to stay warm, hugging myself and turning in all directions just to keep moving.

That's when I see Kensi. Not that it's unusual on a school day, but she's way off in the distance already heading toward Rosslyn Village, arm-in-arm with—well, I can't make out who it is, but I know it isn't Quince.

The light finally turns green and I walk as fast as I can, which it turns out isn't very fast at all, considering I'm wearing about ten extra pounds of clothing and carrying a sixty-pound backpack.

I have to find out who Kensi is with this time, since I assume Mr. College Guy has gone back to wherever he came from. Gradually I close the gap between us, aided by the fact that the two of them keep stopping to look in store windows.

Connor Stevenson! No way!

Just like before with the other guy at the mall, she's leaning her head on his shoulder, cooing in his ear, and smiling that seductive smile at him. I sort of feel bad for Ashleigh, but I'm really angry at Kensi for treating Quince like that. Mostly I just feel bad for Quince.

While I'm standing there trying to decide whether or not I should tell him, I realize I can't feel my hands, so I hurry into Peterson's to warm up. Megan, Emma, and Ashleigh are already at a table. They wave at me and I walk over to join them.

"Did you see Kensi?" I ask, dropping my coat and book bag in an empty chair.

"Yeah, headed for the bus right after school. Why?" Emma blows on her hot chocolate before taking a sip.

"NOT headed for the bus," I correct her. "She's strolling through Rosslyn Village with Connor Stevenson."

"Connor!" Ashleigh exclaims. "He's supposed to be—"

"Don't start thinking of him as a boyfriend," I warn her. "He's not a one-woman man."

"But he's so cute—and smart." Ashleigh frowns.

I shake my head at her.

"Study date?" Emma suggests, a hopeful smile on her face.

Megan nearly chokes on her hot mocha latte. "Yeah, right. Kensi never studies, and NEVER does her own homework if she can get someone else to do it for her."

"Where were they going?" Ashleigh cranes her neck to catch a glimpse of them out the window.

"I don't know, but it looked just like when we saw her at the mall in December, except a different guy."

"What's this about December?" Ashleigh looks from one of us to the other. I guess no one ever told her about what we saw.

"That girl is the biggest cheat!" Megan suddenly exclaims. "Sorry, Ashleigh. Kensi was all over some college guy at the mall, and now Connor. Poor Quince."

"Okay, did we mess up by not telling him what she was doing at the mall?" I ask.

"Should we tell him now?" Megan asks.

Before we can decide, Quince and Kevin walk into Peterson's, rubbing their hands together for warmth as they head to the counter to place their orders. That's when I realize I forgot to place my order, so I walk over to the counter and get in line behind them.

"A cup of hot mint tea," I tell the barista when it's my turn. I smile at Quince and Kevin when they finally notice me. I pick up my tea from the counter, carefully holding it by the heat-guard handle, and rejoin my friends.

Quince and Kevin join us at our table, pulling up a couple of extra chairs and forcing the rest of us to scoot over. Megan turns directly to Quince and asks pointedly, "Where's Kensi?"

Quince shrugs. "She said she had cheerleading practice."

Oh, sure, the old after-school practice excuse. Megan and I exchange knowing glances. How can this guy be that obtuse?

He looks from one of us to the other. "What?"

"Oh, nothing. Hey, there's Jeremy," Megan says, waving to him across the room. "Emma, you and Kevin coming?" The look on Megan's face emphatically tells them they're moving to another table. Behind Quince's back, Megan jerks her thumb at him, letting me know she expects me to tell him.

"Ashleigh, you don't have to go." I'm pleading, not just being polite.

"I've got a violin lesson." Ashleigh gathers up her books in a huff, puts on her coat, and leaves the coffee shop.

I clear my throat and debate my options. Quince is looking as uncomfortable as I feel.

"Got a lot of homework tonight?"

"Yeah," he responds. "You?"

"Tons, but I'm on my way to my mom's store to help out till closing."

"What kind of store is it?" he asks, blowing on his coffee, his gaze wandering around the shop.

"Metaphysical book store," I mutter.

Quince looks at me in that way kids do when they think I'm into witchcraft or something.

"So you're into that stuff, huh?" He looks like he's trying to slide as far away from me as possible.

"Well, yeah, sort of." I take a packet of sweetener, shake it and pour it into my tea.

We sit there in silence awhile, sipping our drinks and fidgeting. Finally Quince speaks up.

"Is that why you said what you said at the carnival last fall?" he asks, his gaze on the stir stick he's tapping on the table.

I thought we'd moved past that. "Well, no, not really. I just heard your grandp...I mean—"

No No NO! You don't tell people that stuff!

"Here we go again," Quince groans. "You're just way weird." He gets up to go join Kevin and Emma.

I want to crawl under the table, but I figure that would draw even more attention to me, so I abandon my half-full mint tea, gather my belongings, and walk out of the coffee shop.

"Remember to be true to yourself," a familiar voice says in my ear as I walk toward Mom's store.

"You're clueless, Uncle Omar. Most kids just don't get someone like me."

I hear laughing in my head.

Maybe I should feel self-conscious talking out loud to myself, but it's so cold that people are moving pretty quickly and not paying attention, and anyway most of my face is covered with the hat and scarf. My voice is muffled and I guess everyone thinks I'm muttering about the cold. At least I hope so.

****

A couple of hours later I've almost forgotten about my conversation with Quince because I'm busy with customers in the store. On a cold day when it gets dark early, it seems lots of people want to snuggle up in front of a warm fire with a book, but first they have to buy the book. There are still a few customers dawdling in the store, but I really don't think I'm going to sell anything else this near to closing time. I busy myself straightening the counter and watching the clock tick toward six o'clock.

So imagine my surprise when the door bell jingles and in walks Quince Adams! I hesitate, not knowing whether to approach him or not, but he solves that problem by walking right over to the cash register.

"Megan talked me into coming in here," he says, a slight flush on his cheeks. "She said this store wasn't any weirder than about half the shops in Rosslyn Village, and I should come see for myself."

Thank you, Megan.

"Can I show you around or anything?" I ask him, hoping I won't say anything stupid if he says yes.

"Who are Starshine and Sybil?" he asks me, indicating the names on the door.

"My mom and her business partner."

Quince frowns, looking back at the door. "So is your mom named Starshine or Sybil?"

"Neither. Bethany Alderson and Sybil Smythe. Starshine is like a stage name."

"Oh."

Quince seems unconvinced as he wanders off to look around the store. He walks over to the bookshelves and browses awhile, and then makes his way through the shelves of candles, tarots, icons, and the jewelry display case. I try to concentrate on dusting the sales counter (which isn't dusty) and pretend that my big crush hasn't just walked into the store. After a few minutes, he comes back and my heart begins to pound fast.

"Interesting stuff," he says, with a shrug.

"Um, thanks." I hope he doesn't notice I'm blushing. I try to think of something to say but my mind is blank. The guy just makes me forget about everything else when he's near.

Quince is gazing over my head and I turn around to see what he's looking at. It's a large, framed photograph of a rainbow. My mom actually saw it in Houston after a thunderstorm and captured it on film. She's not a bad photographer and the picture turned out pretty well, so she had it framed.

"You like rainbows?" I ask.

Quince nods. "I saw one after my grandfather's funeral, and it hadn't even been raining. He used to take me fishing when I was little, and a few times we actually saw rainbows over the lake."

I smile. I can picture Quince as a cute little boy in a fishing boat with his grandfather, beaming as he pulls a big one out of the lake. His kindly grandfather must have sent him that rainbow at the funeral as a sort of comforting sign that he's okay, a reminder of their time together. Quince probably thought it was just a coincidence.

"You've got to tell him the truth about his girlfriend," says a disembodied voice in my ear.

This time it isn't Uncle Omar, it's Quince's Grandpa Adams, pipe and all. It might be good timing for *him* to show up again, but for me it's all wrong.

"No!" I say a little too loudly.

"What?" asks Quince.

I shake my head and smile at him. "Nothing," I say, trying to act normal. It doesn't work.

"You're always doing that, Caryn," he says, a slight curl to his lip. "Talking to yourself. It's creepy."

"Sorry," I say, trying to smile.

A chill shivers down my neck as Quince's grandfather hovers closer.

"He needs to know," Grandpa Adams says insistently.

I try to brush him away but my hand only meets ice-cold air.

I know he isn't going to leave me alone, so against my better judgment I speak up.

"Uh, Quince, there's something I need to tell you and I've been arguing with myself about it." I know that's lame, but maybe Quince will think it explains why I was talking to myself—this time anyway.

"Yeah?" He regards me with narrowed eyes.

"Where's Kensi?" I ask, my heart thudding in my chest.

"You asked me that earlier. Why do you keep bringing her up?" He shoves his hands in his pockets and frowns at me again.

I gulp hard and dive in. "Because…because she's cheating on you."

At first, Quince's mouth drops open wide enough to let an elephant fly in, but soon his face reflects every bit of anger I know he's entitled to feel. Unfortunately, that anger isn't directed at Kensi where I think it belongs.

"Why would you say such mean things about her? You don't even know her!" He says, leaning across the counter.

"Yeah, but—" I can't even think how to tell him

what I saw.

"But what?"

"Quince, I swear I'm not making this up. I saw Kensi hanging all over some college guy at the mall in December and today I saw her holding hands with Connor Stevenson."

"You're lying because you're jealous!" he practically shouts, jabbing a finger at me.

Okay, fair enough, I'm jealous, but it's the truth.

Quiet discussion is out of the question because Quince's loud voice is attracting attention. The few customers still in the store look up from their book browsing to see what the commotion is all about. I lower my voice.

"I'm telling you the truth about Kensi, and if you don't end it with her, she's going to break your heart and end up in some serious trouble."

"Says who? YOU? You and your stupid predictions. You're crazy, Caryn Alderson!"

And with that, Quince storms out of the store.

I stare after him and feel like kicking myself. Great. My one chance to talk to Quince like a normal fifteen-year-old girl and I blow it.

I shake my fist at the ceiling. "Gee thanks, Mr. Adams." No response. NOW he's silent?

Later, when I tell my mom what happened, she gives me a hug and says, "Caryn, you told him the truth, even if he didn't want to hear it. You can't be less than who you are."

Mom has always been my biggest fan. She's never contradicted me when I tell her stuff, even when I was a little kid and most moms would have written it off as an overactive imagination. Not my mom. She accepted everything I predicted as if it were already a fact.

"That's what Uncle Omar said," I say with a sigh.

Mom raises an eyebrow and then hugs me even

tighter. "He's right. Be yourself. If this boy Quince doesn't accept you for who you are, then he isn't the boy for you."

Easy for her to say.

Chapter 8
Sunny Valentine

Winter in Indianapolis is cold—at least it is to me. This is my first experience with real winter, so I come to school bundled up like an Eskimo most days, even when the other kids think it's warm outside. In Houston, a day in February with a temperature of sixty-five degrees is considered winter, but here, everyone thinks it turned summer.

That's what is happening today—Valentine's Day. It's a mild day with a record-setting temperature pushing the seventy degree mark. I'm wearing my usual jeans and hoodie sweatshirt, but most of the kids came to school dressed like they're headed to the beach. Emma is wearing a thin cotton skirt with a belted sleeveless white-eyelet blouse and high-heeled sandals. Very fashionable for June actually, but it isn't June. Ashleigh, usually the sensible one, has on jean shorts and a ribbed scoop-neck top. Megan looks pretty conservative in tight-fitting jeans, T-shirt, and flip-flops, but I'm sure her mother had something to say about her wardrobe.

Other girls around school are wearing outrageously short skirts, short shorts, or sundresses, all of which make me shiver with cold just to look at them. Even the guys have gotten into the spirit of the unexpectedly warm weather by wearing cutoffs and tank tops.

And don't get me started on Kensington Marlow's outfit. She prances into Mrs. York's class wearing, well, not much really. It's a jean skirt that barely skims the top of her thighs, a cotton shirt that bares her midriff and displays her cleavage, and four-inch sandals that most girls wouldn't be able to wobble around in. Needless to say, jaws drop as she parades into the classroom first period and slides into her seat.

Mrs. York is cool, though, and she doesn't say anything to Kensi about her daring outfit.

"Let's open our books to Act V of *Romeo and Juliet*," she says, looking ready-for-summer herself in khaki linen trousers and a white blouse.

"Isn't it kind of a cliché to be reading *R&J* on Valentine's Day?" Janae asks.

"But that's the point of this class, Janae," says Mrs. York. "We're studying the great love stories of literature, and as tragic love stories go, *Romeo and Juliet* is the best there is."

"They kill themselves," Quince says with a snort. "What's so romantic about that?"

Mrs. York gives that some thought. "It's not their tragic end so much as their deep love that makes it such a moving story. Why do you suppose people are still reading and performing this play over four hundred years after it was written?"

No one answers. I look around the room and see students struggling with the concept, but then Harris raises his hand. You can almost hear the silent groans.

"Yes, Harris?" Mrs. York has been pacing up and down in front of the classroom, but she stops patiently to listen to Harris's question.

"Is it because Romeo and Juliet are kids like us, and we can relate to them?"

I see him glance at me seeking approval and I deliberately look the other way. No sense encouraging him.

"Partly, but there are other reasons," Mrs. York says.

Emma raises her hand. "I think it's because

their deaths accomplished something their love couldn't. It united their families."

"Good point, Emma," Mrs. York says with a smile. "Any other comments?"

"Like Romeo and Juliet have a lock on true love," Kensi mutters, and casts a seductive look at Quince making him blush.

UGH! Is he really buying that?

"Would you like to elaborate, Kensington?"

"Well," she says in a louder voice. "Teachers act like Romeo and Juliet are the only teenagers to ever fall in love."

Mrs. York looks at her indulgently. "Maybe not the *only* ones, but they're certainly the most famous."

Quince beams at Kensi like she said something brilliant, and I want to scream. He seems smart enough to know when someone is playing him, yet he falls for her games every time. I wish I'd kept my mouth shut about her since it hasn't changed anything at all.

After lots of groveling on my part, he and I are almost back on speaking terms after my ill-advised blurt last month. But Quince barely even acknowledges my existence when Kensi is around. And he still doesn't believe she's been unfaithful to him.

Here it is February 14, and the love of my life is making goo-goo eyes at a half-dressed girl who has another guy (or two!) on the side. And to make it even worse, I did something this morning before school that I already regret and now want to take back.

I wish Kensi wasn't here.

"Mrs. York," says a woman's voice on the PA. "Could you please send Kensington Marlow to the office?"

Hmmm. Was that a psychic hit on my part or is

the Universe granting my wish? Either way, who cares?

"Certainly," Mrs. York answers, nodding at Kensi.

Kensington picks up her books and walks out the door like she's headed down a fashion runway. Come to think of it, she sort of is, considering how all the guys gawk at her until she's out of sight.

"What do you suppose that's about?" Janae whispers.

"Her outfit," I answer, then quickly add, "I'll bet."

Now I'll readily admit that anyone could've figured out Kensi would be in trouble for how she's dressed, so the fact that I know her mother is waiting in the office for her, I keep to myself. But I don't need to tell Janae that Kensi is about to get sent home, since Janae will figure it out soon enough and spread it all over school by lunch. Problem is, Kensi isn't the only girl at school dressed inappropriately today, so I suppose the administrators are making an example of her since she's so popular.

Mrs. York tries to redirect her students. "Shall we continue?"

I steal a glance at Quince who has pulled out his folder and is now taking notes. Once his focus is off Kensi, all he appears interested in is academics.

If only he'd look at me the same way he looks at her. I'm starting to hate Valentine's Day.

****

The school cafeteria is a hotbed of romantic activity. Everywhere you look there are red heart-shaped balloons, pink and red teddy bears, Valentine's cards (both store-bought and homemade), candy hearts, and of course, chocolate galore. It's enough to give a person a stomach ache from the sugar rush.

Confessions of a Teenage Psychic

I sit down at our usual table next to Emma, Ashleigh, and Megan, uninterested in my lunch and dreading their discussions about what their boyfriends got them.

"Kevin gave me this," Emma says, proudly displaying a heart necklace.

"Very pretty," I say.

"I got a huge box of chocolates from Jeremy," Megan gushes. "Anybody want a piece?"

She pops a piece of chocolate in her mouth before passing the box around the table. I take a piece of chocolate-covered caramel and stuff it into my mouth. *Can you drown your sorrows in candy?* I don't know, but I think I might try.

"Ashleigh," I say with my mouth full. "Who gave you the teddy bear?"

"Connor Stevenson."

I nearly choke on the candy thinking of Connor and Kensi.

"Connor's going to be valedictorian this year, so I guess he doesn't want to hang out with the likes of Kensington 'Bottom of the Junior Class' Marlow after all." Ashleigh has a triumphant smile on her face.

"I'd say he traded up." I swallow the sticky candy, wishing the chocolate would do its mood-enhancing magic.

"What about you, Caryn? Anything from Mark?" Ashleigh helps herself to a piece of Megan's candy.

"Mark? No way, not that I care. I'd rather get a card from Harris Rutherford."

Well, not really. And don't even get me started on my unrequited love for Quince Adams.

Ashleigh looks genuinely surprised that I've been left out of the love-fest, like she's just now realizing I don't have a boyfriend.

"I didn't even get a pity card. I'm too much of a freak to attract a boyfriend." I'm feeling pretty sorry for myself, so I cram another piece of candy in my mouth.

"That's not true," Megan says sympathetically, swallowing the last of her chocolate. "You just haven't met Mr. Right yet."

Yes I have, and he's attached to Miss Wrong.

"Did anyone see how Kensi Marlow was dressed this morning?" Emma asks, changing to her favorite subject, fashion. "She was really pushing the envelope."

"Pushing her luck's more like it." Megan takes a swig of apple juice. "I heard she got sent home."

I nod as I swallow the chocolate. "I can't believe how some kids dress for school. When I enrolled in September…"

"You got here late and it was already getting cooler," Megan says. "You should have seen the fashion parade in August. My mother wouldn't let me wear half the outrageous stuff the other girls were wearing."

"Who are you calling outrageous?" Emma demands.

"Not you, Emma. I'm talking about Kensi and her crew. Like how she looked today," Megan says.

I'm trying to listen to this discussion, really I am, but my mind is on Quince sitting at the guys' table across the room. I allow my thoughts to drift away from fashion and onto the unrequited love of my life.

Quince: Oh, Caryn, I've been a fool to believe all Kensi's lies. Will you forgive me and be my girlfriend?

Caryn: Of course, Quince. You know how much I care about you.

(Organ music reaches a crescendo in the background!)

While Emma is babbling on about fashion faux pas and I'm daydreaming, Quince gets up to take his tray to the back of the cafeteria. Dirty lunch trays are anything but romantic and I snap back to the moment just in time to realize he's stopped at our table on his way. My stomach lurches, either in anticipation that he'll speak to me or nausea from the candy, I can't tell which.

"Okay, I know you all love me, but which one of you ladies taped that anonymous Valentine card to my locker?"

He looks each one of us in the eye. I lower my head and pretend to take a bite of my now-cold hamburger.

"Not me!" Emma is the first to speak up. "I've got a boyfriend." She turns to each of us in succession. "Megan? Ashleigh? Caryn?"

She had to name me last, which leaves everyone staring at me, expecting an answer.

"It was probably Kensi," I say, not making eye contact with him.

"Nope, not her. This one was hand-drawn, and Kensi can't draw for squat. Besides, she already gave me my Valentine." Quince blushes and then grins as if remembering it.

TMI! I close my eyes and try to shut out the image of the two of them kissing.

"What'd it look like?" Megan asks. "The one on your locker, I mean. I pretty much know all the kids in the art program. I could take a look at it."

She must see the look on my face, because she hastily changes directions, "Or maybe it'll just have to stay a mystery."

She smiles innocently at Quince and I silently mouth, "Thank you."

Quince shrugs. "Well, whatever, but it's really cool, with a heart in the middle of a rainbow. Tell *whoever* drew it that I liked it."

He winks at us and then goes to dump his tray. I'm about to faint.

"Ohmigod, Caryn!" Megan turns to me when he's out of earshot. "*You* put that card on Quince's locker?"

"Guilty. Please don't tell him." My face feels like it's a blazing red.

"But why? He's with Kensi!"

"Stupid whim, something he told me about rainbows," I say in a mumble, the candy like a lump in my stomach. "Do you think he suspects me?"

"Maybe, but my lips are sealed," Megan says, laughing. "Besides, we all know Kensington Marlow isn't good enough for Quince anyway."

I glance up at the clock and realize the bell is about to ring signaling the end of lunch.

"We've got to hurry and get to class," I tell Megan as I gather up my tray. "We're having an assembly after next period."

"Huh?" Megan closes up her chocolate box and throws her trash onto my tray. "When did they announce that?"

"It hasn't been announced yet," I say, getting up from the table.

Megan does one of her exaggerated eye rolls. "Okay, then, Miss Psychic Know-it-all, what's the assembly about?"

I don't answer but hurry out of the cafeteria. All I know is that a feeling in my gut put a flash into my head, and I'm sure there's more to it than too much candy. I'll just let her and everyone else find out when they get there.

****

Principal MacGregor comes on the PA just after lunch and announces an all-school meeting. Students and teachers are told to come directly to the auditorium with a minimum of conversation. Word on the street—okay, in the school hallways—is that something serious is going down, and all the kids are kind of freaked out.

There are over one thousand students at Rosslyn High School, so the auditorium is filled to capacity, and faculty members are forced to stand in the aisles and along the walls due to a lack of seats. Mr. MacGregor is on the stage glaring at us as we file in. With this many students there's bound to be noise and chaos, and naturally kids are going to try to find a seat next to their friends. Mr. MacGregor is having none of it.

"Students, please take your seats immediately. Teachers, I'm going to ask your assistance in getting the students seated and quiet as quickly as possible."

We all know he means business, so kids begin to sit in any available seat, urged along by teachers who are getting a little grouchy themselves.

"Ladies and gentlemen," the principal begins when order is somewhat restored, "please direct your attention up here immediately."

The school principal isn't one to be ignored and a hush falls over the auditorium. He clears his throat and in a stern voice says, "As you know, we're experiencing unusually warm weather for this time of year, but it's only February. Spring will arrive in a few weeks, and with it will come the desire to wear lightweight clothing."

There's a murmur among the students.

"Today, a number of your classmates came to school in inappropriate attire and have been asked to return home and change their clothes. I'm taking this opportunity to remind you that we have a dress code here at Rosslyn High School and it will be enforced!"

This time the murmuring is very loud.

"Yeah, right!" say some boys on the front row.

"Good luck with that!" More kids join in the clamor.

Principal MacGregor bellows, "This is not a

discussion, it's a warning!"

The kids get quiet again in a hurry.

"Any student arriving at school dressed in unacceptable clothing will face suspension. I do *not* expect to have another day like today, where the moral compass is cast aside in the name of fashion. Rules *will* be followed by all students in this building. You may now return to your afternoon classes."

The grumbling grows louder as we get up to leave the auditorium. Megan catches up to me and pulls me aside.

"You knew we were having an assembly!" For someone whose outfit doesn't even come close to violating the dress code, Megan seems pretty upset. "Did you know what Mr. MacGregor was going to say?"

I nod. "And it's going to get worse."

"How much worse can it get?" Megan says, crossing her arms.

"I don't know," I say with a shrug. "Uniforms maybe?"

Megan stares at me like that's the stupidest thing she ever heard. "They can't make us wear uniforms like in a private school!"

I back off my prediction, because I don't know if this picture in my head is set in stone or just a warning. "They can't?"

"I thought I was done with uniforms when I left Willowby," Megan says with a huff. "Kids will be really mad. *I'm* mad!"

"Megan...Oh, never mind. I'll talk to you tonight!" I try to escape before Megan makes me tell her about the picture that just flashed into my head.

"What do you mean you'll talk to me tonight?" Megan is really puzzled now but I don't have time to explain.

"Caryn Alderson! Tell me what you know!" I

cringe when I realize Janae overheard us.

I whisper to Megan, "*Please* stay out of this."

Trouble is, when Megan sets her mind to something, there's no stopping her, and I can see the wheels in her head turning already. Megan storms out of the auditorium like a woman on a mission.

It's easy to start a rumor in a big public high school, especially with Janae on the case, and now the rumor mill is in full swing. Kids are whispering in hallways and classrooms, "We're not going to be allowed to wear shorts," or "Sandals are being outlawed," or "They're going to make us wear strict uniforms."

All I can hope for is a long, cold spring. Anything to keep kids from dressing like they're at a beach party, because otherwise my internal radar is telling me Rosslyn High School is in for some rough times.

****

When I told Megan earlier today that I'd talk to her tonight I already knew what about, so I'm staying up late waiting for the phone to ring. I guess she's gotten over the wardrobe paranoia, at least temporarily, because she's as bubbly as ever when I answer the phone.

"Guess what, Caryn! You were right. My sister Caroline got engaged today! Valentine's Day—it's just so romantic! And you should see the ring Richard gave her! They're planning their wedding for next summer and she wants me to be a bridesmaid. It's so cool! Mom's so excited! This is one time you can say 'I told you so' and I won't mind at all."

I mentally give myself a thumbs-up. "Tell Caroline I'm very happy for her, and for your family."

Megan tells me all the details and when I hang up the phone, even though it's late and I'm tired, my mind won't quit churning about the day's events. I go into the living room and turn on the TV, find a *Star Wars* marathon playing on one of the local channels, and snuggle down on the sofa to watch.

There's a disturbance in the Force, echoes in my mind as I drift off to sleep.

Luke Skywalker is on a sandy beach, wearing cutoffs and a muscle shirt, fighting Darth Vader who is dressed in swim trunks and flip-flops. Princess Leia is in the background—or is it Kensington Marlow—wearing skintight short shorts, a clingy wet T-shirt, and of course, braided buns on each side of her head.

"A kiss for luck!" Kensington tells Quince.

I sit straight up as my eyes pop open, and then I realize it's only Princess Leia talking to Luke. Heck, even he got a kiss on Valentine's Day—from his sister, but still...

Between the warm weather, the dress code rumors, my sixth sense telling me Megan is heading for disaster, and Kensi cheating on Quince who doesn't seem to care, I wish I could go to that Galaxy Far, Far Away.

I groan, turn off the TV, and go to bed.

Chapter 9
An Ill Wind Marches In

You could say March blew in like a lion, but really it was more like Hurricane Megan.

The rumors about school uniforms died down a little after Valentine's Day, especially since the weather turned cold again and all the kids had to go back to wearing their winter clothes. But Megan wouldn't let it drop. She kept up a running dialogue with anyone who cared to listen—and a few people who didn't care to listen, like me—about how Rosslyn High would be the laughingstock of the city if kids were forced to wear uniforms in public school. Megan single-handedly kept the kids stirred up, despite my constant warnings for her to stay out of it.

This rumor is a tough one to squelch, though, since the story keeps changing all the time. Sometimes there are exaggerations, sometimes there's a grain of truth to it, but most kids just don't know what to believe.

"Mrs. York?" Megan asks the teacher in first period, interrupting the lesson. "Is it true we'll have to wear uniforms next year?"

Mrs. York sighs. "Megan, I really don't know where you heard that, but to my knowledge it's not true."

Megan barely allows Mrs. York to finish before waving her arm in the air. "But Principal MacGregor said—"

"Yes, I know what he said about dressing appropriately, but students have heeded his warning and I think things have calmed down again," Mrs. York says, holding up a hand.

"Yeah, but only because it's cold right now," Kensi whines. "When it gets warm again and we want to wear—"

"Yeah, shorts and stuff," Megan chimes in.

"I believe you students have blown Mr. MacGregor's comments way out of proportion." Mrs. York now has her hands on her hips, exasperation in her voice.

Deana Pruitt raises her hand. "I overheard my dad say something about a stricter dress code."

"Perhaps the superintendent is just planning to enforce the dress code we already have," Mrs. York replies.

"Does that mean only khaki pants and navy blue shirts like I heard someone say?" Janae asks.

"I heard guys would have to wear ties everyday!" Kevin shouts.

There's a lot of murmuring, everyone repeating what they heard like it's a child's game of Gossip. Apparently there are very real threats to our fashion individuality, if you believe the rumors.

Mrs. York's patience is wearing thin. "Class, please, can we get back to work?"

No one is listening to the teacher now. Students are whispering among themselves and the angrier they get, the louder they talk. I hear snippets of conversations punctuated with "no way" and "they can't tell us what to wear" and "my dad will freak" or "uniforms are too expensive." Most of the students have always attended public school and have no idea what it means to wear a uniform. I'm one of those kids, but Megan—straight from Willowby Prep—and a few of the students who attended parochial schools are up in arms.

"Class!" Mrs. York taps her foot until the class settles down. "I think we need to table this discussion and get back to our lesson. We were discussing Shakespeare's *Midsummer Night's Dream*. Does anyone see any similarities in the play-within-a-play about Pyramus and Thisbe, to *Romeo and Juliet?*"

"What I think is important is that Thisbe got to choose her own clothes that supposedly got torn by the lion," Emma says.

Naturally that gets a laugh from the class.

"Anybody have a comment that does *not* pertain to wardrobe?" Mrs. York scouts out a likely victim. "Caryn?"

Nothing like being put on the spot, but since the teacher called on me, I go ahead and make my point.

"I don't know about Thisbe, but if Bottom and all those bogus actors had worn outfits that offended the duke, they'd have been thrown out of Athens."

Okay, I'll admit it's a cryptic remark, but I can't help myself. All the mini-movies running in my head are screaming at me that this problem is going to escalate to a very bad end. If I can believe my gut instincts, everyone needs to back off and quit aggravating the teachers, and more importantly, the principal. Kids are letting what we're wearing to school take on a life of its own.

Quince opens his mouth with a loud, exaggerated yawn, followed by an overhead arm stretch. "Is anybody else as tired of all this dress code talk as I am?"

Megan claps her book closed. "Yeah, well, most of you have no idea how boring it is to wear the same thing to school day after day. I did it for years and I don't want to do it again."

There's a chorus of "me neither" and "so did I" from a few students, but Mrs. York is glaring at the class, so it quickly dies down.

"Please, students, *focus*. Act V..."

The class settles down for the moment, but I

know this is nowhere near over. Megan pulls out a sheet of paper and begins writing furiously.

She's making up a petition!

From where I'm sitting I can't see what she's writing, but I know I'm right and it gives me uncomfortable goose bumps.

****

So it comes as no surprise the next day at lunch when Megan brings in a neatly typed petition with blank pages attached for hundreds of signatures, and begins asking kids in the cafeteria to sign it. Here's what it says:

We, the undersigned students of Rosslyn High School, are opposed to any attempts to require us to wear school uniforms. We believe the current dress code is fine and should be enforced by teachers, administrators, and the school superintendent.

By signing this petition, we students declare that we will NOT cooperate with any forced changes in the current dress code.

It's pretty bold for students to sign their names, saying they refuse to cooperate. Megan walks the petition around from table to table, easily convincing most students to put their signatures at the bottom. She even has to go to a second and then third page as she fills them up. Kids are willing to sign something that at this point is hypothetical, but the petition drive is gaining a lot of momentum and Megan is about to lock herself into a battle of wills with the principal.

I hate the images I'm getting, but they won't get out of my head. Every time I see that petition, alarm bells clang inside my head with a robotic voice chanting *Danger, Danger*. Unfortunately, at this point I can't see how it's going to end. Maybe I don't want to see.

Megan holds the paper out in front of me and tries to shove a pen in my hand. "Caryn, you haven't signed my petition."

I back up, putting some distance between me and that pen. "I don't think it's a good idea. None of it—the petition, challenging the administration—it's just not going to work."

Why do I bother? Megan isn't listening to me. She's too caught up in this new cause of hers to pay any attention.

"Traitor!" She stomps off to find another group of students to add their signatures.

****

"Annabeth, call me when you get this."

I hang up the phone and flip on the TV in the living room. I haven't seen Annabeth since January, although we've talked on the phone since then. I'm thinking she's the one person who might be able to get through to Megan, seeing as how they've known each other since kindergarten.

There's a rerun of *Friends* on one of the independent channels, so I settle in for some mindless comedy.

How come all those characters in that sitcom can get angry with each other and still maintain their friendships? It sure doesn't work that way with the kids I know. Megan is mad at me for not signing her petition. I'm afraid she'll get in big trouble if she doesn't stop, and I'm mad at her for not listening to me. And Quince is still mad at me for accusing Kensi of cheating on him.

I sigh and curl up in a corner of the sofa. I hug a throw pillow and pull an afghan over me while I try to concentrate on the program. Rachel is breaking up with Ross after catching him cheating.

Quince is breaking up with Kensi after catching her cheating. Megan and Monica are in the kitchen cooking pasta while Phoebe and Joey and Annabeth are talking about what to wear to school...

The phone rings and I realize I must have dozed

off.

"Hello?" I'm still half asleep, the television blaring in the background.

"I'm calling you back," Annabeth says. "What's up?"

I sit up and try to get the cobwebs out of my head. I reach for the remote and fumble for the mute button with the phone still in my ear.

"Caryn, you called ME. Are you there? What's so important?" Annabeth sounds oddly impatient.

"Yeah. I'm about half here. It's Megan."

"Megan? You sounded all urgent about Megan?"

"Well, it's what's going on at school."

She's right. Now that I hear myself, it does sound lame.

Annabeth sighs. "Okay, so what's she done now that's got you all upset?"

I sit upright on the sofa, throw the blanket off and try to collect my thoughts. Annabeth knows Megan better than I do, so I'm hoping she has some insights into what might get Megan to back off her single-minded drive to save Rosslyn High School from the dress code demons.

"She's got this petition drive going, trying to stir everyone up about refusing to wear school uniforms. It's gotten, well…"

"Wait, wait. What's this about school uniforms, and what petition?"

"Sorry." I realize I haven't told Annabeth about the principal's threats and the rumors at school. "Megan just won't let this drop."

Annabeth's voice sounds thoughtful. "Yeah, that's Megan, all right. But hey—school uniforms in a *public* school?"

"Well, I don't know for sure, but Megan's acting like it's a done deal."

"Ooooh, interesting." Annabeth puts her hand over the receiver giggling, and I can tell it's nothing

I said. "But, Caryn, if *you* don't know what's going to happen, what do you need me for?"

"Oh, never mind. Maybe I should call you back, since you've got company."

"What? How did you know that?" Annabeth sounds puzzled which is funny since she of all people should know how I know.

I close my eyes and concentrate and see a tall boy with dark eyes and curly hair. "Annabeth, who's your new study partner?"

"Caryn, that's so freaky how you do that," Annabeth says, still in that giggly voice. "Okay, it's a guy in my psychology class and we're studying for a test."

"So that's what you call it!" I say, wishing Quince and I "studied" together. "Does this guy have a name?"

"Yes, he does, but I'm not telling you now. I gotta go. Anything else?" Annabeth puts her hand over the phone and I hear her muffled voice talking to the guy.

I shrug. "I thought maybe you could talk to Megan."

"Well, okay I'll try, but I'm not promising anything. It's *Megan,* you know." She doesn't sound too interested.

"Well, whatever. And have fun with Miguel." I hang up before she can say anything else.

"You can't change the events already set in motion," I hear a voice say to me.

I look around the room and think maybe the TV volume is on, but it's still set to mute. In frustration I grab the remote and flip off the set.

Just your overactive imagination again.

As I yawn, stretch, and head to my bedroom, I come face-to-face with Uncle Omar in the darkened hallway. Well, it should have been dark because all the lights are turned off, but there's this glow around him and I can see him clear as day, grinning at me as usual. At least I've gotten to the place where I don't jump or scream for my mom every time I see an apparition, but I have to admit it still unnerves me.

I put my hands on my hips. "I can't change what?"

"Megan, the petition drive, all of it. It's beyond your control." Why does Uncle Omar always sound so calm?

"But I don't want Megan to get in trouble." I know I sound whiny, but the whole thing has just got me so confused.

Uncle Omar gets serious and says, "That's not what you're afraid of and you know it."

I give that some thought and realize he's making sense for once. But if it isn't Megan getting in trouble, then I still can't focus on what's scaring me so much. I knock my knuckles against my head like that's going to knock the answer loose. Instead it's just giving me a headache.

"Just let things play out the way they're supposed to," he says with that ridiculous grin.

"What's that supposed to mean?"

But then he's gone and the hallway is in darkness again. Without turning on the light I go into my room and collapse on the bed.

What can I do, what can I do, what can I do?

No matter how many times I say it, I don't have any answers. I turn off the lamp next to my bed and decide to sleep on it till morning.

Unfortunately, I forget to set my alarm.

Chapter 10
Late

"Caryn! Why aren't you up yet?"

I open one eye and see my mother standing over my bed. I yawn, rub my eyes, and roll over to look at the bedside clock. Seven thirty! Usually I'm up by six thirty.

I have a morning routine. I shower, dress, and eat a bowl of cereal while brewing my mother's coffee so she can leave for the store by eight-thirty. In a role-reversal kind of thing, I usually wake Mom up just before I leave the apartment to catch the 7:25 school bus. Now I'm going to miss most of my first period class because I overslept.

"I can't believe I forgot to set my alarm. Can you drive me to school, Mom?"

"You know the car doesn't have any gas. I'll give you a note, but you'll have to walk since you missed the bus."

"Is it cold outside?"

"By whose standards?" Mom asks.

I can hear the wind blowing through the trees as their still-bare branches scrape my bedroom window, so I know I'll need a jacket at least. Since it's late March, none of the other kids are wearing their heavy winter coats to school, and not wanting to look uncool, I decide not to wear mine anymore either. Walking the six blocks to school without a coat isn't going to be fun, but my social image is worth the sacrifice. I stumble out of bed and head toward the bathroom.

"Sorry about oversleeping, Mom," I call over my

shoulder as she heads to the kitchen to make her own coffee.

By the time I get close to the school building I'm pretty chilled through, wearing only a hoodie sweatshirt. And then of course I have to stop and wait for that light on the corner, the one that never seems to turn green when I need it to. I jump up and down and try to warm myself, while looking around to see if any other kids are late to school besides me.

Sure enough, off in the distance I spot Kensington Marlow, teetering down the sidewalk in her four-inch heels.

Just my luck.

Now I'm going to have to stand in line at the attendance office with her. But wait—maybe not. Just as the corner light finally turns green, I see Kensi climb into a late-model sports car, then the driver speeds by me and through the light (risking a speeding ticket in a school zone I might add). As the car whips past, I recognize Mr. College Guy—the one she was with at the mall back in December. So not only is Kensi seeing other guys, she's now cutting school with one.

What's he doing here anyway?

"Spring break," I say aloud, slapping my forehead. Colleges take their spring vacations about three weeks earlier than most high schools.

As I cross the street I see another student walking up to the main entrance. It's Quince, and he has a look on his face I've never seen before. I hurry to catch up with him.

"Hi, Quince. You late too?"

Suddenly I'm not cold anymore, and in fact I'm warming up quickly. Just being near Quince makes my pulse quicken.

He doesn't answer and then I know he saw Kensi get into that car. The truth about her is just hitting him, and apparently it isn't the truth that's going to set him free. But he turns to face me and forces a grin.

"Dentist appointment. I might have to get braces, and then I'll look like a geek my senior year."

"You won't—"

His smile fades and he nervously runs his fingers through his hair, frustration pulsating through every move. "It already looks like I'm an idiot. Aren't you going to say I told you so?"

Poor guy. He's miserable and I don't blame him. He just saw what some of us have known for months, and the hurt, anger, and confusion all show on his face.

"No, of course not. Quince, I—"

"Forget it." He cuts me off and heads into school.

We both have to report for late passes, but Quince gets there ahead of me and he's first in line. He never speaks to me again or even makes eye contact with me, hurrying out of the office while I have to stand in line behind two other kids.

"You have ten minutes left in first period, Caryn," says the attendance clerk. "Do you want to go there now or just wait and report to second?"

"I'll go to first, to see if I have any homework."

And find a way to talk to Quince if I can.

I hurry to my locker and then to class. When I get there Quince is already in his seat, staring straight ahead at the chalkboard like he's intent on reading the day's assignment. Since he isn't blinking, just staring, I doubt he's really seeing anything—except red.

I look around the room and notice attendance is a little light this morning. Megan isn't here, Kensi of course isn't, and Emma and Ashleigh are also missing. I slide into my chair and pull out a sheet of notebook paper, quickly scribbling a note to Janae.

Where is everyone?

She scribbles a reply and passes it back to me.

Megan and Emma—office
Ashleigh—college visit
Deana—puking
Quince—late
Kensi? Who cares!
Where have you been?
I scribble back. *Overslept. Megan—why office?*
Petition! Janae scribbles.

Uh-oh, that can't be good. I can almost hear the music of doom playing in the background.

"Caryn, it's bad enough that you've missed most of class, but could you and Janae please stop passing notes and pay attention for what's left?" Mrs. York says.

"Sorry."

I turn my attention toward the front of the classroom. Just as I'm writing down the homework assignment the dismissal bell rings.

****

Since none of the other girls are around at lunchtime, I sit down alone with my food tray at our usual table in the cafeteria. Salissa Pringle is, for whatever reason, sitting at the far end of it trying to appear engrossed in a romance novel. That's fine by me, since she and I definitely travel in different social circles. Normally she sits with Kensi and the other cheerleaders on the far side of the room, but that table is empty today too. I guess Salissa would rather sit with her social inferiors than be seen sitting alone, and I kind of smile to myself at that thought.

I fumble in my book bag for something to read, hoping to appear studious and aloof to anyone who might notice I'm eating alone. While I scrounge through old homework papers, pencils gone astray, and stab myself with a protractor, a food tray slams down next to me.

I look up, startled. "Uh, hi, Megan."

"I'm SO mad I could scream!"

"But you practically are—screaming, that is."

Megan plops down hard in the chair next to me and loudly scrapes its legs across the floor as she scoots herself up to the table. She turns to face me and lowers her voice slightly.

"Aren't you going to say I told you so?"

"That's a popular question today," I say, poking at my food.

But Megan's in no mood for mystery. "Make sense for once, Caryn!"

"Okay, no, I'm not going to rub it in." I take a bite of my lukewarm pepperoni pizza even though my appetite is gone. "What happened?"

"It was horrible!" Megan says, her face flushed. "Someone ratted me out! The principal was there and they even called Mom out of her class, and they made me give up the petition. I had nearly five hundred signatures!" Tears are welling up in her eyes.

I lift my shoulders. "So why are you surprised someone told? At least five hundred kids knew what you were up to."

She shakes her head, fighting back the tears. "Yeah, all the kids knew, but they promised solidarity. So the principal must've found out somehow."

A tear slips down her cheek and she wipes it away with a quick swipe of her hand.

"Megan, I'm sorry. I know how much—"

"It's just so unfair!" Megan slumps down in her chair, her arms folded across her chest.

I remember what Janae wrote in that note earlier. "And what about Emma? Why was she called down?"

Megan pouts her lips. "How do I know? Emma didn't do anything—well, except sign the petition, but so did lots of other kids."

I've definitely lost my appetite and I can't look Megan in the face, so I pick at the cold pepperoni slices with a plastic fork. "So I don't get it. Is the principal going to call in every kid who signed it?"

"I don't know, probably not. Just me."

So common sense—not to mention my sixth sense—tells me that Principal MacGregor thinks punishing the ringleader will squelch this mini-rebellion. But the administration doesn't know Megan if they think it'll be that easy.

I quit playing with my food and face Megan. "What did Mr. MacGregor say to you?"

"That I was setting a bad example, that I'd embarrassed my mother, that I wasn't representing Rosslyn High properly. You know, all that guilt trip stuff," she says, tears welling in her eyes again.

Yeah, I know how adults can be, and the principal's glare and stern voice have a way of making kids wish they'd never been born, let alone disobeyed the rules.

"So did you get in trouble? Detention? What?"

"I have to write a one thousand-word apology to the principal and superintendent before tomorrow," Megan moans.

"That's like three pages long!" No wonder she looks so upset.

"Yeah, and I've got better things to do." Megan takes a sip of her chocolate milk while her gaze wanders around the cafeteria. "Hey, maybe I can get Harris Rutherford to do it for me."

Poor Harris. The only attention he ever gets from girls is when they want something from him—math homework, three-page letters, whatever.

"I thought Harris was better at math than English," I say, hoping to save him.

"Whatever. I'm still gonna ask him." Megan sits there sulking for a few minutes, and then seems to get her second wind. "Well, it's not over, you know!

Just because they took away my petition doesn't mean I'm letting it go!"

I can't believe her, because getting called to the principal's office would be enough to scare most kids—including me—into compliance. Annabeth is right—if Megan has her mind made up, nothing and nobody can change it.

I try a new approach. "Spring break is in a couple of weeks. Got any plans?"

Megan looks annoyed and I know she's about to tell me I can't distract her that easily, but she sighs dramatically before answering. "Sort of. My dad and step-monster are taking me with them for a trip to Vegas. I'm gonna shop and soak up some rays, maybe even see one of those shows they let kids into."

Megan is clearly looking forward to her upcoming vacation, but I instantly know her parents have their own plans for that trip and Megan's invitation to join them is an afterthought, or guilt, or both. An image of Megan watching TV by herself in an expensive hotel room while her dad and stepmom are out on the town flashes into my mind. I'm beginning to understand Megan's need to grab attention any way she can.

"What about you?" she asks me, taking a bite of her sandwich. "Any plans?"

"Nothing much. Just work in the store, maybe hang out at the mall or see a movie or something."

The truth is that I have absolutely no plans for the week-long break, since most of my friends will be out of town. I wish I could afford a plane ticket to go visit Dad, but Mom says that trip will have to wait till summer when she's saved up enough money to pay for it.

We eat in silence for a while. Near the end of the lunch period, Emma comes and sits down with us, a glum look on her face as well.

"So why did you get called to the principal's office?" I ask her.

Emma scowls. "Mr. MacGregor saw my name near the top of Megan's petition. He said I'm supposed to be a role model to other kids, or something like that. He said he has bigger plans for me."

I gulp. I already know what those bigger plans are, but I manage to keep my mouth shut for once. I try another bite of my pizza, but it's ice cold now.

Just when I think we're going to get away from lunch without any more dress code talk, Salissa speaks up from the far end of the lunch table.

"Hey, Megan," she calls out, "what's Plan B?"

Megan narrows her eyes and nods. "I'm working on it."

"Come on, Megan, let it go," I plead. "Nothing good can come of this, I promise you. I mean, *really* promise you. Besides, you're the only one who thinks we might have to wear uniforms. Principal MacGregor never said—"

Megan slaps her drink down. "If you can't support me, Caryn, then stay out of my way!"

After that remark, I gladly pick up my tray as the bell rings, toss my trash and leave for art class. Maybe the whole uniform thing will blow over during spring break and Megan won't get herself into deeper trouble.

"No such luck," Uncle Omar whispers in my ear.

I groan and head for class.

****

I take my sweet time getting to Mom's store after school. I have a lot on my mind and I need time to think things through. And anyway the sun is out and it's warmer than it was this morning. I wonder if Uncle Omar is around to offer me any advice. Now that I'm getting used to him just suddenly appearing, it doesn't seem so weird to ask his opinion about stuff. Unfortunately I haven't heard anything from him since lunch.

I guess I have to puzzle this all out for myself—Megan's determination to challenge the school administrators, Kensi's cheating heart, Quince's anger at her, Quince's coldness to me. It's all too much to sort through, so I decide to stall and do some window shopping on my way.

I peek into Peterson's to see if anyone is in there, and even though the place is as full as ever, none of my friends are there today. I could've used the distraction of kids and their normal high school angst, but it's not to be.

Problem is, I can't quite put my finger on what's bothering me so much. Is it Quince? Megan? Uncle Omar's cryptic remarks? It's giving me a headache.

The sun is shining brightly and all I really want to do is stay outside and enjoy it, but I promised Mom. Reluctantly I walk into the shop, the door bell jangling as I enter. I toss my book bag behind the counter, and look around for something to do to take my mind off things. Sybil isn't around. Mom is over by the book rack, showing a rather attractive older gentleman (okay, about her age) a few copies of something or other. She looks up and smiles at me.

I lean over the counter and grin at her, sensing her attraction to the man, and then realize I really should do the dusting, since my sweater is covered in dust bunnies when I stand up. Before I even get two steps in the direction of the backroom and the feather duster, though, I hear the front door jangle and turn to see Quince walking in.

"Hi!" Boy, am I surprised.

"Hi, yourself. I owe you an apology." The frown on Quince's face says he's still in a bad mood, but he *sounds* contrite.

"You do?" My palms begin to sweat. True, he cut me off this morning when I tried to talk to him, but I didn't expect an apology.

"Yeah, I'm sorry about the way I talked to you this morning, like it was your fault or something. I was just really mad. Seeing Kensi with that other guy and all." He looks down at the floor, pretending to scrape something off his shoe. "You tried to tell me about Kensi before and I wouldn't listen."

I grasp the edge of the counter to keep myself from jumping across to hug him. "I'm sorry you had to find out like that—seeing her in that college guy's car."

"College guy?" Quince's eyebrow shoots up and I hope he lets that one pass, because I don't want to talk about how I know that.

I clear my throat. "I just thought you should know what kind of girl Kensi really is."

He doesn't say anything for quite a while, and I wonder if he's still mad at me. "You were just being straight with me, Caryn, which is what friends do. Sorry I went off on you."

Friends? He said we're *friends!* I'm so happy I want to do a little dance, but he's standing here looking at me all serious and stuff, so I force myself to contain my enthusiasm. "Quince, you know you can always count on me."

"It's kind of funny if you think about it," he says, but he doesn't look amused. "I had a feeling for a long time that she just wasn't into me as much, but I wouldn't admit it. Nothing like finding out the hard way."

I *so* want to reach out and squeeze his hand, but I resist the urge. "Yeah, that's gotta hurt."

Quince shrugs, then zips up his jacket, pulls the hoodie up, and gives me a wide grin.

"Well, I need to go. Baseball practice, and Coach'll have me running extra laps if I'm late."

"I'm glad you came by, Quince. See you tomorrow?" All right, I know I'll see him at school, but what I'm really hoping is that I'll see him AFTER school—like for coffee or something, and not just in a group of kids.

Quince nods, hesitating. "Uh, Caryn..."

My heart is pounding, hoping my wish is about to be granted. Now that Kensi is out of the way...

"This morning you said something and I cut you off." He's frowning again, rubbing a finger across his lower lip.

Yes! Of course! I'd love to go to Peterson's with you after school tomorrow.

"You know, about my trip to the dentist."

The dentist. Oh yeah. Back to Earth. "Right. The dentist." *Wake up, Caryn. He said we're FRIENDS, not a couple.*

I try to look casual, which isn't easy with my pulse racing and my imagination on overdrive. I swallow hard. "I was going to say you won't look like a dork, because you're getting those invisible kind of braces."

Quince shrugs and shakes his head. "I think my original word was 'geek,' and I don't get how you know that stuff, but that's a relief anyway." He winks at me as he leaves.

I close the door after him and think about our conversation. Maybe Quince didn't mean to ask me a psychic question—even in a roundabout way—but he didn't make fun of me this time either. Maybe he's ready to accept the real me, warts and all!

Mom has a funny smile on her face as she brings the man she's been chatting with to the register to ring up his purchase. She takes a little too long handing him his change and giving him her business card, and then walks him to the door. As for me, I practically dance to the back room, grab the feather duster, and proceed to dust the counters with vigor. It seems the Universe has brought both of us interesting conversations with attractive men.

****

The next day Kensi's name is on the school's cut list, which means she has to report to the dean's office first thing in the morning. I figure she'll be suspended from school for a few days, Quince will have time to cool down, and I won't have to look at her smug face in first period.

But *no-o-o-o*, that girl lives a charmed life. Kensi is back in class in record time, smiling as she hands her pass to Mrs. York. She then triumphantly crosses the room to her seat by the window, and casually turns her back on the teacher to begin a conversation with Salissa that they take no pains to keep private.

"I thought you'd be suspended," Salissa says in a too-loud whisper.

"Me? No way. I just told the dean that my brother came to pick me up because I had *female* problems. He turned all kinds of red, wrote me the pass, and here I am!" Kensi shakes her hair back with a laugh.

"You don't have a brother," I mutter.

"Did you say something, Caryn?" Mrs. York asks.

"Uh, no, sorry."

But it really makes me angry that Kensi cut school, lied about it, AND got away with both. She has such a self-satisfied look on her face I want to scream!

The class is whispering among themselves about Kensi's nerve, when Mrs. York briskly gets everyone back on task.

"Ladies and gentlemen, today we're beginning our study of *Pride and Prejudice* by Jane Austen. Let's examine women's roles in the nineteenth century. Shall we open our books?"

Gladly.

I'd much rather talk about Elizabeth Bennet

and Mr. Darcy than think one more minute about Kensington Marlow and her flavor-of-the-month boyfriend. I steal a glance over at Quince as he pretends to listen to the teacher, but I know he's really brooding about Kensi. My heart goes out to him, and naturally I wish I could be the one to ease his hurt feelings.

No one in class, except maybe Harris, is paying very much attention to Mrs. York. Megan is intently sketching something in her journal, Kevin is "reading" *Pride and Prejudice* propped up on his desk with a baseball statistics book hidden inside it, while Emma doodles his name dreamily on her notebook. Deana's asleep as usual, Janae is staring out the window, and Salissa and Kensi still have their heads together giggling and whispering.

I sigh. One more week till spring break.

****

The Friday before spring vacation, Quince catches up to me in the hall before first period.

"Hey Caryn! Wait up!"

Ever since our conversation at the store, Quince has actually started acting like we're friends, just as he said. He talks to me in classes and in the halls during passing periods, and sometimes we don't only talk about school stuff, but about other things we have in common. Like baseball—we found a connection in our mutual love of the sport.

"Hi, Quince!" I smooth out my hair, which is curled and hanging loose around my shoulders, and hope he notices I took pains with my appearance this morning.

His baby blue eyes are sparkling and I can barely breathe. "Hey, how 'bout those Astros! Did you see the game on ESPN?"

"Yeah. Oswalt pitched a no-hitter!" I exclaim.

"It was amazing! Hey, I was wondering, since you're such a baseball fan and all, if you're planning to come to our game tonight. Turnout's been kinda light the last few games, and Coach says to bring our friends."

I haven't been to any of Rosslyn High's baseball games yet, since in my opinion late March is still too chilly to be outdoors, but this is Quince asking.

"Sure, I'd like that," I say, hoping he can't hear how loud my heart is pounding. "What time?"

"Six. Stop at the dugout and say hi!" And with a wave, he's gone.

Well, by the time my pulse returns to normal, I realize the tardy bell has rung and I just hope Mrs. York lets me into class without a pass.

Quince invited me to his game!

Maybe spring break won't be so boring after all.

Chapter 11
Spring Is Breaking

With the exception of that Friday night Wrangler's baseball game (which we won by a score of 5-4), my spring break is a bust. As eager as I was for it to start, I'm more than ready for it to be over.

Megan is in Las Vegas, just like she said. She called me late one night our time, although it was early evening in Nevada, to tell me she was watching pay-per-view in the hotel room and waiting on room service, since her dad and stepmother were in the casino with friends. I sighed, sorry my earlier vision had been right.

All my other friends are gone too. Quince is on the beach in Florida with his family, Emma is spending every waking minute at the mall, Ashleigh is taking special violin lessons in Chicago, and Annabeth's school break isn't until next week. Except for sleeping later in the mornings, my routine hasn't changed one bit. There are only two days left till school resumes, and I haven't done anything except watch old sitcoms and movies.

It's Friday evening and Mom has just come home from work grinning like she has some huge secret. I try to get a read on it, but for some reason I can't pick up anything. She waltzes into the apartment, humming a tune as she glides into the kitchen and begins rummaging around in the fridge for something to cook for supper.

"Why are you so cheerful?" I throw myself onto the sofa and reach for the TV remote.

"No reason," she answers.

I guess it isn't cool to call your mother a liar, but I know she's holding something back. As I sit there trying to puzzle out what she's up to, she calls out to me from the kitchen. "Is spaghetti okay for dinner tonight? And, Caryn, dear, answer the phone!"

What? Answer the phone? That's MY trick!

And even though it doesn't feel like the phone is about to ring, sure enough it does about five minutes later.

"Hey! No fair! How'd you know that?"

"It's for you, and you're not psychic about yourself, remember? Now answer it before the machine picks up."

I'm really puzzled. "Hello?"

"Hey, Caryn, it's Annabeth. What's up?" Annabeth sounds bubbly and a little giggly.

"Hey, Annabeth, what's up?" Annabeth always seems to appear just when I need her most. But what I can't figure out is how my mom knew she was going to call.

"Are you doing anything tonight?"

"Well, no, just having dinner with my mom," I say, and hear a snicker from the kitchen.

"What if I come over and pick you up and you spend the night at my house? Say eight o'clock?"

"You got your new car!" I shout that out almost at the instant I flash on a picture of her dad handing her the keys to it.

"Darn it, Caryn, you're such a killjoy." I can almost see Annabeth rolling her eyes, one hand propped on her hip. "I can't get anything by you."

"No, really, I *am* surprised."

"Uh-huh," she says.

"Well, then, I'm happy for you," I say, trying not to laugh at her annoyed tone. "And sure. Eight would be fine."

As I hang up I see Mom giving me the thumbs-up sign. I grin back at her, having figured out

Confessions of a Teenage Psychic

already that she's in on this. After dinner I pack a few overnight things in my backpack and go out front of the apartment complex to wait for Annabeth.

It's a lovely evening in early April. Sunset comes later now, and there's a warm, gentle breeze blowing that gives me a fuzzy, nostalgic feeling as I sit on the front steps. I think of Houston this time of year, how warm it is, flowers in full bloom, and remember taking long after-dinner walks with my dad. I wonder what he's doing right now.

I don't have too much time to dwell on it, though, because Annabeth pulls up in her brand new compact car—one of those hybrids that's supposed to get such great gas mileage—and honks the horn.

"Wow! Is this cool or what?" I open the passenger door and slide in, tossing my backpack on the floor between my feet.

"Sure is," she says, shifting into gear. "My parents bought it for me last week after—"

"—you made Honor Roll!"

Annabeth blushes. "Yeah, like you told me New Year's Eve. And no 'I told you so's,' okay? So do you like it?"

What's not to like? It has leather seats, GPS, CD player, Onstar—in fact everything a rich girl from the suburbs is expected to have.

"It's really nice." Okay, I admit it, I'm envious, but I try to sound enthusiastic.

"Come on, Caryn, don't go all weird on me." Annabeth makes a scowly-face and I can't help laughing. "Anyway, I can't wait for you to meet my folks. Ready?"

I fasten my seatbelt and off we go, windows rolled down to catch the breeze, CD blaring. I've never been to Belford, even though it's just over the county line, and I'm amazed at the change in scenery in a mere thirty minute drive from Rosslyn Village to the wealthy suburbs. Don't get me wrong—I've seen big houses before. They've got them in spades in Houston, but it's just that I never knew anyone who lived in one. And boy does Annabeth live in a big house! We pull into her driveway and she parks the car behind a late-model Lexus, which is parked next to a Mercedes convertible.

A picture pops into my head of a house a lot like this one in a nearby neighborhood, and I realize it's the house Megan used to live in. I can see Megan swimming in the backyard pool, running through the half-acre yard playing tag with her sisters, and a whole extra outdoor kitchen in the backyard for entertaining. I now understand what a culture shock it must have been for her to move from one of these sprawling mansions to their little home in Rosslyn Village.

I'm gawking as I stumble out of the car, dragging my old backpack. I follow Annabeth in the back door to the kitchen which is bigger than our entire apartment. The house must have over 10,000 square feet, and every inch is decorated luxuriously.

"How many people live here?" I ask, trying to keep my jaw from dropping.

"Just the three of us right now. My brother's away at college back East."

A house this huge for four people. It boggles my mind. "Wow," is all I can think to say.

"Come on, let's put your stuff in my room." Annabeth leads me down a hallway, through a dining room that could seat a dozen or more, past a couple of living rooms, and finally to a winding staircase that goes up to the bedrooms. At the top of the stairs there's another well-appointed hallway with thick plush carpeting and so many closed doors I lose count. Annabeth finally opens one of the doors and as I look into her bedroom, I nearly burst out laughing.

"Did the maid forget to clean in here?"

She has a canopy bed with a black-and-white toile top, a painted-white antiqued dresser and armoire, a matching desk with a laptop computer on it, and a cushioned window seat under a large picture window. But every square inch of the room is covered with clothes, shoes, tennis equipment, schoolbooks, papers, crumpled bath towels, makeup, hair styling equipment, and stuffed animals. Suddenly I don't feel so out of place.

Annabeth shrugs. "I don't let her in my room. She just messes up my stuff trying to straighten up and then I can never find anything."

We both giggle and I toss my backpack on the cluttered bed.

"I've got a surprise for you," Annabeth says, waggling her eyebrows at me.

"I thought the car was the surprise."

"You weren't surprised by the car," Annabeth reminds me.

"Sure I was." I widen my eyes, trying to look convincing, but Annabeth isn't buying it.

"Anyway, your mom says you can't predict stuff in your own life, so this is going to be so cool!"

Mom is in on this mysterious surprise? I wrack my brain trying to figure out what the two of them have cooked up, but I can't do it.

I blow out a breath. "Okay, I guess you got me this time. So when do I find out?"

Annabeth does that thing where she pretends to lock her lips and throw away the key.

"Come on, I'm starved," is all she says, pushing me toward the door.

We go downstairs to the kitchen and she rummages through the food pantry and refrigerator pulling out soda, potato chips, chocolate chip cookies, and pretzels.

"Annabeth, that's too much junk food," says an attractive woman in her forties who is wearing a black, floor-length sheath with ropes of pearls around her neck. "The maid prepared some veggies and dip and put them in the refrigerator. I'd prefer you eat that."

"But Mom," Annabeth says, waving her hand toward the loaded countertop. "What's the fun of a sleepover without junk food?"

"Eat the healthy stuff first," her mother admonishes with a twinkling smile in my direction. "You can have some frozen yogurt later."

Annabeth groans, but pulls out the prepared veggie platter from the fridge and exchanges the sodas for bottled water.

"Caryn, this is my mom," she says, sliding the tray onto the counter. "I guess you never really met at church last Christmas."

I smile and try not to stare too obviously at the pearls around her neck. "Nice to meet you, Mrs. Walton. Thanks for having me."

"You're more than welcome, Caryn," she says smiling again.

I instantly like Mrs. Walton as much as I instantly liked Annabeth.

"Your dad and I have that charity auction at the country club tonight, remember?"

"Yeah, I remember."

"My dad volunteers for the Humane Society too," I say, reaching for a carrot stick and forgetting yet again to let people tell me stuff instead of blurting it out.

Annabeth covers her mouth and stifles a giggle when she sees the look of surprise on her mother's face.

"Well, yes. Did Annabeth already mention that?"

Annabeth just winks at me. "Have fun, Mom. We're gonna take our food and go watch TV in Dad's study."

Annabeth grabs the veggie tray, hands me the

bottled waters, and leads me down another hallway. We go past what appears to be a game room with a bar, a black leather sofa to one side, and a pool table right smack in the middle of the room. I crane my neck to see more.

"Come on, Caryn, no gawking. We're on a schedule here," Annabeth says, hustling me down the hallway.

"Why?" I ask, but her sly smile is her only answer. I follow her into what must be her dad's private study, but looks more like an office in some luxury high rise.

"Wow!" I need a new vocabulary, but there just isn't any other way to describe the opulence in this house.

She puts the food down on the dark wood desk and says, "Okay, ready for your surprise?"

"This is driving me nuts, Annabeth," I say, depositing the water bottles on the desk, hoping they won't harm the polished surface. "What's going on?"

"You'll see," she says in a singsong voice.

She sits down in the large, leather armchair, pulls the TV remote from a desk drawer, and flips on the widescreen television that's roughly the width of our apartment's living room. There's a baseball game on and it's really loud, so Annabeth mutes the sound. Then she boots up the laptop on the desk which has one of those extra-wide monitors.

"You know how you can predict phone calls?" Annabeth is fiddling with the mouse pad.

I nod, trying to peek around the computer to see what she's doing.

"Well, now it's my turn," Annabeth says, a grin spreading across her face. "In about five minutes, this phone's gonna ring."

"*That* phone?" I point to the multi-line phone on the desk. "Isn't that your dad's business line?"

"Well, yeah. It's not...Oh, never mind. Make

yourself comfortable." She pushes away from the laptop and turns up the sound on the TV.

What IS going on?

I sit down on the leather loveseat she indicates but I can't relax. My fingers are cold and I tuck them under my legs, trying to pay attention to the game.

"Great base hit!" Annabeth swivels a complete 180 in the desk chair.

I roll my eyes. "Is this what you're being so mysterious about? Baseball?"

She doesn't answer me. We sit there in silence for several minutes watching the game while I tap my toe on the ground, not sure why there are tingles chasing each other up and down my spine. And then the phone really does ring.

"Hello?" Annabeth says, snatching it up on the first ring. "Yeah, we're all set." She clicks a few keys on the laptop then waves at the screen.

"Hi, honey! It's so good to see you!" A familiar voice is coming from the laptop.

I jump up and run over to the monitor and that's when I notice the webcam on top of it.

"Dad!"

Yes, it's him, sitting next to Michael in what looks like their favorite Internet café in downtown Houston.

"Dad!" I exclaim again, feeling tears stinging my eyes.

"You don't have to shout. It's just like a regular phone, except with video," he smiles at me.

It's so good to see his face. He looks a little thinner than when I saw him last September, but other than that, Dad is the picture of health.

"How did you..." Seeing him after all these months brings a tightness to my throat and chokes off my voice.

"Your mom called me and told me how sad you were that you couldn't come visit during spring break, so we figured out a way for us to see each other anyhow, with your friend's help," he says, smiling, although his voice wavers a little bit, as if he's choked up too. "What do you think? Your old dad's pretty clever, huh?"

"I love you, Dad," I say, trying to choke back sobs.

Annabeth tiptoes out of the room once she's sure we're all set, waving as she pulls the door closed behind her. Dad and I talk for about an hour. I tell him all about school, Mom's shop, my encounters with Uncle Omar, and my crush on Quince. Dad and Michael tell me some of the plans they have for our summer vacation once school lets out in June and I can fly to Houston.

After Dad and I finally hang up, Annabeth peeks in the door with a huge grin on her face. "Well...?"

I'm overcome with emotion. "You're a great friend!" I give her a big hug.

I'll bet no kid at school had a better spring break than I did.

Chapter 12
Full Circle

So now it's mid-April and everything at school is a mess, mostly thanks to Megan. I haven't seen her since her mother pulled her out of Love of Lit class this morning.

Megan's book bag is still in the classroom, so I pick it up when the bell rings and head off toward her locker, which is right next to mine. I stand there hoping she'll show, juggling both her bag and mine as I search up and down the hall for her. Finally she comes around the corner with an exasperated look on her face.

"What'd your mom say?"

She rolls her eyes. "Stuff about my sister's wedding."

"Megan, seriously, you don't expect me to believe that, do you?"

"See you at lunch," she says, taking her book bag from me and hurrying off down the hall.

Rumors about the dress code have gone from bad to worse since we got back to school after spring break. Warm weather is here to stay and I'll be the first to rejoice about that, but honestly, the way some of these kids come dressed for school, it's enough to make a stripper blush.

Take Kensi, for instance. Today she's wearing a midriff-baring blouse with a jeans skirt that someone could mistake for a large belt. The boys all have their tongues hanging out of their mouths, and even though she and Quince broke up in March, I'm scared it's not going to stick. He could take one look at her half-naked body and forget she was cheating on him all winter.

Not to mention how it makes the rest of us feel. Especially me, in my consignment store jeans, faded T-shirt, and off-brand tennis shoes. I'm beginning to see the wisdom in Principal MacGregor's strict dress code idea. At least if kids weren't allowed to come to school dressed like Kensi is, I'd have a fighting chance at getting Quince's attention.

I'm bored out of my mind in English class today as we review for a grammar test. I keep thinking about seeing Quince in the hall before school this morning. He smiled and winked at me, but hurried to his locker before we could have a conversation.

The lunch bell rings, jarring me out of my latest daydream, one where I imagine Quince is admiring my fashion sense and is turned off by Kensi's suggestive clothing. But my stomach is growling so I head to the cafeteria, wondering what fresh mischief Megan has gotten into since first period.

I get my tray and find I'm the first to arrive at our regular table, so I sit down and open my bottle of juice. Naturally it squirts out and I end up with orange juice all over the front of my Houston Astros T-shirt. As I'm wiping it off, Megan plops down in the chair beside me.

"You're supposed to drink that stuff, not wear it," she says, smirking at me.

I throw the sopping paper napkin down and reach for a fresh one. "Gee, I didn't know."

Megan laughs, and starts eating as if her mother hadn't just dragged her to the principal's office for stirring up trouble.

Emma soon joins us at the table, looking glum. "Caryn, why didn't you tell me I was going to flunk that algebra test this morning? You said..."

"I wished you good luck, like you asked," I say, shaking my finger. "But I knew you weren't going to pass it."

"Then why didn't you say so?" Emma thrusts her test paper in my face, showing me a big, fat F circled in red at the top.

I brush it aside. "Because you didn't ask me. It's not my fault you were texting Kevin last night instead of studying."

Emma turns to face me and her mouth drops open. "How did you...? Never mind." She shoves a bite of sandwich into her mouth. "And where did your mom drag you off to?" she asks Megan.

Megan rolls her eyes but instead of answering, makes a big show of biting into her chocolate chip cookie.

I try again. "So exactly what did your mom say to you this morning, Megan? And don't tell me wedding plans, because I know that's not what she wanted to talk about."

"You're so psychic, you tell me," Megan says with her mouth full of chocolate chip cookie.

"Megan, I can't read your mind!"

She swallows the last of the cookie and shrugs. "Okay. Mom says the principal is on her case because I'm still keeping all the kids stirred up about the dress code."

Which I know she is. I've seen her huddled with kids in the halls, whispering and glancing around over her shoulder, and the rumors are running wild throughout the building. Janae has been on the case too. Every time she sees Megan with a group of kids, she shoves her way into the conversation and then tells everybody what she heard.

"So are you?" Emma says, pointing her milk straw at Megan. "Keeping kids stirred up, I mean?"

"No comment," Megan says, stuffing potato chips in her mouth.

That uneasy feeling about how this will turn out is nagging at me again. "Megan—"

"I'm not talking about it anymore." She takes a big gulp of chocolate milk. "But come over to my house Friday after supper."

"Huh? Friday? What about going to your dad's?" Megan hardly ever spends time at her dad's house, so I'd think she wouldn't want to miss out on an opportunity.

"Now I'm not going till Saturday morning," Megan says impatiently. "Dad and Sharlene—"

"Who's Sharlene?" Emma asks.

Megan gives an exaggerated sigh. "My stepmonster. They have some social thing to go to Friday night."

"So then Friday—what's going on at your house?" I don't like the feeling in my gut one bit and Megan won't look me in the face, which I take as a bad sign.

"Just a little get-together."

"And where's your mom gonna be?" I ask, trying to get a read on the situation.

"Out with Patrick." Megan pauses in her junk-food fest and grins. "Mom's got a serious boyfriend, if you can believe."

I can tell she likes this guy, Patrick, but it must be weird that her mother is going out on dates like she's some schoolgirl.

I force myself to refocus. "So, Megan, you're telling me that something's going on at your house Friday night and your mom won't even be there? That's not cool."

"My sister Allie will be there," Megan says, still not making eye contact with me.

"No, she won't. She's going to a concert." Megan frowns at me so I know I'm right.

"She'll be home—eventually," Megan argues. "Besides, we'll all be in the backyard, not in the house. Come on, Caryn, we need your help."

"Help with what?" *Why can't I "see" what she's*

planning? "And who's 'we'?"

Megan smiles at me. "Just be there."

"I don't know..." I have serious misgivings about all her covert activities, and from what little she's telling me, this backyard thing could be worse than the petition drive.

Before I can say anything else, the dismissal bell sounds. Darn that lunch bell. It always seems to ring just when things are getting interesting.

****

Well, after wrestling with my conscience all week, I decide not to miss whatever is going on at Megan's house. So this morning before school, I tell Mom I have to leave the store early to get ready for a party at a friend's house. Okay, it's a bit of a white lie, but I figure it's better to stretch the truth than to tell Mom that Megan is stirring up a revolution.

Mom seems not to notice my fib, though, and readily gives me permission. Honestly, I think there's something else on her mind lately.

The day turns into the kind of spring evening that makes me want to be outside anyway, so I don't mind the mile or so walk from my apartment to Megan's house. Flowers are starting to bloom and the fragrance is divine. The air is cool with just a hint of warmth—enough to need a light jacket, but not enough to give me shivers. The days are getting longer too, so I don't have to worry about walking in the dark.

"Hey, Caryn!"

I whip my head around looking for whoever is calling me, but no one's there. I shudder but keep walking, this time a little faster.

"Hey, Caryn," the voice says again. "You need to get on board with what's goin' down."

Okay, only one person I "know" would use such dated slang. "Uncle Omar, I'm not talking to you if I can't see you." I keep walking.

"Okay, have it your way."

And there he is, standing in front of me on the sidewalk, hands on his hips, a big smile on his face.

Maybe I should've thought that through, because now I'm talking to a man no one else can see, and there are plenty of people out tonight in Rosslyn Village, walking on this very sidewalk. There's a mom pushing a baby in a stroller right behind me, two joggers who each go around me like I'm a light pole, a group of guys in their twenties dressed for a night on the town, an elderly Asian couple strolling arm-in-arm. You know, just a regular Friday evening with lots of people out-and-about enjoying the spring weather. They must think I'm a freak—or worse, insane—since it looks like I'm talking to myself.

"Say what you have to say and go, because people are staring," I say, trying to move my lips as little as possible as I talk.

"Just doing what you told me—in your face," he teases, waving his hand in front of my eyes.

"What do you want?" I repeat a little too loudly. The Asian couple is staring at me, shaking their heads with pity as if I'm some kind of mental case.

"I just came to give you a heads-up," Omar says, nodding to the elderly couple as if they can see him.

"About what?" I smile at them, almost like I expect them to acknowledge Uncle Omar's greeting. They shake their heads and keep walking.

"About some really groovy, far-out stuff that's gonna go down!" Uncle Omar's still grinning at me and it's annoying. So is that outdated vocabulary.

"The 70s are over, Uncle Omar! And anyway, what are you talking about?" I look around the street as I talk, as if I've just stopped to figure out which direction I should take. If only Mom would let me have a cell phone, these public conversations with Uncle Omar would be a lot less embarrassing.

"You'll figure it out. Just roll with it, and never doubt yourself," Uncle Omar says, pointing both index fingers at me.

I roll my eyes. "Uncle Omar, if you can't say something straight out then leave me alone."

But he's gone. I look all around to see if he's standing somewhere else, but he isn't. I roll my eyes again and hurry on to Megan's house.

"I'll walk you to your friend's house," his disembodied voice says.

"Gee, thanks." I walk on toward Megan's, feeling Uncle Omar's presence at my side the whole way. It's kind of comforting, really, knowing that I'm not totally alone out here, but a little creepy too.

When I arrive at Megan's I can see that there are quite a few cars parked nearby, and if there are that many cars then there must be lots of kids in her backyard. I can't see anyone from the front of her house, but their voices carry and they're laughing and talking loudly, so I know something is going on back there. She had to do lots of planning to pull this off with both her mother and sister out of the house, and it's pretty amazing, but still—an unsupervised party? My mom would kill me if she knew. I almost turn around and leave, but my curiosity gets the better of me. I walk up to the front porch and let myself in through the unlocked door.

When I get to the backyard I stare speechless at the commotion. There's Megan surrounded by dozens of Rosslyn High students, all working diligently on posters, banners, and what look like signs for picketing. She looks up and sees me gawking at all the activity and waves me over.

"Hey, Caryn! It's about time! Grab a marker and get busy. We need all the help we can get!"

I walk over to where Megan is creating a rather colorful—and artistic, if I'm honest—banner which is stretched out on a picnic table under a large tree.

She's lettered "NO UNIFORMS AT ROSSLYN HIGH!!!" next to an image of a student dressed in a parochial school uniform inside a circle with a slash across it.

Megan tosses a marker to me. "What we're trying to do here—"

"It's pretty clear," I say, letting the marker fall on the table. "How did all these kids know to come here anyway? I didn't hear a word at school."

"E-mail," Megan replies, with a lifted eyebrow. "You should try it."

Ouch. Yeah, I'm definitely out of the cyber-loop. But I'm sort of surprised that she asked me at all—in person, no less—knowing how I feel about all this underground stuff.

I look around her backyard and see Emma and Kevin with their heads together, looking rather cozy as they color a poster, giggling all the while. Ashleigh claims she's not very artistic, but she's adorning the picket signs with crepe paper, all the while listening to her iPod and occasionally playing air violin. Over by the flowerbed I see Janae working side-by-side with Deana Pruitt of all people. Deana must be here on the sly, because if her father knew she was working in the enemy camp, he'd probably ship her off to some rehab for people with eating disorders. Janae and Deana are decorating a second banner that reads "ONE TWO THREE FOUR, WE WON'T WEAR A UNIFORM!!" which I guess they consider poetry. Next to them are several members of Coach Edgemont's baseball team decorating posters that read "WE ONLY WEAR *BASEBALL* UNIFORMS!!!"

And then I catch sight of Quince and Kensi in the far corner of the yard by a huge oak tree, definitely *not* working on posters. I blink twice, hoping I'm not seeing what I think I'm seeing.

Can it be? Can they really be making up and getting back together? There she is, wearing skintight jeans and a sweater cut so low you can see...I look away in anger. And just when I thought I had a real chance with Quince.

I want to run over there, grab him by the arms and make him he see reason. What if...

Caryn: Quince, you know Kensi's only going to break your heart again.

Quince: Hi, Caryn! Don't worry 'cause Kensi's just leaving anyway. Besides, it's YOU I want to talk to!

I shake off the fantasy, gather up my courage and walk over.

"Hi Quince! And Kensi," I say, trying to smile, be cool, and hide my Kensi-hatred, all at the same time.

"Look, Quince, it's that new girl in Mrs. York's class." Kensi flashes an insincere and very smug smile at me.

Okay, maybe I won't worry so much about hiding my reaction to Kensi. "I'm not NEW! I've been here since way last fall."

"Sure she has, Kensi. Remember?" Quince gives me a wink, but he only glances at me a moment before focusing on Kensi again.

"Um, Quince, could I talk to you a minute?" I ask.

"Well, I..." He frowns at me a moment before smiling at Kensi again. "Kensi, do you mind?"

Kensi heaves a big sigh, rolls her eyes at me and purrs to Quince, "Don't be too long, babe." She walks off toward Ashleigh and Deana.

"What did you want?" Quince's eyes follow Kensi all the way across the yard.

Hello? I'm right in front of you! I'm the girl you've been talking to in class and discussing baseball stats with for the last couple of weeks! Remember me?

I widen my eyes at him, hoping to get his

attention. Not happening. Clearly I'm not the girl he wants to be talking to at the moment. "Quince, I thought you and Kensi broke up. You told me—"

"Well, we did," he says, a slight flush on his cheekbones. "But she told me how sorry she was about that college guy."

"And you believed her? She's still a..." I start to say "liar and cheat" but think better of it. "She's playing you."

His cheeks get a little redder and now he's frowning at me. "We're cool now. I'm over what happened before spring break, so you can quit worrying."

Is he kidding? A fake apology and a few winks and he forgets all she did to him? Why are guys so gullible about girls like Kensi?

"Quince, please don't let her suck you back in," I say, trying not to sound like a jealous girl who's crushing on him, which unfortunately is what I am.

He steps away from me. "Caryn, you're a good friend, but you need to stay out of it."

There's no mistaking the warning note in his voice. UGH! Can't he see I want desperately to be more than just friends?

A thought flashes into my head and before I can stop myself I blurt out, "You'd better watch out, Quince, because Kensi's going to embarrass you big time, and then she'll break your heart. Again!"

He doesn't even spare me another glance. "Thanks for the warning, Caryn, but I trust her."

Tears of frustration well up in my eyes as he walks away. Although I don't know exactly when or how, I'm positive what I said about Kensi is true. I should feel sorry for Quince getting hurt by her again, but right now I'm just really mad at him.

I walk back over to Megan and whisper, "Are Quince and Kensi really back together?"

Megan shrugs. "Who knows with those two? But

this is a work party, so get busy and start making a poster or something."

I look around at the signs and all my laughing, happy classmates. "I don't know, Megan."

Megan slaps a hand to her hip. "Then why did you even come?"

"You told me it was a friendly get-together!"

Megan nonchalantly goes back to work on her drawing. "It is, with a purpose. Do you want to help or not?"

I don't have an answer for that one. Should I stay and get involved when my instincts tell me not to? Can I even stand being around Quince and his renewed relationship with Kensington Marlow for one more minute? I look over at them again, all cozy under the large shade tree, and I fight back the tears.

"And what do you plan to do with all this stuff?" My anger vibrates in my voice, even though Megan has nothing to do with what's really bothering me.

"Be prepared," is all Megan says.

Prepared for what? Maybe I'd rather not know. "Your sister's gonna be home in a couple of hours, right?"

Megan doesn't even look surprised. "Like I said, tick, tick, tick..."

I groan and walk over to Ashleigh, deciding I'll pretend to look busy when I know in my heart I can't really bring myself to help out. But from where Ashleigh's working, I've got an excellent view of Quince and Kensi. She has her arms wrapped around his neck and he's hugging her around the waist as they lean against the tree trunk. I never noticed before, but when she wears those three-inch boots, she's taller than he is, so she's scrunched down slightly in an attempt to make him feel like the big man. I can hear her cooing in his ear, and the stupid grin on his face is enough to make me barf.

"I've gotta go." I wave goodbye to Ashleigh as I walk away.

"But you didn't even..." I hear Ashleigh call out to me.

As I rush into Megan's kitchen and out through the front door trying to catch my breath, I wonder if this is what Uncle Omar was trying to tell me, about all my hopes for a relationship with Quince.

"Is that it, Uncle Omar?" I ask, addressing the sky, like I'd expect to see him floating up there or something. "Were you trying to tell me to quit fighting Quince's attraction to Kensington?"

"Big picture, Caryn," I hear him say. "Don't worry, things will work out the way they're supposed to."

"NOT helping!" I shout.

Zipping up my jacket as I notice a sudden chill, I head home.

****

"Hi, hon, you're home early," Mom says as I slam the front door. "And clearly, you're not in a good mood. I thought you were going to a party."

"Some party," I say, not even glancing her way.

I go straight to my bedroom for some serious sulking. I throw myself onto my bed while trying to make sense of all the chaotic thoughts going through my head. Quince is back with Kensi when I hoped he and I were getting closer, and then there's Megan. When I close my eyes I still see that image of her chanting and carrying a picket sign somewhere, sometime in the future, surrounded by lots of people. I feel uneasy as I replay that vision in my head. I decide to call Annabeth and get her take on all this.

I grab the phone but after several rings I get the inevitable, "Hi, this is Annabeth. Leave a message and I'll get back to you."

AARRGGHH!!

"Hey, Annabeth, it's Caryn. I just wanted to talk

to you about what's happening at Megan's. Give me a call when you get this."

I lie back on my bed and stare at the ceiling. I try to focus on what I should tell Megan but all I can see are Quince and Kensi snuggling together under the tree. I'm trying not to scream in frustration when Mom knocks on my door and peeks in.

"What's up?" she asks, peering around my room as if she thinks there's some clue hidden here.

"Nothing."

"Don't try to fool me, Caryn Alderson," she says, coming over to sit on the edge of the bed. "I know you too well. What happened at that party tonight?"

I flop an arm over my eyes. "Megan—she's up to no good."

Under my arm, I see Mom's eyes suddenly get very wide and I know she's imagining all kinds of *no good* a teenage girl could get into, so I set her straight.

"No, it's just that she's got kids at her house making signs and planning a protest in case Principal MacGregor decides on a uniform policy."

I see Mom exhale in relief. "Oh. Actually, I don't know that parents have been informed of a new dress code. I do read the PTA newsletter, you know."

I sigh. "I didn't say dress code, Mom, I said *uniforms.*"

"Caryn, nothing's been said about uniforms at all." Mom is using her soothing voice which somehow makes me want to scream more. "Absolutely nothing."

"Well, Megan's going ahead like it's all settled." I drop my arm and stare out the window.

"So what exactly is Megan doing?"

"She's got kids making all kinds of banners and posters. I left before she could tell me what her real plan is. I just don't know what to do."

"Caryn, I think you're taking way too much on

yourself," she says, patting my leg. "I know she was your first friend here, but if Megan Benedict is determined to get herself into trouble, all you can do is stay out of it."

She tugs at my chin until I'm facing her, then searches my eyes. "What else?" Mom knows me too well.

I roll over on my side and face the wall, fighting back the tears. "I thought I had a chance with Quince Adams, but tonight I saw him with that cheating Kensington Marlow."

"Ah," says my mother. "So you're concerned about Megan, but you're really upset about seeing the boy you like with another girl."

That was pretty much it. Mom has a way of getting right to the bottom line.

"Mom, the phone," I say between sniffles. "It's for me."

She passes me a tissue and gives my shoulder a squeeze, just as the phone rings in the living room. Mom hands me the receiver and I hear Annabeth's voice on the other end.

"Hey, girl, what's Megan up to now?"

I breathe a sigh of relief and start explaining all the events of the evening to her. It's so cool to have a friend like Annabeth. I can talk to her about anything—Megan, Quince, Kensi—and she listens and doesn't judge. With Annabeth I can just be myself, making me feel like that normal teenager I so want to be.

And I would be normal, if only I could get rid of these stupid psychic insights...*and* the talking spirits.

****

There's this huge conspiracy of silence at school after the weekend. No one mentions Megan's poster party, almost like it never happened. At lunch time I confront Megan while we wait to get our food.

"Megan, where did you stash all those banners?"

"SHHH!" She looks around to see who might be listening.

Nobody is, since the kids in line in front of us are more intent on deciding between mystery meatloaf and grilled cheese sandwiches.

Megan lowers her voice. "We're waiting to see if the principal makes it official about uniforms next year. And I stashed all those posters at my dad's house in a closet in a guest room. I told the maid to stay out of there because I was storing some school art projects."

Oh, brother. "Megan, how do you think hanging posters or making banners is going to change the principal's mind?"

"Don't be stupid, Caryn, I'm not dumb enough to think that's the *only* thing that would make a difference."

"Then what?" I realize the cafeteria lady is glaring at me because it's my turn to order and I'm holding up the lunch line. "Grilled cheese," I tell her with a smile she doesn't return.

By the time I get my lunch card punched, Megan is already sitting at the table and deep in conversation with Emma. I've been having some weird vibes about Emma all morning, and as I join them it all comes into focus. "So, Emma. Running for student council?"

Emma's eyes widen and her mouth drops open, but she quickly regains her composure. "I most certainly am not. I told you last winter I'm not into politics."

"But Mr. MacGregor thinks otherwise, doesn't he?" I say, pointing a grilled-cheese triangle at her.

Emma fidgets in her seat, takes a big gulp of her bottled water, adjusts her headband, and finally says, "Well, okay, he did call me into his office this morning and say something like that. But I told him no!"

"Uh-huh," I say, biting into the sandwich.

"Caryn, cut it out, I'm not kidding. I told him I'm not running and that's all there is to it!"

We'll see.

Emma is frowning at me so I take another bite of my sandwich, wishing I could remember that normal teenagers don't go around predicting stuff and then saying "I told you so" all the time. If I want to have any friends at all, I need to quit antagonizing them.

If I can just hold on till June.

****

I'm staring into my locker at the end of the day trying to remember if I have homework and if I do what books I need or where I've stashed them. Just as I'm about to give up and slam the door shut, I feel a tap on my shoulder and turn around to see Kensi towering over me. I briefly wonder how tall she really is without those spike heels, but I can see from the look on her face that this isn't a social call.

"Hi, Caryn," she says in a saccharine tone.

"Hi." I bite my lip trying not to tell her exactly what I think of her cheating ways. Kids around us are staring, probably wondering why Miss Popular Cheerleader is talking to the hippie girl.

Kensi folds her arms and smiles at me. "Quince tells me you've been such a good friend to him. We're both so fond of you, being new and all."

I hate that snarky *we* she uses, like she and Quince are joined at the hip or something. Mostly I'm just wondering why she's talking to me at all, especially in the main hall where everyone can see.

I return her phony smile with one of my own. "Kensi, I've been in this school for months."

"Well, of course you have," she says, patting me on the shoulder like I'm in kindergarten or something. "And you've tried hard to fit in, really you have. Hanging out with that other new girl, Megan, and buddying up with that freshman kid. What's his name? Henry? Herbert?"

I shrug her hand off my shoulder. "I'm pretty sure you didn't stop by to talk about Harris Rutherford."

"I'm just trying to be a friend to you," Kensi says, lifting both hands in the air.

Does she think I'm stupid? Friends—with me?

Kensi gives me another fake smile. "I just wanted to tell you that even though Quince and I had a little disagreement last month, it's over and we're back together."

Little disagreement? She cheats on him—twice—and that's a *little disagreement*? And why is she telling me this? Because she knows I like Quince? Is it that obvious?

I can feel my cheeks flushing as I say, "Quince is too nice a guy to be sucked in by you, Kensi."

"Excuse me?" Her fake smile disappears and she puts her hands on her hips as her voice rises. "Hello? Me—cute, popular, fashionably dressed. You—consignment store clothes, no makeup, and that stupid braided hair. For heaven's sake, Caryn, get a makeover or something."

This is getting us nowhere, and unless I walk away I'm afraid I'm going to smack her. I guess she can't resist one last dig, though, because as I turn on my heel she calls after me.

"Caryn, I'd love to help you get a date with Harris!"

I turn back to her and shout, "Enjoy your time with Quince because it won't last!"

"Says you!" she says with a wave of her hand.

"Yeah, says me," I say, walking back toward her. "You're about to do something even stupider than you've done all year, and this time you're not going to get away with it!"

She snorts. "What are you, some kind of psychic? You don't know my business!" And with that, Kensi sails off down the hallway.

"As a matter of fact I am!" I call after her, but she's long gone and now the few students left in the building are staring at me.

I must look pretty ridiculous yelling taunts at one of Rosslyn High's social elite, so I duck my head and hurry out the front door of the building.

But I know I'm right. Kensi is headed for a fall and part of me can't wait to see it.

Chapter 13
Showdown at Rosslyn Corral

It's May! Warmer weather, longer days, and the school year is in the home stretch. Kids all have spring fever, and it seems like the teachers do too, because no one can focus on schoolwork anymore. Even in my favorite class, Love of Lit, things have slowed to a crawl. Maybe that's because Mrs. York is distracted, glowing the way pregnant women always are, and facing a group of mostly uninterested teenagers in an elective class is more of a challenge than she needs right now.

I walk into the room and smile at her as I take my seat. I'm always one of the first students to arrive, so the room is empty except for the two of us.

"Good morning, Caryn," says Mrs. York.

"Good morning. You look nice today," I say, taking out my assignment.

She blushes, smiles, and adjusts the oversize blouse she's wearing. Technically we students aren't supposed to know Mrs. York is expecting, but she's just so happy that even the most clueless among us must know something is up.

Harris Rutherford walks quietly into the room and kind of waves at me as he heads to his seat in the back corner of the room. He pulls out his advanced algebra book and starts working, which is his way of avoiding conversation. Or maybe all that studying is why he's so good in math. Maybe I should ask him for some help.

Kensi strolls into the room with Salissa at her side, both of them dressed in unbelievably short denim skirts, high-heeled sandals, and in Kensi's case, a low-cut, clingy T-shirt.

"Hi, Caryn," she says, giving me a condescending smile. "Early again? You're just such a devoted student."

I hate her.

She and Salissa glide into their seats by the window, put their heads together and start giggling and whispering with occasional glances in my direction.

How obvious can they be? *I know you're talking about me.* I try to ignore them and pretend to study my homework.

There's a lot of bustle out in the hallway, since all of the buses have arrived and the five-minute warning bell has sounded. Through the door come Ashleigh, Emma, and Janae. They all call out "hi" or "good morning" to no one in particular and hurry to their seats.

"Did you hear about Emma?" Janae asks me, as Emma rolls her eyes.

"Hear what?"

"Mr. MacGregor is insisting she run for student council president. Isn't that crazy? Emma? Who would've known?"

Me, that's who. But I try not to gloat as I turn to Emma. "Are you going to?"

"I don't know. I had plans to attend this fashion design camp in July, but Mr. MacGregor called my mom and got her all excited telling her he wants me to go to some week-long teen forum thingy in Washington DC." Emma's shoulders slump.

I shrug. "Why can't you do both?"

Emma's brows lift but just as she opens her mouth to respond, Megan blasts into the room. Okay, maybe a little exaggeration, but Megan never does anything low-key, and today there's something about her behavior that says "look out world." She slams her books onto her desk and plops herself into her chair with a huge sigh.

Mrs. York looks up from her desk, startled. "Something wrong, Megan?"

"No!" she says, without even looking up.

Yeah, right. Brace yourself.

Most of the students have arrived now, including Quince who winks playfully at me but gives Kensi a love-struck smile, then sits down in front of me and gets ready for class. I stare wistfully at the back of his head as the tardy bell rings and Mrs. York steps from behind her desk.

"How are we doing with our love sonnets, class?" she asks, her cheeks flushing a little as if she's love-struck herself. "Is anyone having trouble writing theirs?"

More than a few students are squirming in their seats when Megan pokes her hand in the air. "How can anyone have time to write stupid love poems when this school is in crisis mode?"

"Crisis?" Suddenly Janae is on high alert. "Megan! Spill!"

"You know—about the dress code, uniforms, whatever," Megan says with a flap of her hand.

I groan inwardly.

"Oh, Megan, get over it," snaps Janae. "That's old news. You're all wound up over nothing."

"It's not *nothing*." Megan says, her voice rising. "Wait till morning announcements."

I'm wondering how Megan knows about morning announcements when even I don't have a sense of impending doom. Then it comes to me. The chain of information from Superintendent Pruitt to Principal MacGregor, Mr. MacGregor to the faculty (including Megan's mom), and then Ms. Benedict to Megan. This can't be anything good, coming all the way from the top.

"Megan, if you don't mind, we're starting a

lesson now, and we'll hear the announcements later in the class period," Mrs. York says firmly.

Megan opens her mouth as if she's about to argue, but she apparently thinks better of it and says nothing.

"Now, class, back to our sonnets. Does anyone have one they'd like to share?"

Of all people, Kensington waves her hand in the air. "Mrs. York, Quince has written a great one and I think he should read it." She ends with a giggle and a flirtatious look in his direction.

Quince turns about three shades of red. I slump down in my seat wishing I was invisible, because both Megan and Emma are staring at me like I'm going to burst into tears or something. Well, I'm not going to cry, but it's pretty humiliating when my friends know I'm crushing on a guy who's crazy for another girl.

Quince is clearing his throat and fiddling with his notebook and I think I'm really going to have to hear his poetic praises of a girl I despise, when Harris raises his hand.

Mrs. York points to him. "Yes, Harris?"

"I have a question"—his voice cracks, so he swallows hard and tries again—"about sonnets."

I think maybe he's just trying to save Quince from embarrassment, but he really seems all intent on asking this question about poetry.

He flips open his book. "Aren't they always supposed to end in a rhyming couplet? If they don't it messes up the mathematical equation, but sometimes Elizabeth Barrett Browning's sonnets don't end right."

Harris's question temporarily distracts everyone, and I breathe a sigh of relief because I really don't want to listen to Quince's "Ode to a Cheating Girlfriend." Quince seems to relax too, thinking he's off the hook.

Kensi, who figured she was about to become the center of attention, now makes a display of boredom with Harris's question, yawns, and resumes her not-so-quiet conversation with Salissa.

Mrs. York tries to get us kids back on task. "Well, class, that's a very interesting question. And the answer is that Shakespeare's sonnets are always twelve lines followed by the couplet, but Barrett Browning was writing in the Italian form."

"I'd still like to hear Quince's sonnet," Salissa says from across the room. She gives Kensi two-thumbs-up like she's being subtle or something.

"I don't want to read it aloud," Quince mumbles.

"Aw, come on, Quince, suck it up."

Gee thanks, Kevin. Emma shoots him a dirty look and he shrugs. Guys can be so clueless.

"Yes, John, I'd like to hear it," Mrs. York agrees.

Reluctantly Quince stands up, paper in hand, clears his throat, and reads his sonnet aloud. He's patterned it after that famous Barrett Browning sonnet, and it's not too bad actually—if only it weren't dedicated to Kensington Marlow.

"'How do I love you? Let me calculate the ways...'"

I love Caryn with the depth, strength, and height my arms can reach...I love her to the end of the school year, I love her to distraction...

I snap back to attention when the rest of the students applaud his efforts and Kensi preens as if they're applauding her. Quince blushes and sits down. *Now* I feel like crying.

"Very nice, John. Any comments from the class?"

Emma raises her hand. "Anyone can write a love poem. It's a lot harder to write a poem about the loss of love. Isn't that what Shakespeare's later sonnets are about?"

Emma is trying to change the subject, and I'm grateful, but talking about loss of love is not making me any less miserable. I lower my head, pick up my pencil, and pretend to be engrossed in my own sonnet writing.

Mrs. York nods. "Very insightful, Emma."

The teacher glances at the clock, but then Deana's hand flies up. Mrs. York doesn't even question her by now.

"Yes, Deana, you may be excused," she says with a sigh.

Deana runs out the door, grabbing the hall pass on her way.

The next interruption is from Principal MacGregor over the PA. Everyone looks at Megan, whose expression shouts, "I told you so."

The tone of Principal MacGregor's voice says his comments aren't going to be the usual club meetings, social activities, and athletic practices. Even Mrs. York seems to be holding her breath as the classroom falls silent.

"Good morning, Rosslyn Wranglers. This is Principal MacGregor with some very important news from Superintendent Pruitt concerning your lack of compliance with our current dress code. Starting next school year, all Rosslyn High School students will be required to wear uniforms. Specific information can be found on the school's website or in the PTA newsletter. Please tell your parents to read the instructions carefully, because no exceptions will be made. That's all. Have a nice day."

And with that seemingly simple announcement, the battle lines are drawn.

****

Not much schoolwork gets done for the rest of the day, and considering it was only first period when Mr. MacGregor dropped that bombshell, it makes for a very long day for everyone. Teachers can't get any work done since all the kids want to talk about is school uniforms, and every teacher has to listen to the same arguments from students, class after class.

"It's going to stifle our creativity" or "uniforms are too expensive" or "we'll all look like robots" pretty much sums up the gripes kids have. I feel bad for the teachers who seem just as frustrated as the kids over the news.

Finally the last bell of the day rings and I make it a point to be one of the first students out of the building, trying to put as much distance between me and all that emotional upheaval as possible. I pick up on so much stuff from people around me anyway, but today it's like my head is going to explode. For once, Sybil and Starshine's seems like a refuge, not just a place to work.

I arrive much earlier than usual, much to Mom's surprise. But she isn't the only one surprised.

"Mom!" I stop so suddenly, the door almost hits me in the back of the head. "Why are you all dressed up?"

She's wearing a new, pale-green pantsuit with a matching camisole underneath, and beige sling-back heels. Her curled hair is held back from her face by a jeweled comb, instead of tucked into a pencil bun, and she's wearing eye makeup. Definitely not her usual work clothes.

"You say it like I'm usually a mess," she says, brows lifted.

"Sorry," I say, letting the door close as I step inside. "You look nice."

Mom smiles and seems to fairly float around the store.

I stare at her for a minute and then it hits me. "You've got a date!"

Mom smiles condescendingly, or so it seems to me. "I know I can't put one over on you, Caryn, but I really was going to tell you."

I'm in shock. She hasn't had a single date since

we've lived in Indianapolis, and not too many the last year or so we were in Houston.

"That's cool." But I'm so far from cool about it. Who's she dating? And why don't I know about it? "Anybody I know?"

"Mr. Desmond!" says Sybil from across the store.

That's when I remember the nice-looking gentleman Mom was helping here in the store a couple of months ago.

"He's become a regular customer, and a good friend," Mom says, a little smile on her face as she sorts through some invoices.

"Does Mr. Desmond have a first name—or a job?" I say, knowing I sound like the parent instead of the child. But really, someone needs to call attention to the fact that she's blushing like a lovesick schoolgirl.

"George. And he's a pharmacist, but he's actually into herbal remedies as well as pharmaceuticals, so he's been purchasing books on the subject."

I put my hands on my hips and say sternly, "Mom, don't be stupid. He doesn't care about herbal remedies."

This guy's been coming to the store for weeks to spend time with her, not buy books, and I've been so involved with my own problems I never even noticed. I feel a little guilty, but Mom looks so happy and excited (and pretty!), that her enthusiasm is almost enough to bring me out of my doldrums. Almost.

I force myself to relax a little. "Where are you going?"

"He's picking me up at six and we're going to a vegetarian restaurant downtown."

"Well, tell him to have you home at a reasonable hour."

Mom laughs. "Caryn, this is quite a role reversal."

"I don't care, Mom. I have to actually meet this guy face-to-face before I know he's okay for you."

Mom shakes her head. "Turn off the psychic radar, Caryn, and just trust my judgment."

I roll my eyes, which makes me think of Megan doing the same thing. "Oh yeah, I have to tell you something about school."

Mom frowns at my tone. "Did something happen?"

I shudder at the memory of the commotion at school and my psychic reactions to it. "Yeah, and it's been crazy all day. You've got to get on Rosslyn High's website because they're posting the new required uniforms for next year. Mom, I just know it's going to get ugly."

Mom raises an eyebrow. "Uniforms? Isn't that a little unorthodox?"

I nod. "Yeah, you'd think so. Public school and all."

"And what do you mean by 'ugly'?"

"This is what I've been afraid of for months, Mom. This is what Megan's been plotting about, and it's going to be awful."

I go to her and bury my head on her shoulder like I used to do when I was little. But I'm not little now. I'm nearly as tall as she is, and I don't want to mess up her nice clothes. I try to be mature about it even though inside I'm all tied up in knots, my sixth sense on overdrive.

Mom puts her hands on my shoulders and looks me directly in the eye. "Do you *know* know, or just think you know?"

"What I *know* is that something big is gonna happen, and I can't stop it. That's what Uncle Omar said."

"Omar?" Mom's mouth drops open as she releases me.

Sybil suddenly takes an interest in our

conversation from across the store. "You mean Bethany's dead brother?"

Mom looks at me for confirmation and I nod my head. "Caryn, have you been having conversations with him?"

I guess I'd forgotten to mention how often I chat up my dead uncle.

"Oh my!" says Sybil, seeming only slightly surprised by what most people would call startling news.

"So exactly what has Omar told you?" Mom shakes her head. "I can't believe I just asked my teenage daughter what my deceased brother said to her."

I could almost laugh at her expression, but all this uncertainty is zapping my sense of humor. "Uncle Omar keeps saying that whatever's 'going down' as he puts it, it'll happen. I can't stop it, *and* it's supposed to change my life."

Mom taps a finger on the counter for a minute, a frown between her brows. "That's a lot to take in."

"Which part?" I ask with a shrug. "His prediction or the fact that I can talk to dead people?"

"I guess I need some time to process all this." Mom still looks disbelieving, but then she smiles again. "There must be a reason Omar is communicating with you, so you have to pay attention to what he says."

"But Mom, listen, here's what I *know* know—Megan's gonna get in trouble, and Quince is gonna get hurt by Kensi, not that I care about her, and something bad that I can't figure out is gonna happen at school. I...I don't know what to do."

Tears begin to roll down my cheeks despite my best efforts to stop them. So much for acting mature. I didn't realize how frustrated I was with all this—whatever it is—until just now as I tell Mom about it.

Mom puts her hands on my shoulders and gives

me a little squeeze. "Messages-from-Beyond notwithstanding, you're only fifteen years old, Caryn. You aren't expected to fix everything. Let the adults handle it, even Megan."

"What you do," interjects Sybil coming out from behind the counter, "is forget all this nonsense for a while and let me take you out for a nice dinner. There's a Tex-Mex restaurant up in Belford that's supposed to be pretty good and I've got a craving for tacos."

Mom seems relieved that I'll be in good hands while she's out on her date.

I smile at Sybil through my tears. "Do you think I could ask my friend Annabeth to come too? She lives up there."

"The more the merrier, I always say," Sybil says grinning.

I go to the phone and dial Annabeth's number. Maybe between the two of them they can help me forget about Rosslyn High, and school uniforms, and impending disaster—at least for one evening.

****

"Caryn, I've SO got to talk to you," says Annabeth as she slides into the booth at the Mexican restaurant. "Pass the chips and salsa. I'm starved."

Sybil is studying the menu and tells the waiter to bring two diet sodas and an iced coffee, then carefully puts a chip overflowing with salsa into her mouth.

Everything in this restaurant seems so normal. Families with kids eating dinner, couples chatting over margaritas, three single women munching chips and studying the menu, you know—normal. And the smell of food coming from the kitchen is heavenly and makes me feel right at home, like we're back in Houston at my favorite family-owned Mexican place. This is definitely the distraction I need to get my mind off non-normal stuff, like talking to dead uncles and premonitions of chaos at school.

"You won't believe who called me last night!" giggles Annabeth conspiratorially.

I grab a chip from the basket and don't even bother looking at her before I answer, "Ken."

Annabeth pauses in the middle of dunking a chip in salsa. "Ken? Who's Ken?"

I shrug. "Well, I can't remember his real name, but the first day I met you at Peterson's, you were with some guy and I thought you two looked like Barbie and Ken."

"Oh," she says, laughing. "It's Josh Kennedy, that's his name, and you're right—he called me last night!"

"And...?" I ask, even though it's obvious from the way she's almost bouncing on the seat that she's got good news.

"And—he wants us to get back together! Can you believe it?" Annabeth beams at me, her eyes sparkling.

I dunk another chip, wondering about that break-up scene at Peterson's. "What about that other girl he was seeing?"

"Oh *her*!" Annabeth waves a hand. "Well, she dumped him a couple of months ago, and then I started hearing rumors at school—"

"Don't you two go to different schools?"

"It's a small town." Annabeth looks exasperated, and then goes on, "—rumors that he wanted to get back with me, and then last night—"

"Once a man cheats he'll do it again," warns Sybil as she pours another packet of sugar into her iced coffee. "And I should know about that, dear, especially at my age."

Annabeth frowns at us both. "Well, that's what I wanted to ask you, Caryn. Is he being honest with me or am I just a rebound from the rebound?"

I shake my head with a snort. "I don't get boys. They never do what you expect them to do." I think about Quince and how he hurt me when he went back to HIS cheating Significant Other.

Annabeth grabs my hand and gives it a shake. "Caryn, focus. Do you see this working out for me or not?"

I stall for time as I stuff another chip in my mouth. I know what kind of answer she's looking for. She wants my *psychic* opinion, but I just want to push those feelings away for once and have a peaceful meal.

I take my time swallowing my food. "I don't know, Annabeth. Most friends would just tell you to be careful if you give Josh another chance."

"You're not 'most friends.' You're psychic," she says, in a voice that seems very loud to me.

"SHHH!" I look around to make sure no one heard her. "Being—you know—makes me feel like I'm from another planet or something. I just want to be normal."

She points a finger at me. "This *is* normal, for you."

"Quite true," Sybil says. "You've been this way all your life, Caryn. You wouldn't know how to be any other way."

Annabeth taps a spoon on the table. "Listen, you know how Megan is such a good artist?"

I nod. "What's that got to do with it?"

"Well, she's got a gift, you know? She can draw just about anything and that's normal for her. It doesn't make her any less of a regular kid, does it?"

"No, but Megan's talents don't make people look at her funny all the time."

"But Caryn, hon," Sybil interjects. "Your friend here is right. That's just who you are."

"Besides, I think you're way paranoid about what kids think." Annabeth sits back in the booth and crosses her arms, tilting her head at me.

Are they serious? I've spent my entire (admittedly short) life trying (and usually failing) to avoid any public display of my abilities because of the reactions I get from both kids and adults. I know I haven't imagined that people think I'm weird or crazy or both when I blurt out something I shouldn't know. Is Uncle Omar right? Does being psychic make me strange, or is it just one part of the whole me?

"Then why do kids act like I'm crazy when I—know stuff?" I ask Sybil.

"Other kids don't know who they are right now any more than you do, dear. It's easy to make fun of someone who's a little different."

I take a big swallow of my soda, scoop a huge serving of salsa onto a chip, and take my time nibbling while I think about this. I figure Sybil is going to support me no matter what, because she's Mom's friend and she cares about me. But when I look at Annabeth, I realize she's being straight with me, as always. This is the first time it's ever occurred to me that maybe I'm not just the freaky kid who has to hide in the background.

"Do you really think I'm normal? Really?"

"Duh," Annabeth says, rolling her eyes. "That's what I've been telling you for months."

And it's true. Annabeth not only accepted me but encouraged me from day one.

"So you don't think I'm weird?" I ask for the umpteenth time.

"Caryn, get over yourself," Annabeth says. "You take all this way too seriously."

I smile, feeling almost giddy from this new revelation. Annabeth makes it sound so simple. *I'm a normal teenager—with a special talent!* So does that mean I don't need to hide who I am? That I can just be myself?

Annabeth taps the spoon on the table again. "So, back to my question. What's going to happen with Josh?"

"Depends on his birthday," Sybil answers. Annabeth looks at *her* funny this time.

I tilt my head in Sybil's direction. "Numerology."

Annabeth's eyes widen and she leans toward Sybil, but the waiter arrives with three steaming plates on a tray for our table and interrupts whatever she was about to say. The smell of spicy meat and cheese reminds me how hungry I am, and I dig in as soon he places our dishes in front of us.

"Be careful, plates are hot," he warns in his thick Hispanic accent.

I giggle as I take a bite of enchilada and lean over the table like I'm just sharing gossip with a friend, but of course it's not gossip but soon-to-happen stuff.

"Well...Josh thinks he's got you back, just by being sorry—and he *is* sorry—and he won't cheat on you again. But what he doesn't know is there's serious competition! You know that guy Miguel you were studying with last winter? And remember when I said you'd have a choice to make? Well..."

****

Nobody at Rosslyn High is talking much about uniforms, or anything else for that matter. In fact, there's an eerie silence around the place. School gets out in about ten days, so I'm sure all the kids are hoping this whole uniform thing will go away over the summer. In the meantime, there are all the usual end-of-school rituals to be gotten through, like elections, exams, prom.

I didn't go to prom, of course, because it's only for juniors and seniors, but the week after the dance, everyone was talking about how Quince and Kensi were not only there as a couple, but were crowned king and queen.

I'm trying not to think too much about them, since I can't stand the thought of Quince with a girl so unworthy of him, but I guess I need to accept it and move on. I'm also still sure Kensi is headed for a fall, I just don't know when or how. But I can't say it doesn't hurt when I see them together.

It's Monday morning after prom, and Principal MacGregor uses the PA to announce the results of the election for next year's student council officers. They are:
Kensington Marlow—President
Emma Cartwright—Vice President
Ashleigh Ko—Treasurer
Kevin Marshall—Recording Secretary
Harris Rutherford—Sophomore Class Representative
Megan Benedict—Junior Class Representative
Salissa Pringle—Senior Class Representative

No one is particularly surprised at the outcome except me. I've been so sure that Emma is going to be president, I seriously question how my sixth sense could be that far off. I also don't understand how Kensi got more votes than Emma. In my opinion the girl just doesn't have the brains for such an important office, but I guess I'm underestimating her popularity. And Principal MacGregor—well, since Emma is his hand-picked candidate, he sounds more than a little upset as he makes the announcement.

When I see Emma at lunch she looks relieved, so I ask her how she feels about being vice president.

"It's great! It means I've got an office that'll look good on my college resume, but it's a no-brainer. I don't have to do anything except be on call in case Kensi gets sick or something. And now I can attend that design camp this summer!"

I'm happy for her, but still a little uneasy. I just can't figure out how I've been so wrong about the outcome of the election. All day I wrack my brain and can't come up with a single reason why I'm so psychically off base.

Pretty soon my head aches from all the mental exertion, so I decide not to think about school stuff anymore and focus on my own summer plans—visiting Dad in Houston. Unfortunately, I don't get to dwell on my plans for too long, because Principal MacGregor sends a letter home to all parents about the required clothing for next year. And all hell breaks loose.

****

By Tuesday morning, Megan has rallied her anti-uniform troops. I hear rumors and whispers all over school about a protest or walkout or something like that, and my stomach—not to mention my sixth sense—lurches at the very thought.

"Caryn, *it* is happening after lunch tomorrow, so are you with us or not?" Megan asks me in the hallway, checking over her shoulder for teachers.

"What is *it?*" I ask, trying to look unconcerned.

Megan rolls her eyes. "If you're joining us, just be ready after lunch," is all she says as she walks off.

I see her standing in the middle of a group of kids—the ones who were at her house last month making all those protest signs—their heads together like they're in a football huddle. That creepy feeling is all over me now.

I just can't be a part of this—whatever it is—and I decide to make myself scarce tomorrow.

****

"Caryn, did you forget to set your alarm again?" asks Mom standing in the door of my room. "You're going to miss the bus."

I roll over and look at the bedside clock and smile to myself. My plan is working, sort of, and now all I have to do is convince my mother to let me stay home.

"I'm sick," is the first lie that pops into my head.

Mom isn't easily fooled, though. She feels my forehead, looks in my eyes and down my throat, and then shakes her head.

"Get up, faker. You're definitely not sick."

"My stomach hurts," I say, sounding a little whiny, even to myself.

"For heaven's sake, Caryn, are you five?" Mom sits on the edge of the bed. "What's this all about?"

I sit up. "I can't go to school today. Megan has some protest march or walkout or something planned, and I don't even want to be there when it all happens."

Mom arches a brow at me. "That's pretty drastic, isn't it? What does she hope to accomplish by all that?"

I grab my pillow and hug it tightly. "Force Mr. MacGregor's hand about the uniforms, I guess. Please don't make me go to school."

Mom thinks for a minute, and to my relief agrees with me. "Okay, you can stay home for today, but it's only because I'm relying on your good sense to stay out of whatever Megan's plotting. I still have to go to work, though, so will you be all right at home?"

I nod and give Mom a big hug, deciding it's in my best interest not to remind her I'm not a little kid anymore. I roll over, pull the covers up, and try to go back to sleep. Maybe when I wake up all this will be over and I can finally quit worrying about it.

I'm walking barefoot on a beautiful beach at sunrise, feeling the warmth of the summer air on my face. Off in the distance I see a man approaching me and run toward him, hoping it's my father. Instead of Dad, it's a reporter with a microphone that he sticks in my face. "Miss Alderson, what is your psychic opinion of all this?"

Okay, I'm awake. That was truly a nightmare,

only I realize it isn't night. I try to shake it off as I look at the clock. Noon.

I'm starved, so I kick back the covers and head for the kitchen to pour myself a big bowl of cereal. I plop down on the sofa with my breakfast and pick up the TV remote and flip through channels, looking for something besides soap operas. I'm about to give up and turn off the television when I hear a voice say, "It's time, Caryn. Listen to your instincts."

I nearly drop my cereal. "NO!" I shout to the air.

I turn up the volume and flip through the channels again, this time landing on a local newscast that's broadcasting a live remote.

"Again, this is Michael Simons, coming to you live from outside Rosslyn High School, where there's a protest going on. It seems the students have all walked out of the building carrying posters and signs, and now are marching in protest against a new school uniform policy set to be implemented at the start of next school year."

The camera pans around the front lawn of the school building and there are hundreds of kids out of classes—yelling, chanting, waving signs and banners, and some just mugging for the cameras. In addition to all the students outside, there are administrators, teachers, police, and the fire department. And naturally there are news reporters of all kinds swarming around, trying to be the first to get the story. It's what they like to call a media circus, and it's definitely what Megan must have had in mind all along. I suddenly feel guilty for not being there.

Without even thinking, I throw on some jeans, a clean T-shirt, and tennis shoes and race out the front door, locking it behind me. I run the entire six blocks to school and arrive, breathless, to find myself tangled in a group of onlookers trying to get a look at all the action.

It's like I'm on autopilot. I'm searching for Megan, even though I'm not sure why I'm even here or what I'll say when I find her, but something compelled me to come. However, in this crowd, finding her seems almost impossible.

"Look over by the Channel 2 news crew," someone whispers in my ear.

For once, I'm grateful for the assist. "Thanks, Uncle Omar."

I head off toward the satellite truck emblazoned with a giant red "2" and find Megan at the center of the firestorm. She's jumping up and down, waving her banner, and the Channel 2 reporter is holding a mike in front of her face. I wonder how the news media even got wind of this, but I guess it isn't that hard to leave an anonymous message on a reporter's voice mail. I push past some upper-classmen trying to grab the spotlight for themselves and stand close enough to Megan to hear her give the reporter the story he came for.

"And what is your name?"

"Megan Benedict. My dad's Daniel Benedict, CEO of Truitt Wellness Corporation."

I kind of feel sorry for her dad being called out on live TV, but Megan looks very proud of herself for adding that important piece of info.

The reporter nods and smiles, appreciating the scoop he just got. "Are you the organizer of today's protest march?"

"Yes, I am. We're all out here today to demonstrate against school uniforms in a PUBLIC school!"

Megan lets out a whoop, and of course all the kids around her begin shouting too, waving their signs in the air like it's a pep rally or something. Just as the crowd noise subsides, Megan is jerked aside by Ms. Benedict with Principal MacGregor at her side. The reporter gives a throat-slashing signal to his cameraman, who lowers his camera.

I make my way toward where they've dragged Megan, although I have no idea what I'm going to say to her when I get there, but she doesn't see me anyway. Turns out her mother and the principal have plenty to say.

"Megan Benedict, what are you thinking?" Ms. Benedict has a very grim look on her flushed face.

"I'm *thinking* that none of us want to wear school uniforms!" Megan says, waving her banner.

"Young lady, you are in a great deal of trouble," says Mr. MacGregor. "It appears that every student in the school is out of class right now!"

"Don't be silly, not EVERY student," Megan says. "I happen to know for a fact that Deana Pruitt's in the second floor girls' bathroom throwing up her lunch."

Ms. Benedict nods knowingly to Mr. MacGregor, lowering her voice. "The superintendent's daughter is a notorious bulimic. She's in there every day after lunch."

Mr. MacGregor looks almost as shocked at this news as he is about the walkout, which just shows how out of touch he is with his student body.

"Megan is right, though," continues Ms. Benedict. "Not all students are participating, Mr. MacGregor. Ashleigh Ko, Harris Rutherford, and several other gifted math students are at the Economics exhibit downtown. Emma Cartwright is doing an internship for her clothing design class, and the boys' baseball team is on a bus headed for an out-of-town game with Coach Edgemont."

"See?" Megan says, tapping her foot. "Not everybody!"

The principal gives her a severe look, silencing her for once. Megan notices me and waves excitedly.

Mr. MacGregor sees me at about the same time and exclaims, "Caryn Alderson! I thought your mother called you in sick today! So you were involved in this as well? Frankly, Caryn, I thought you had better sense."

"Um, well, I…" I swallow hard.

Suddenly I wonder what made me even come here when I had determined to stay out of it. It's like something—or *someone*—was propelling me here.

Then before I can stop myself, like an idiot I blurt out, "You should answer your cell phone, Mr. MacGregor. It's the superintendent and he's not happy."

Mr. MacGregor looks at me like I'm nuts, turns back to Megan, and then stops as his cell phone rings. He doesn't seem too surprised until he flips it open and looks at the caller ID. "Yes, Superintendent Pruitt?" he says, with a raised-eyebrow look at me. "We certainly are trying to get the situation under control, sir." The principal steps away from the crowd to finish his conversation.

"Caryn Alderson, is it?" asks someone behind me. "How did you know the phone was going to ring, or who it was going to be?"

I turn around and find myself face-to-face with Michael Simons, who not only has his cameraman at his side but his microphone stuck in my face.

"I…I…uh…"

"She's a psychic!" announces Megan, smiling directly into the camera.

AAARRRGGGHHH!!!

Chapter 14
Candid Camera

I stand there speechless, staring at Megan and feeling like the wicked witch must have felt when the house dropped on her. Instead of a house, though, it's my world that just came crashing down on me.

Please, Universe, tell me she didn't just say that on live TV.

Why couldn't she have just said "she's psychic," like it was a big joke someone could laugh off? No, she had to say "She's *a* psychic," which conjures up visions of a crystal-ball-gazing gypsy.

The reporter looks as stunned as I feel, but he's a pro and recovers quickly, sticking the mike back in my face. "Is that true? Do you have psychic abilities?"

Now, honestly. What am I supposed to say to that? If I say no, it's a lie and my conscience (to say nothing of Uncle Omar) will haunt me forever. If I say yes, I'm dooming myself to social isolation. I look around for a way out of this predicament, an escape route, anything to keep from having to answer that question. I blink once, then twice, and wouldn't you know it? I see Uncle Omar in the flesh—or, well you know—leaning against the school's marquis, his arms crossed, and a smirk on his face.

"Don't even think about denying it," he says, grinning at me.

Michael Simons repeats his question. "Are you psychic, Miss…?"

Megan leans over and shouts into his

microphone. "Her name is Caryn Alderson!"

I'm still sputtering, fumbling for words, shooting dirty looks at Megan, and trying to pretend I don't see Uncle Omar, when I hear some kids from the crowd shouting, "Hey, look at the cheerleaders!"

Relieved to have the focus anywhere but on me, I turn with everyone else to see what Kensi and the other cheerleaders are up to. They've formed one of those human pyramids with Kensi at the top. She's precariously balanced on two other girls' shoulders and she's holding a sign over her head that reads "ROSSLYN HIGH SCHOOL STUDENTS *WILL NOT* WEAR UNIFORMS!!!"

Once she's sure the cameras are all on her, she throws down the sign shouting "Fashion freedom for all!" and—*removes her shirt!*

That's right, in front of cameras, students, administrators, and various onlookers, Kensington Marlow takes off her shirt, revealing her black bra decorated with red ribbons—*school colors for a striptease?*—and the word "Uniform" written in bold black ink on her stomach, inside a red circle with a slash mark across it.

Of course the camera gets a close-up of her and just as the kids start cheering, she loses her footing and topples off the top of the pyramid. Now mind you, in addition to being without a shirt, Kensi is wearing very tight shorts that ride low on her hips, and as she falls, everyone in the Channel 2 viewing area gets an up-close look at her hot pink underwear. The other five girls manage not to fall down after her, but once Kensington hits the ground unhurt, she stands up smiling and waves at the camera, which once again gets a close-up of her bra and decorated bare midriff.

I can't stand it anymore. I push my way through the crowds of people gawking at the cheerleaders and head for home. Unfortunately, when I get there

I realize I've locked myself out of the apartment in my hurry to get to school, so I slowly walk to Mom's store.

I'm feeling pretty miserable and extremely mad at myself for having ever left home, so when I see Uncle Omar on the sidewalk up ahead, it's just one more irritation in a lousy day.

"Come to say 'I told you so'?" Right now I don't even care if anyone sees me talking to the signpost.

He laughs. "Not exactly, but I did tell you that certain events had to happen."

"That's 'I told you so' if I ever heard it," I grumble. "My life is over."

"Your *true* life is just beginning," he says cheerfully. "Everything's copasetic. Don't worry."

And he's gone. *Copasetic?*

"Easy for you to say," I yell at the air, and a mother pushing a stroller crosses to the other side of the street to get away from me.

I slink into Sybil and Starshine's, embarrassed and ashamed of myself, and see that Mom is on the phone. I sit on the stool behind the counter, dreading what I have to tell her.

"No, George, I haven't seen any television today," she's saying. "We don't have one here in the store, you know. Has something happened?"

Mom's eyes get bigger and bigger as she listens to Mr. Desmond, and she casts a few wide-eyed glances in my direction.

"Uh-huh, I see. Well, yes, she's here now and I guess I need to speak with her. Thanks for calling, George. You too."

Mom hangs up the phone. For a minute, neither of us can say a word. Finally, I break the silence.

"How's Mr. Desmond?" Okay, I'm stalling.

"Pretty surprised, actually."

"So you heard about the stuff at school?" It's like I'm out of my body again, floating up near that dusty light fixture and hearing myself say the dumbest things. "Stuff at school" barely scratches the surface.

Mom puts her hands on her hips. "Caryn, explain to me why you went to school today when you begged me to let you stay home."

I feel all the humiliation coming back to me, and tears flood my eyes. "I'm so sorry, Mom. It's just that when I turned on TV and saw all the news cameras at school—"

"—you suddenly decided you wanted to be part of it after all?"

A big tear rolls down my cheek. "I just didn't think."

Mom softens a little, but I can tell she's still not happy with me. "What's this about you being interviewed on camera?"

I wipe my eyes with the back of my hand. "It was just awful. Does Mr. Desmond think you have a freak for a daughter?" Before Mom can respond to that I sniffle and add, "Pick up the phone."

Of course the store's phone rings and Mom reluctantly answers it.

"Sybil and Starshine's New Age Bookstore." Glancing over at me, she says, "Yes, she's here." She hands the phone to me. "Annabeth."

I'm relieved it's an ally. "Hi, Annabeth."

"OHMIGOD! Caryn!" Annabeth's voice is high-pitched and a little envious. "That is so crazy what happened at Rosslyn today! Megan planned all that?"

I sigh and hold the phone away from my ear. "I told you she was up to something."

"No joke," says Annabeth. "Are you okay?"

"Me? Why wouldn't I be?"

"Because that interview with you and Megan is on all the teasers for the six o'clock news! That and Kensington Marlow's striptease," she adds with a snort.

Despite my misery, I find that pretty funny. "Who knew my prediction that Kensi was headed for a fall meant *literally* falling?"

Annabeth laughs. "Well, at least you were right about that. But then there are all the sound bites of you looking like a deer caught in the headlights."

I groan, then take a deep breath. "The news cameras were all focused on the walkout until Megan opened her big mouth about me."

"Yeah, the walkout's the big story, but you're in there too. Just be prepared, okay?"

That would've been pretty good advice if I'd known what to prepare myself for.

As soon as I hang up the phone from Annabeth, it rings again and I pick it up without thinking. "Sybil and Starshine's New Age Bookstore, Caryn speaking."

"Hello?" It's a woman's voice I don't recognize. "Is this the Caryn Alderson who was interviewed by Channel 2 at Midday?"

"Uh, I guess so. Who's this?"

"This is Serena Farrell with *The Indianapolis Star*. Can I ask you a few questions?"

"NO!" I slam down the phone, my heart pounding.

A newspaper reporter? Seriously, this is all way out of control. I find myself hoping that there's a major development over in the Middle East, or gas prices take another huge jump, or the president trips over a potted plant—anything to get the local news media's attention off me. What I can't figure out is why they're interested in me at all. They should be focusing on the all-school walkout in protest of school uniforms. THAT was the story, not me.

****

I borrow Mom's apartment key and walk home, feeling all the weight of the world on my shoulders. As I toss the keys on the table just inside the door, I see the blinking light on the answering machine and notice that there are fourteen messages. I hit play, ready to delete the usual nuisance calls, but nothing could have prepared me for what I heard next:

BEEP! *This is Mrs. Smith from school. I am not your personal secretary and I am tired of fielding calls from reporters, so I'm giving them your home phone number!*

BEEP! *Hello, Caryn, this is Serena Farrell from* The Indianapolis Star. *I was hoping to get an interview with you. The school secretary suggested I try your mother's bookstore if you aren't home.*

BEEP! *This is a message for Caryn Alderson. Michael Simons from Channel 2 News calling. I'd like to finish the interview I started with you earlier today.*

BEEP! *Caryn Alderson, please call WXXZ radio station and ask for Bob Parker, or e-mail me through the website.*

BEEP! *Sandra MacKenzie from* The Belford Daily News *calling for Caryn Alderson. Please call me back.*

BEEP! *Tom Harrison from* Eyewitness News. *I'd like to interview Caryn Alderson about her so-called psychic abilities. Give me a call as soon as possible.*

BEEP! *Caryn Alderson, why in the world did you bail on me today? It's Megan. Call me back NOW!*

BEEP! *Miss Alderson, this is Matthew Gains with the* Paranormal News Weekly. *We'd like to tell your story in our next edition. Please call me at your earliest convenience.*

BEEP! *Hey, Caryn, Jeremy. Is it true about you being psychic? Weird!*

BEEP! *Caryn, it's Kevin Marshall. Wait till I tell Emma! Or does she already know?*

BEEP! *Caryn, it's Emma. I just got a call from Kevin and he told me about the walkout and you being on TV. Call me!*

BEEP! *Caryn, girl, you've given me a month's worth of gossip to spread around school. It's Janae, by the way.*

BEEP! *Hi Caryn, it's Ashleigh. Well, the cat's outta the bag now, girlfriend. Look out!*

BEEP! *Uh, hi, Caryn? This is Harris Rutherford. You know, in your Love of Lit class? Um, I was wondering if, uh, well, could you give me some advice? I mean, you being psychic and all. I'd pay you. Call me back.*

HUH? Harris wants to pay me for a psychic reading? And he sounds serious. He's not laughing at me or anything, which is good, but it's Harris and I know I can't judge what the other kids are thinking based on him.

It's just all so weird, though. Suddenly I picture myself sitting in the back room at Mom's store, dressed like Madame Wilhelmina again, staring into a crystal ball and giving psychic readings. I shudder at that image, hope it's just my overactive imagination, and collapse on the sofa. I'm overwhelmed and exhausted, so I close my eyes and drift off into a fitful sleep.

I'm on the Houston Astros' baseball field. The stands are deserted, the players are nowhere in sight, but the scoreboard keeps flashing "Caryn the Teenage Psychic—Now at Bat."

Just like it's my own little field of dreams, Uncle Omar appears from nowhere, not dressed in his usual army fatigues but in an Astros uniform. He pitches me a ball which I catch with a mitt I got from somewhere in dreamland, and then he suddenly doubles over in laughter.

"*What are you laughing about? This isn't funny!*"

"*Sure it is! The joke's on you, kid! Here you were thinking everything was about Megan, when it was really all about you!*"

I sit up, wide awake. I rub my eyes and try to clear my head. And in that moment, it's like a lightning bolt hits me. Not being psychic about my own life, I had no way of knowing I'd be more profoundly affected by this protest rally than Megan, since this whole time all I'd done was worry about *her*. The uneasy feeling I'd had for months was about me, not Megan. And now my secret is out and as much as I hate to admit it, it looks like Uncle Omar was right all along. He was pitching the facts to me and I just now caught his meaning.

In the middle of my breakthrough, Mom walks in the door. She puts her purse on the coffee table, looks through the mail—you know, the usual stuff she does when she gets home from work every day—and checks the answering machine. I watch with apprehension as she grows more and more amazed listening to the calls, and I seriously wish I'd deleted them.

"Have you listened to all these messages, Caryn?"

"Duh," is my brilliant response.

"Well, then, what do you plan to do?"

"I plan to move to a deserted island and live there for the rest of my life."

Mom points to the answering machine, like I've forgotten what's on there, and then sighs. "Be reasonable, Caryn. This isn't going to go away, and these reporters will keep hounding you if you don't do something."

I sit up. "Do what? Give an interview to a reporter? About being psychic of all things?"

She drops the mail and kicks off her shoes. "Caryn, I know it's been a tough day, but you were outed on local television. Information like that is what the news media like to call a human interest story. They aren't going to leave you alone."

I sink back onto the sofa and bury my face in a

throw pillow. "But I'm already an outcast at school. If I talk to a reporter about being psychic, it's like committing social suicide!"

"You *are* psychic." Mom sits down next to me and strokes my hair. "Instead of letting kids and the media make up stories about you, why not take control and tell the story of the real you?"

I sit up and blink tears out of my eyes. "Are you saying—give an interview?"

"Exactly." Mom makes it sound so simple, but to me it's anything but simple.

"But what would I do?"

"Well, for starters, return one of those phone calls. Let the reporter come interview you with me sitting by your side, and we can put this all behind us. Believe me, honey, your fifteen minutes will be up before you know it."

There's a strange kind of logic to what Mom is saying. If I give just one interview—with Mom right there—maybe I can get this all to go away with the least amount of damage to my reputation. School is almost over anyway, and I'm sure kids will forget over the summer.

I let out a huge sigh. "Okay, I'll do it. Which one do I pick?"

"How about the newspaper reporter? That might be less threatening than more TV exposure."

I nod and give her a big hug. But before I grant any interviews about my psychic abilities, I have to do one thing.

"I need to call Dad, to tell him about what happened today before he sees it on YouTube or something."

Mom smiles and hands the phone to me so I can dial his number. It rings three times, and just as I figure it's going to voice mail, my father's voice is on the other end.

"Hi, Dad," I say, tears welling in my eyes again.

"You won't believe what happened at school today!"

****

I don't usually read the newspaper in the mornings—okay, never—but the neighbor across the hall subscribes, and his paper is lying open in front of his apartment door when I leave for school this morning. I can't help but see the glaring headline: "SHOWDOWN AT THE OL' ROSSLYN CORRAL! Rosslyn High School Wranglers stage protest rally!"

I shudder and walk to school just hoping to get this day behind me. The newspaper reporter agreed to meet me this afternoon at Mom's store, so I've got all day to worry about that. In the meantime I have to make it through the day at school, hopefully with my nerves and reputation intact. My stomach is all butterflies as I walk in the main entrance, but no one seems to notice me.

What they *are* doing is standing around in clusters, talking in hushed whispers. And it doesn't take a sixth sense to know they're talking about yesterday's walkout and today's fallout. I briefly worry that I might be in trouble, since being on camera could make it seem like I was in on the whole conspiracy. But I ignore that thought and head to my locker. My goal is to get to Mrs. York's class as quickly as possible and hide out.

Quince is standing in front of my locker.

My heart skips a beat, or two, or three. I hesitate, wondering if I should just go to my locker like it's the most normal thing in the world for him to be standing there, or say something, or—

"Hi, Caryn," he says before I can decide. "I was afraid you weren't coming to school today."

"Um, really? I, uh..." Why am I always so tongue-tied around this guy?

"Yeah, and before you say anything"—(like I could get the words out anyway)—"I just wanted to tell you I'm sorry I didn't listen to you about Kensi.

Maybe I was just too stupid to see who she really is, but you were right and I messed up big time. We—you know, the team—we got back late last night from our game and when I went home and turned on TV, there she was on the eleven o'clock news. Man, I couldn't believe it. A girl I thought I knew! Well, anyway. So I called her right then and told her it was over between us, and she said it wasn't her fault, it was Megan's, or yours, or the TV crew, or whoever. Kensi can't ever take responsibility for herself, and now she's trying to blame everyone else."

Quince stops for a breath, and I can tell he's hurt. My heart goes out to him, so to speak, because of course he already has my heart. But what I mean is that he looks so pitiful about being stung by Kensi yet again.

"So can you forgive me for being such an idiot?" Quince smiles at me sheepishly.

It's more words at once than I've ever heard from him—even better than one of my dreams—and I can't think of a thing to say. Can this be for real? Is Quince telling me without a doubt that he finally broke up with Kensi?

"Okay, you're still mad and I get it," he says, with a shrug. "You don't have to say anything."

"No, that's not it, I..." Quince is looking at me expectantly, so I'd better spit something out and quick, before he walks away. "I never was mad at you. I just hated to see Kensi hurt you."

"I wish I'd listened to you way back last winter. Could've saved myself a lot of grief." He looks a little better after getting all that off his chest. "Anyway, I'm glad we're still friends, and I was wondering if you'd go to Peterson's with me after school one day."

Quince smiles at me, and I suddenly realize he's just asked me for a date. After all these months—finally! I feel like I'm floating on a cloud.

"I'd like that." Now *there's* an understatement.

"Great," says Quince, heading off toward class. "I'll call you."

I can barely breathe over my heart palpitations, and then he calls over his shoulder, "Hey, Caryn, you looked cool on TV yesterday!"

My literature book slips out of my hand and bounces off my foot and I don't even care. Quince saw me on television in my biggest moment of shame, and he still wants to go out on a date with me! I must be the luckiest girl on the planet.

****

Attendance is pretty light at school today. As I look around Mrs. York's classroom, I notice quite a few empty chairs. Kensi is absent, for one, and Salissa and Megan aren't here either. The seniors are gone anyway, since graduation is coming up and they're pretty much finished for the year. I'm wondering how bad things are going to be after the walkout yesterday, but Mrs. York clearly has more important things on her mind.

"Ladies and gentlemen," she says, rapping on her desk. "I know everyone is still reeling from yesterday's activities, but I'd like to make an announcement of a different nature."

She's going to tell us about the baby!

I absentmindedly wonder why she picks today of all days to talk about it, but Mrs. York's face is glowing and it's impossible not to smile back at her.

"This is my last school year here at Rosslyn." There's a murmur in the room, and all the kids look puzzled, including me. "My husband has accepted a new job in Chicago, and we're moving right away."

Moving? Not coming back next year? That's not what she's supposed to tell us.

Before I can stop myself, I ask, "But what about the baby, Mrs. York?"

She looks surprised at first, but then she smiles

at me. "I started to ask how you knew that, but then I remembered your TV appearance yesterday." To the whole class she says, "Yes, Mr. York and I are expecting our first child, and *he* will be born next December. The doctor has suggested that I rest as much as possible, so I plan to take it easy once we're settled into our new home."

There's a great deal of giggling and chatter among the kids, with various shouts of "cool" and "congratulations" and stuff like that. Mrs. York blushes with pride and happiness.

"Mrs. York?" interrupts one of the school secretaries over the PA. "Could you please send Caryn Alderson to the principal's office?"

Everyone turns to look at me, and I want to hide under my desk. Me? Why me? Even Mrs. York seems surprised that I've been summoned, but she nods at me to go. Quince gives me a big grin, so at least he's still in my corner if I'm in trouble.

I swallow hard as I pick up my book bag and head out the door.

****

Everything seems pretty normal in the principal's office—phones ringing, the secretary working at her computer, kids coming in for late passes. I sit in the waiting area trying not to fidget. Just a regular day, almost like yesterday never happened. But my internal radar is going off and I know there's more going on than just being questioned by the principal about the walkout.

"Caryn," says the principal's secretary. "You may go in now."

I muster up all the courage I have (which isn't much), and open the door to the principal's office to see—Mrs. Renfrow! The head of the English Department is sitting in Principal MacGregor's chair, and looking very comfortable behind his desk. She smiles warmly at me and motions me to a chair opposite the desk. I hesitate, wondering what's going on.

"Caryn, I'm sure you're confused at the moment," Mrs. Renfrow says.

She can say that again.

"Where is Mr. MacGregor?" I ask, dropping into one of the room's vinyl chairs.

"He's been reassigned," she says in a neutral voice.

I instantly get an image of a tiny building in a rundown part of town. "To an elementary school?"

"Well, yes," Mrs. Renfrow answers with a surprised frown. "The superintendent was displeased about yesterday's activities in general and Principal MacGregor's handling of it in particular."

What she means is *mis*-handling, but for once I keep my mouth shut. Someone coughs and I realize Megan, grinning widely, is sitting on a sofa on the back wall next to Ms. Benedict, who doesn't look happy at all. A frowning man in a pinstripe suit is sitting on the other side of Megan, studying the screen of a large phone.

I'm wondering who he is when Mrs. Renfrow claims my attention. "I'm the acting principal of Rosslyn High School now, Caryn, and I'd like to begin by assuring you that you're not in trouble. I'm just looking for answers."

So why am I here?

As if in answer to my unspoken question, Ms. Benedict says, "I know you were accidentally caught on camera, Caryn, but I also know you weren't really involved. I've told Mrs. Renfrow that yesterday's activities were Megan's choices, not yours."

"I just want you to tell me in your own words what happened," says Mrs. Renfrow. "We're trying to piece together the events leading up to the activities and see to it that the appropriate persons are held accountable."

I can't figure out why all the grownups keep calling the walkout "activities" like it was a field trip or something. But Mrs. Renfrow is looking at me expectantly, and unfortunately I can't form a single coherent thought. Why is she asking me? The silence in the room is eerie. And something else is distracting me. Who's that man? *OH! Of course! Megan's father!* He's here to make sure Megan doesn't get into too much trouble.

I realize Mrs. Renfrow is still waiting for my reply. "Well, I...I..." Seriously, I've got nothing.

"No one blames you for anything, Caryn, but somehow you managed to attract a great deal of media attention, and naturally I'd like your version of things. As the new administrator, I must make students aware that walking out of the building in the middle of a school day is an inappropriate way to address certain issues."

"Well, sure, but I..."

Mrs. Renfrow closes a file folder on the desk in front of her. "Why don't you just write down your version of the activities, Caryn—in correct essay form mind you—and turn it in to me by tomorrow?"

I cringe. Mrs. Renfrow's not only expecting a detailed account, but she's going to be grading my spelling and punctuation.

"What about the uniforms?" Megan asks.

Mr. Benedict shoots his daughter a warning look. "That's quite enough, young lady."

But Megan just shrugs. "Dad, it was just a question."

"I've spoken with Superintendent Pruitt," Mrs. Renfrow tells her. "And a decision will be made soon concerning the school dress code. In the meantime, Megan, I believe you have something you need to say to everyone."

Megan grins at me, gives me a subtle thumbs-up

sign, and says, "Hey, Caryn, any psychic predictions about uniforms?"

Ms. Benedict groans and Mr. Benedict looks like he'd like to throttle his daughter.

Megan seems to have won this round.

Epilogue
Summertime

Today's the last day of school! Just counting down the minutes till the final bell makes me giddy with anticipation. Still, I've learned more in the last week than I did all year, except it wasn't lessons from a textbook, it was stuff about the real world.

Lesson #1: Being psychic isn't all that bad.

After the episode in the acting principal's office last week, I went to Mom's store to meet *Indianapolis Star* reporter Serena Farrell. She turned out to be a young woman fresh out of college and eager to impress her boss with a good human interest story. The Rosslyn High School walkout was still big news, so Serena said she felt lucky to get the interview with me, considering all the offers I'd had.

Serena had a bubbly personality and I felt comfortable with her, but once she turned on her tape recorder she was all business.

"How were you involved in yesterday's protest march against Rosslyn High School?" Serena began.

"I really wasn't involved at all. I just got caught on TV by accident," I said, while Serena scribbled notes on a pad, which kind of freaked me out.

"You were seen on camera predicting a phone call from the superintendent, correct?"

"Uh, yeah, I guess."

She looked up from her note-taking, almost like she was surprised at my answer even though the whole point of this interview was my psychic coming-out. "Is that something you do a lot?"

I looked over at Mom and she nodded

encouragement.

"I've been doing it since I was a little kid."

"And your friend Megan Benedict told the Channel 2 news reporter that you're a psychic. Is that true? Are you psychic?"

"Yeah, it's true," I mumbled.

"Can you speak up, Caryn? I don't think the recorder will catch that." Serena moved the device closer to me.

I remembered that the reason I was here in the first place was to finally admit who I am, so I sat up straight, looked Serena directly in the eye, and spoke in a firm tone. "Yes, it's true. I'm psychic."

"So, predicting phone calls—is that the only thing you do, or are there other things?"

"Oh, yeah, lots of other things. I get strong feelings or sometimes pictures in my mind." I didn't mention talking to dead people. I figured she was getting enough ammunition as it was.

"And Ms. Alderson," Serena said. "What's it like living with a psychic daughter?"

Mom paused a moment. "Well, I suppose it was a surprise at first, when she was so little and started making predictions. But now it's just a part of who she is and I don't think about it very much. Sometimes her abilities come in handy." Mom winked at me.

"In what way?"

"Oh, this and that. Most recently she insisted I wait a few days before buying a new handbag I had my eye on, and sure enough the next week it went on sale."

Serena nodded but didn't smile. "How accurate are your predictions?"

I shrugged. "Most of the time I'm right. Except for when it's stuff about me. Then I don't have a clue."

"Then you're not psychic about your own life?"

I shook my head, but then I remembered the tape recorder and said, "No, I guess I just have to figure out stuff on my own without any extra help."

"But she's pretty accurate about other people's lives," Mom said smiling.

Serena nodded again. "Can you give me an example? Some sort of psychic insight about me, for instance?"

Okay, I didn't anticipate having to prove myself. I paused longer than I needed to, so maybe she'd think I was giving it some deep thought. Actually, once I focused on Serena's life I got a pretty quick hit. Finally I said, "Well, you're moving out of that tiny apartment you live in and you'll be sharing a bigger house with two other women. And you'll be getting a raise soon." I sneaked a glance at Mom, who lowered her head and smiled to herself. She knew I was dragging out my answer for effect.

Serena's eyes got real wide. "Amazing! It's true I'm moving in with friends, but the raise? In this economy?"

I shrugged. "Call me back in about a week after this story hits. It'll happen."

After Serena turned off the recorder, she said she'd do a follow-up story if she got a raise. I told her she'd have to call me in Houston, because that's where I'd be for the summer. And actually, I enjoyed making that happy prediction for her and I'm looking forward to her phone call at my dad's.

Serena had brought a photographer with her and the story was in the Metro section the next morning, accompanied by a fairly large picture of Mom and me smiling broadly. We're standing in front of Mom's store with the sign visible behind us, which was Mom's idea to get some free publicity from the story.

Of course the interview stirred up the whole psychic story about me all over again. Kids at school were buzzing with the news.

"Hey, Caryn!" I saw one of the senior girls waving at me from way down the hall, running to catch up to me. I didn't even know her name. "Can you tell me if I'll meet a new boyfriend when I start at Purdue in the fall?"

"Uh, yeah...?" I walked down the hall shaking my head.

"So what's my future career going to be?" I looked behind me and a freshman girl I barely knew, Angie Morrison, was standing right there.

I was surprised she even knew who I was, but said without thinking, "Interior design."

"Uh, Caryn." It was Mark Evans, who'd barely said two words to me since the Christmas dance, shuffling up to my locker with his hand in front of his mouth. "Uh, do you see me getting...braces?"

I almost laughed, but I guess it wasn't funny to him. "Not for another year, but then it's going to make all the difference."

He even smiled a little before he hurried off down the hall.

"Yo, Alderson! Tell me how I did on that AP exam!" I turned around yet again and there was Connor Stevenson, yelling at me from down the hall, his arms spread wide.

I don't know why I saw what I saw, because I don't know anything about AP scores. But suddenly there was a cartoon "5" dancing in my head, complete with top hat and walking stick. "Five." *Whatever that means.*

It must have been the answer he was looking for, though, because he gave me a double thumbs-up and strutted down the hall, calling out to everyone he saw, "I got a FIVE!"

"Caryn, girl, you gotta tell me what it's like to be you." Janae Thomas was leaning against the locker next to mine wearing stonewashed jeans, stilettos, and a rhinestone-studded T-shirt, her hand on one hip.

I sighed. "To be me? What are you talking about, Janae?"

"Being psychic. What's that like?"

I lifted a shoulder. "Well, it's hard to explain. But it's kinda like watching words and pictures on a computer screen all going by really fast, except it's happening in my head."

Janae smiled and I could just see the wheels turning in her head. She thinks she has the inside track on all future goings-on at Rosslyn High, with me as her personal psychic hotline for gossip.

"Girlfriend, any time you get a preview of anything juicy about to happen, you call me first, okay?"

"Okay, Janae." But since she's usually the first to get the news anyway, she probably doesn't need my help at all.

So the day wasn't half as bad as I'd imagined it would be. I went straight home after school the day the newspaper story hit, eager to tell Mom my social life wasn't over after all.

But by the time Mom got to the apartment she was fried. I guess the phone had been ringing off the hook at the store all day and she couldn't take down the messages fast enough.

"Thank goodness you're home, Caryn. Here, start returning these phone calls."

I looked through the slips of pink paper she handed me. "Who are these people?"

She shouted to me from the kitchen where she was raiding the refrigerator. "They all saw the newspaper story this morning and now they want to make an appointment with you for a reading."

I shuffled through the stack. There had to be thirty messages. "Reading?"

"Yes. People want to pay you money to predict

their futures."

"Predict their futures?" I repeated, dropping the messages on the table.

Mom stepped back into the living room, a frown on her face. "It's called a reading, Caryn."

"But, Mom, I've never given one before." Was she serious? For total strangers? How could I?

Mom stared at me like that was the most ridiculous thing she'd ever heard. "Sure you have, Caryn. Not a formal one maybe, but you do it all the time."

"Yeah, but these people would expect me to, you know, be accurate." I picked up the messages and tried to give them back to her.

Mom put her hands behind her back "Yes, and you usually are accurate, Caryn. Why don't you give it a try and see if you like it?"

"Oh, Mom, I just couldn't."

Mom looked at me pleadingly. "We should take advantage of the publicity. These are paying customers, honey, and it could be really good business for the store too."

People not only wanted me to give them my psychic insights, but they were willing to pay for it? I kicked the thought around in my head for a few minutes. On the one hand, I'd have to rev up my psychic abilities to give people their money's worth. On the other hand I could also pick up a little cash that would come in handy on my visit to Houston this summer. On the other hand...

"You're only entitled to two hands!" said a laughing voice in my head.

I stifled a giggle. Mom raised her eyebrows at me, so I said, "Nothing. Just Uncle Omar."

She just shook her head.

"How much do you think I should charge people?" I asked, trying to remember how much Astros tickets cost. "Ten dollars?"

"Ten dollars?" Mom said, pausing on her way back to the kitchen.

"Too much?"

"Not enough! At least twenty. You're worth every penny."

I flopped my head back on the sofa trying to take it all in. People wanted *me* to tell them about their futures. Offering to pay me for my advice, and yet only a few days ago I was still pretending I made lucky guesses all the time. Things had changed so fast I could barely catch my breath. But I liked the idea of having a little money of my own, not having to depend on my parents all the time.

So I returned some of the phone calls and actually set up a few appointments. Just three for starters because, well, I'm a kid, and I also want to do normal stuff.

When I got to the store the next day after school, I couldn't believe what I saw. The store was packed with customers, which of course was a good thing. But I didn't know if I should help wait on people or go start my readings like Mom and I had agreed. I caught her eye and waved both of my arms over people's heads. Mom didn't have time to spare, but she pointed to the back room and then continued waiting on customers near the bookshelves. Sybil had a line of people at the cash register waiting to pay for their merchandise, so she couldn't stop to talk either.

I smiled politely at people as I squeezed my way past them to the storeroom where I was supposed to begin my career as a professional psychic. I was nervous enough already, but all those people set my fears into hyper-drive. What if I gave someone bad advice? What if more of them wanted readings than the ones I'd counted on? Maybe this wasn't such a good idea after all.

Too late to back out now, though, since I'd

already made appointments. Mom had set me up in a corner of the storeroom with a dinette table, two chairs, and a floor lamp. She even used Grandma's white linen tablecloth to make it more attractive. It was pretty cozy and private, actually. But I was still nervous.

I sure could use some help right now.

I heard Uncle Omar laughing. "You'll be G-R-E-A-T!"

I dropped my head in my hands but couldn't help laughing too. "Uncle Omar, no one does that tiger thing anymore. It's the twenty-first century now!"

But his joke helped me relax.

The lamp next to the table had a low-wattage bulb which cast a soft light, and on the table was a deck of playing cards.

Mom knows I don't need props to read people so it must be for effect only, but since I didn't know what else to do, I picked them up, shuffled, and dealt out a hand of solitaire.

"Uh, Caryn?" I heard a familiar voice call out.

"Back here!"

My first customer had arrived—Harris Rutherford! He grinned at me shyly, shook my hand, sat in the chair opposite me, and fidgeted for a moment before finally speaking.

"Um, are you going to read my future with cards?"

"No," I said, stacking the cards back into a deck. "I was just fooling around. Now, what do you want to know?"

I guess what he wanted to ask was really important because he looked me in the eye and blurted out his question without waiting another second. "Why don't the girls at school like me?"

Talk about a loaded question. I didn't want to hurt his feelings with the truth, and I didn't want

Harris to think I wasn't taking his question seriously. So I thought for a minute and focused really hard on his problem.

Finally it came to me like a lightning bolt. "Remember last October when I told you to concentrate on getting good grades?"

He nodded and his shoulders slumped like he already knew what I was going to say, but I was sure he didn't.

"Well, all that hard work is going to pay off, Harris. You're going to some kind of camp this summer where there'll be lots of other brainiac kids like you. All because of that 4.0 you earned this year."

His smile was crooked, but he didn't seem very happy with that answer. "Yeah, I just got accepted to a science camp held by some local pharmaceutical company, but that's not—"

"Who's Jenna?" I interrupted him.

He frowned and then shrugged. "I don't know any Jenna."

I smiled, because I liked this particular vision. "You will. You'll meet her at that camp this summer, and she'll become a good friend. The two of you will have lots in common. You know, science stuff."

I saw a whole roomful of geeky kids like Harris, all engrossed in their science projects, and I knew he'd fit right in and be happy. And Jenna? She's shorter than Harris, has curly brown hair and wears thick-rimmed eyeglasses that actually suit her. She's cute and has that intellectual type of humor that most kids don't get, but Harris does. I knew he'd like her.

Harris looked skeptical, though. "Do you really think so? I mean, so far girls,.." He didn't finish and even without psychic powers, I knew what he wanted to say.

"Trust me, Harris, this girl Jenna's really gonna

like you."

A smile slowly crept onto Harris's face. He's kinda cute when he smiles like that. "Well, thanks, Caryn. How much do I owe you?"

It just didn't seem right to charge him money, and I remembered something I'd told myself last month in Mrs. York's class. "About three or four math-tutoring sessions next fall should do it. Maybe. I'm really bad at math," I said.

Harris beamed. "Okay, great! I'll call you in August."

He stood up, shook my hand again, and walked away with more swagger than I'd seen all year.

And that was my first professional reading!

It was way past the store's usual six o'clock closing time when I finished my last reading—a college student who wanted to know if the guy she was dating was *Mr. Right* (he wasn't!)—and I felt a rumbling in my stomach as I made my way out of the darkened back room and into the brighter lights of the shop. Standing near the cash register, with a big smile on his face, was Quince. Hello, butterflies!

"Hi, Caryn!"

I managed to smile back at him. "Hi, yourself."

"I know I said something about coffee, but I'm famished and wondered if you'd like to go get a burger with me instead."

Wow! Quince Adams was asking me for a date, and all I had to do was open my mouth and accept. But of course, I was speechless.

"But if you're busy..." he said, after a lengthy pause.

"No! I'd love to go!" *Congratulations, Caryn, you did it.*

"Great!"

Quince held the door open for me, and as we strolled out into the warm, early-evening sunshine, I saw Uncle Omar leaning on a parking meter. "Told ya so," he said with a wink.

"Thanks, Uncle Omar," I said under my breath.

"Did you say something?" Quince asked.

I looked up again but all I saw was a car parallel parking next to that meter. I smiled at Quince. "Oh, just telling myself how lucky I am to be here with you."

Quince smiled back at me and took my hand as we walked down the street to the fast-food restaurant.

Lesson #2: It's okay to stand up for what you believe.

I never was in favor of Megan's protest march against the administration for trying to force kids to wear school uniforms. But this time it looks like the kids won.

The news media have stayed all over the big walkout story and been following up on it for days now, with interviews of school administrators, parents, PTA officers, and even the superintendent. Their slant is that Rosslyn High School will be the laughingstock of not only the city, but the state and possibly the country (slight exaggeration but it sells newspapers), if they force public school students to wear uniforms, as if Rosslyn is a private school. According to Janae, Superintendent Pruitt is getting hundreds of phone calls and e-mails from angry parents and embarrassed community leaders, including the mayor of Indianapolis.

So today, the superintendent caved under all that pressure and issued a statement that in the future, students will be strictly held to the current dress code, but uniforms will not be required. Cha-ching!

Lesson #3: Sometimes people get away with things and sometimes they don't.

Take Megan Benedict, for instance. She's the Teflon Kid. Despite being the ringleader, all she officially got was a slap on the wrist and a stern talking-to. Mrs. Renfrow assigned her to three days in DLC—Directed Learning Center—which is supposed to make kids think they're in an educational environment instead of serving in-school suspension. She also had to write a letter of apology to the superintendent, which she did, but in a final act of defiance she sent off a copy to the newspaper. They gladly published it on the "Letters to the Editor" page. Here's what it said:

Dear Superintendent Pruitt:

I'm a sophomore at Rosslyn High School. I led the student body in the protest march last week against school uniforms, which brought lots of publicity to the school. As a student, I'm sorry I had to disobey school rules in order to get this issue out in the open, but no kids got hurt by being out of the building for a couple of hours. I'm also sorry for embarrassing you, Mr. Pruitt, but it was worth it for the administrators to see what a huge mistake they were making. Thank you for changing your mind about making us wear uniforms.

Sincerely,

Megan Benedict

Some apology, huh? What really saved her, though, was her dad making a huge cash donation to the school. Janae's been happily spreading the news that next year we'll have all new computers in a renovated lab, thanks to Mr. Benedict's generosity.

But on the other side of the getting-away-with-it spectrum is Kensington Marlow. She probably wouldn't have gotten in much trouble at all if she hadn't taken her shirt off and displayed her underwear for the TV-viewing public. Kensi was asked—no, TOLD—to go home and not return for the rest of the school year, even though there were only a few days of school left. That means she didn't get to take her final exams, so her already-low grade point average took an even bigger nosedive. Next year, according to Janae, Kensi will be assigned to an alternative school. No cheerleading, no student council, just Kensi and some other at-risk kids in a converted elementary building somewhere in downtown Indianapolis, doing lessons on computers all day.

The ironic thing about Kensi's downfall—sorry, it was too good to pass up!—is what it did for Emma's political career. She's been bumped from vice president to president of the student council after Kensi's removal, much to Emma's amazement and to my relief, because I'd seriously begun to doubt myself. I guess everything happens for a reason though, and there's no timeline for psychic predictions.

The day after the protest, Mrs. Renfrow summoned Emma and Janae Thomas to her office, where she informed them of her decision to promote Emma to president and Janae to vice president.

Afterward, Emma came storming up to me in the hallway. "Caryn, can you believe it! Now I have to be student council president just because Kensi couldn't keep her shirt on!"

"Well, Emma, I said—"

"Oh, don't go all 'I told you so' on me," she said, hands on hips. "This is going to ruin my summer!"

"It is not," I insisted.

"Because now I have to go to that student council forum after all. Talk about a waste of a whole week! And what about the design camp I really wanted to go to?"

I shook my head. "Wow. A week in Washington DC at the school's expense. Tough luck, Emma."

Her shoulders slumped. "But you know how I feel about political stuff! I really want to go to that clothing design camp."

"You'll do both," I said.

"How do you know?" Emma frowned, like she really expected a logical answer. Then she rolled her eyes. "Oh. Well, you don't have to be so smug about it!" And she flounced off down the hall.

****

So here's how things are shaping up for the summer for everyone:

Megan's sister Caroline told her she could invite a few friends to her wedding so that Megan would have the company of kids her own age. She decided on Jeremy Harper for her date, and Emma and Kevin, and then she invited Quince and me, officially recognizing us as a couple. I'm thrilled to be invited, especially since Mr. Benedict is shelling out big bucks for his daughter's wedding. It's going to be held outdoors at some big country club up in Belford, and Megan tells me the whole thing was mostly planned by her stepmother. It's pretty cool getting to go to such a romantic event with the guy who's been my crush all year. There will be an actual orchestra—not just a DJ—and I'll have to do some practicing ahead of time, because Quince is a very good dancer. I wonder if Uncle Omar could teach me some moves? Nah! Too 70s.

After the wedding, Megan's off to Ball State University where she'll be attending a camp for future architects. I guess they have some prestigious architecture school up there, and supposedly high school kids who are invited to attend the camp have a good shot at being admitted to the university when the time comes. Miss Emerson, the art teacher, recommended her for the camp which means Megan really has talent.

Annabeth is off to her family's summer house on Lake Michigan. She promised to call me often while I'm in Houston, and we're definitely getting together as soon as we both get back to town in August.

Ashleigh and Harris are each attending smart-kid camps—Harris to that science camp and Ashleigh to some month-long camp in New Hampshire for gifted math kids. I guess that's their idea of a good time, but it makes my head throb thinking about spending the summer doing equations.

I was a little worried about my mom being lonesome while I'm down in Texas, since every other time I've stayed at my dad's she was only a few miles away across town. I asked her if she'd be okay here by herself.

"Honey, don't give it a thought. I have the store and Sybil, and George has promised to keep me occupied while you're away."

So I guess Mom and Mr. Desmond are becoming a hot item. Who would've thought old folks could still enjoy romance?

Then I started worrying about being away from Quince while I'm out of state, and wondering if he'd find a new girlfriend over the summer. I guess I'm still pretty insecure where he's concerned.

"Caryn, give me some credit," he said, tugging on my ponytail. "It took me all year to realize you were the girl for me, and I'm not backing down from it now. And did I tell you I'll be in Houston in July?"

I was thrilled. "Houston? Really?"

"Yeah, I'm attending a weeklong baseball camp at some university down there. It's gonna be pretty hot out I guess, but there are a bunch of professional ball players running the camp, and I could really learn a lot." He took my hand and melted my heart with a smile. "Do you think we could get together?"

I felt almost giddy. "Are you serious? I wouldn't miss it! And I can introduce you to my dad."

Quince got a funny look on his face, and it occurred to me that being introduced to the girl's father isn't every teenage boy's dream.

"Unless you'd rather not."

"No, I'd like to meet your dad."

Okay, I'm not totally convinced, but it's still cool I'll be able to see him some while we're both in Texas.

"I'm so glad that school's over. It's been a long year," I told him.

"Yeah, and by the way, I've been meaning to ask you..."

I smiled. "Ask me what?"

"Remember last October? And we'd just met—"

Uh-oh.

"—when you told me about my mother's diabetes. How did you know that?"

"Just a lucky psychic guess," was all I said.

Someday I'll get up the nerve to tell Quince that I can also talk to spirits, but today isn't that day. I just smiled at him, squeezed his hand, and looked up into those smiling blue eyes of his.

And speaking of spirits, what about Uncle Omar? I still see him everywhere, or sometimes I just hear his voice when I don't actually see him. I'm kind of getting used to having him in my life—almost as if I wasn't talking to a dead dude. He gives me good advice sometimes, and other times it's like having an extra parent to correct me.

"Are you going to Houston with me?" I asked him one day.

"You kidding? Sun, surf, hot chicks. I'm there!"

He's still got his sense of humor.

I can't wait to see my dad. I fly out of Indianapolis the day after Caroline Benedict's wedding, and I'll be in Houston until mid-August. Dad has promised to take me to baseball games, the beach, a new art museum that's opened, and picnics in the park near their apartment.

Want to hear something crazy? I'm dreading the hot, sticky weather down there. Maybe I'm becoming a Hoosier after all.

****

It's late in the afternoon on the last day of school and the hallways are filled with kids who mostly haven't been in a classroom since lunchtime. We're all watching the clock tick down the minutes until summer vacation begins, almost like we're ringing in a new calendar year instead of ending the school year. As I look around, I finally feel like I fit in here. I've gone from being a self-conscious loner to having friends who accept me for myself—psychic abilities and all.

The final bell rings loudly. There are notebooks and trash all over the floor where kids have cleaned out their lockers and couldn't fit stuff into the overflowing wastebaskets. All the signs and posters have been pulled down in the hallways, exposing bare walls painted an institutional green. Locker doors are hanging open, and someone dumped an algebra book in the water fountain. A "Goodbye Mrs. York" sign has fallen halfway off her classroom door, and someone walks by and rips it the rest of the way off.

I wave goodbye to Emma and Kevin as they walk out of school arm-in-arm. Ashleigh calls across the hallway to me, saying she'll see me next fall. Janae runs down the middle of the hall high-fiving kids and shouting to everyone that summer is finally here. Megan and Jeremy are in a rush to leave, so she breathlessly reminds me that I'm invited to her sister's wedding in a couple of weeks, like I could forget. And then Quince appears by my side.

"Ready to go?" he asks, grinning at me.

"You bet."

I have one last look around, take Quince's offered hand, and we walk out the door together.

I feel like a pretty normal kid.

A word about the author...

I live in Carmel, Indiana, just north of Indianapolis, with my two cats Molly and Phoebe. My children, Robert and Caroline, both live in Indianapolis and I enjoy a close relationship with them.

Thank you for purchasing
this Wild Rose Press publication.
For other wonderful stories of romance,
please visit our on-line bookstore at
www.thewildrosepress.com

For questions or more information,
contact us at
info@thewildrosepress.com

The Wild Rose Press
www.TheWildRosePress.com